BAYONETS IN NO-MAN'S LAND

Len Levinson
writing as
Jonathan Scofield

SAPERE
BOOKS

BAYONETS IN NO-MAN'S LAND

Published by Sapere Books.

20 Windermere Drive, Leeds, England, LS17 7UZ,
United Kingdom

saperebooks.com

ISBN: 978-1-80055-631-7

To my father, Samuel William Levinson, who served with the Second Division during World War One, and was wounded at Château-Thierry. He carried a roundish scar approximately three centimeters in diameter on the left side of his forehead for the rest of his life.

To be able to say, when this war is finished, "I belonged to the Second Division, and I fought with it at the Battle of Blanc Mont Ridge," will be the highest honor that can come to any man.

Major General John A Lejeune
United States Marine Corps

PART 1

CHAPTER 1

The band played "The Stars and Stripes Forever" as the doughboys marched through sunny Paris on July 4, 1917. The boulevards were lined with Frenchmen, all anxious to see the American soldiers they hoped would win the war for them.

The doughboys had arrived only six days before, and many had not yet recovered fully from their sea voyage, but they held their heads high, marching proudly to the beat of the drums as they made their way through the cheering throngs. They were from all over the United States, from all walks of life. Two-thirds of them were green soldiers who'd been civilians only a couple of months before; the rest were grizzled old regular army men who'd served with the cavalry on the Mexican border, and some of the old sergeants and officers had fought in the Spanish-American War.

The French tossed bouquets of flowers at them and held out bottles of champagne, but the doughboys kept their eyes straight ahead and continued to march, their wide-brimmed campaign hats slanted low over their eyes and their high-buttoned collars tight around their necks. They carried Springfield rifles at right-shoulder-arms, and their boots beat a steady tattoo on the street as they marched toward Lafayette's Tomb.

Fifty yards in front of the doughboys, in the rear seat of an open automobile, sat Major General John J Pershing, their commander, with French General Ferdinand Foch and Field Marshal Joseph Joffre beside him. Raymond Poincaré,

President of the French Republic, sat in the front seat beside the American ambassador William Sharp, who was translating.

General Pershing smiled and waved to the crowds, astonished and touched by the enthusiasm shown for him and his men. He looked back at the advancing columns of doughboys. With all the blooms and confetti showering down on them, they looked almost like a moving flower garden.

Poincaré leaned toward Pershing and touched his shoulder. "The people are indeed happy to see you," he said.

"We shall not fail them," Pershing replied, although he knew his doughboys were not yet ready for war. America had only two hundred thousand men under arms when she declared war on the Central Powers, and that many could be killed in a week on the Western Front. It would be a tremendous job to build an army that could defeat the mighty Germany; Pershing figured he would need around three million men to do the job.

A garland of blood-red roses fell into Pershing's lap. Field Marshal Joffre chuckled, picked them up and placed them around Pershing's neck. The crowd roared its approval as the limousine advanced down the Champs-Élysées.

While Pershing was waving to the crowds, General Foch studied him, trying to size up the man. Pershing was the most famous officer in the American army, a fearless combatant and close friend of former president, Teddy Roosevelt. Tall and broad-shouldered, with superb military bearing, General Pershing was obviously a born leader of men, but had never commanded a unit larger than a division in combat. Could such a man mold and lead an army to victory against the most devastating war machine the world had ever seen?

People leaned out of tall buildings and waved at the doughboys. Gendarmes struggled to hold the crowds back, but little boys broke through and ran alongside the Americans, touching their uniforms and gazing at them in awe. The women in the crowd blew kisses, while the older men and women waved tiny American flags on sticks.

Pershing's staff officers marched behind his car in two solid ranks, and in the middle of the second rank was Second Lieutenant Everett DeWitt of New York City. Tall and slender, with fair skin and blond hair, he looked out of the corners of his eyes at the fabled buildings of Paris as flowers and confetti rained down upon him. Twenty-two years old and a member of one of the most distinguished families in America, he knew this was a momentous day in his life, a day he would talk about to his grandchildren, for he was keenly aware that he was marching across the stage of history.

"You're out of step, Ev," muttered the officer to his right, Captain George S Patton from Virginia.

DeWitt looked down and saw that he was indeed out of step. He'd been daydreaming and had forgotten the soldier's most elementary task, to stay in step. He skipped once and got into step with the others.

The doughboys marched into Picpus Cemetery, where a platform had been erected behind the white marble tomb of the Marquis de Lafayette, who had fought for America during its Revolutionary War. The open car stopped beside the platform, and French soldiers rushed forward to open its doors as the doughboys marched into battalion formations in front of the tomb. Poincaré, Pershing, Foch and Joffre got out of the limousine and ascended the steps to the platform. They were followed by Pershing's staff officers, and greeted by various dignitaries of the French, British and American governments.

Tens of thousands of French pressed against the gates of the cemetery, wanting to see everything, to hear every word. A battalion of bearded French combat soldiers stood to the side, wearing blue uniforms and helmets, holding rifles with long bayonets, examining the American doughboys, who in turn were examining them.

The sun shone brightly on the platform as General Pershing shook hands with the dignitaries, and the crowds shouted and cheered. Paul Painlevé, the French Minister of War, took Pershing by the arm. "You must speak now," he said.

Pershing shook his head. "I'm not much of a speaker, sir. I've designated Colonel Stanton to speak for me."

Painlevé's eyes widened. "I am afraid that is impossible, *mon général*. You are the commander of the American soldiers here. You are the one who must deliver the address."

"But I haven't prepared anything."

"Surely you can say something."

Pershing looked to the American ambassador, William Sharp, for help, but received a stern look in reply. "I think you'd better say something," Sharp said quietly.

Pershing knew he was on the spot, but he'd been in tighter spots than this, with bullets flying and artillery shells exploding. He advanced to the podium with no idea of what he was going to say. A hush fell over the crowd, and everyone listened eagerly.

Pershing looked down at his doughboys, then at the French soldiers to the side of the tomb. Behind them he could see crowds of French people and the skyline of Paris in the far distance. Everyone was waiting for him to speak, but his mind was blank.

Pershing looked down at the tomb of Lafayette, cleared his throat, and then, suddenly, like gifts from God, the words fell into his mind. Holding the sides of the podium, he gazed solemnly at the tomb and said in his deep booming voice, "Lafayette, we are here!"

CHAPTER 2

It was late afternoon, the sun setting over the Western Front. High in the sky, in the cockpit of a Spad S.13, Sergeant Blake Langley Hunter looked down at the battlefield on which hundreds of thousands of men had died since 1914. The earth was brown, interlaced with thin black lines that Blake knew were long coils of barbed wire. He saw the deep scars of trenches and the men moving around inside them.

It was quiet down there; there had been no heavy action that day. He'd taken his Spad up in the hope that he might find a lone German observer plane or fighter trying to make its way back to German lines. Four of his confirmed kills had been on late-afternoon patrols, and he hoped today would be another of his lucky days.

He was American, twenty-four years old, from Virginia. His squadron was the Lafayette Escadrille, composed of Americans flying for France. His Spad had an Indian head painted on both sides of the fuselage, the insignia of the escadrille.

A speck in the distance caught his eye. Squinting between the struts of the wings, he saw that his Spad was not the only aircraft in the area.

Blake pushed the stick to the side and banked his plane so that it would head west. He wanted to get the sun behind him, making it difficult for the pilot in the other plane to see him. The Spad's 210-horsepower Hispano-Suiza engine roared as the biplane angled to the side. Blake peered at the lone plane in the distance to see if it altered its course or behaved as though it knew it was being stalked. It continued unswervingly toward

German lines, and Blake knew it must be a German plane: an Allied plane would not be heading toward Germany at that time of day.

Blake maneuvered his Spad so that it floated behind and above the other plane. At the same time he searched the skies around him to make sure he wasn't being lured into a trap. Cold windstreams whistled through struts of his wings and washed his face. His heart always beat faster, and his perceptions seemed finer, when he was closing in for a kill. He was slowly gaining on the other plane. Soon he would know whether or not it was German.

It reminded him of when he was a boy, hunting squirrels in the forests of Virginia. He'd crept up on them the same way, gained a favorable firing position, and aimed carefully. Hunting was the same whether the prey was a small forest creature or a lone airplane in the sky over France.

He looked around him again, then checked his compass, airspeed indicator and radiator thermometer. His cockpit was fitted with a Camel joystick that he'd rigged with an apparatus enabling him to fire both his Vickers machine guns with one trigger. Drawing closer to the other plane, he pushed the stick forward so he could dive down and get a better look.

The front of the Spad angled downward as Blake began his dive. He smiled as the black crosses of the German air force came into focus on the wings of the other plane; he'd found what he'd been looking for. Then he noticed that it was a two-seater, with a machine gunner behind the pilot. It would be deadly to try to take them from above and behind as he was attempting.

Blake pulled back his stick and angled to the right. His Spad climbed into the air and rolled out, its Hispano-Suiza engines snarling. He heard machine guns beneath him; the German gunner had seen him and was trying to bring him down, but Blake was speeding toward the earth at a terrific speed, rolling to the side at the same time.

The wind rushed into his cockpit and he held his stick tightly with both hands, feeling the sick, empty feeling in his stomach as he plummeted to earth upside down. He heard machine gun bullets whistling through the air, and one of them shot through the fabric on his upper wing, but he was a fast-moving target and it would take a tremendous stroke of luck for the German to disable him.

Glancing to the side, he looked at the German plane and saw that it was a Halberstadt, which was used as a fighting plane and scout. Blake dived below it and pushed his stick all the way to the right. His Spad rolled over and came out upright again.

Now he was underneath the Halberstadt, heading toward it at an angle from the front. Aiming his twin Vickers, he gave the Spad some top rudder and took off a bit of aileron. He climbed toward the Halberstadt, aligning it dead ahead. Unconsciously clenching his teeth, he pushed his trigger button, and lightning darted from twin Vickers mounted on the Spad's cowling. The machine guns chattered, and Blake saw his tracers making long red lines that disappeared beneath the fuselage of the Halberstadt.

The German plane tried to climb, but that only exposed more of its belly. Blake held his trigger down and sprayed hot lead into the Halberstadt. He was closing fast with it but kept his Vickers firing until the last moment. Then he pushed his stick forward and dived underneath the plane. Looking behind him, he saw a trail of smoke underneath the Halberstadt. *I got him*, Blake thought. *He's hurt.*

Now Blake was exposed. The rear gunner on the Halberstadt swung his machine gun down and fired at the Spad. Blake eased off his throttle, banked to the left, turned around and attacked the Halberstadt from below again. The German gunner in the rear seat continued firing down at him, Blake's Spad twitching as bullets ripped through its fabric.

The Halberstadt had slowed considerably. Blake opened fire. His Spad trembled with the fire of the machine guns, and Blake saw bits of material flying into the air beneath the German aircraft. The smoke became blacker and more voluminous. Blake roared past the Halberstadt and looked back. It seemed to be going into a dive.

Blake turned the Spad around and climbed into the air. Bullets zipped around him as the German rear gunner opened fire again. He leveled off and looked down. The Halberstadt was steady in the air, but it had evidently lost power and was gliding to earth. It would crash within a minute or two, and Blake would have another kill to his credit, provided the kill could be confirmed.

Glancing down, he thought he was over French territory, but wasn't sure. He leaned out of his cockpit and saw the Halberstadt coasting toward the ground. Blake thought it might land safely and be damaged instead of destroyed. He decided to make one more pass and finish it off. Turning to maneuver underneath the Halberstadt again, he heard a German machine-gun bullet ricochet off one of his machine guns. *You son of a bitch,* he thought to himself.

He pulled back the stick, the wings and struts of the Spad straining as Blake climbed into the sky. The sun was sinking toward the horizon behind him and the brown earth below glowed the color of gold. He looked at the stricken Halberstadt and saw black smoke trailing from its tail. "So you want to trade bullets with me, eh?" he muttered, pushing the stick forward and to the side.

The nose of the Spad lowered and dived out of the sun at the Halberstadt. It wasn't considered wise to take a two-seater from above this way, but Blake had the sun behind him and knew the rear gunner couldn't see him well. Moreover, the Halberstadt was in trouble, and its crew under deadly strain.

The German gunner fired valiantly at Blake, who smiled as he fixed his angle of descent and pressed his trigger button. The twin Vickers chattered loudly and Blake smelled gunpowder as bullets streamed down at the Halberstadt. The German rear gunner fired back, but his aim was wide. Blake's bullets stitched up the fuselage of the Halberstadt, then the German rear gunner fell away from his weapon and clutched his chest. Blake's bullets tore up the Halberstadt and the German pilot turned around fearfully to see what was behind him. Blake was close enough to see the German's face transformed into a mask of blood, to hear the Halberstadt's engine whine as it went into a tailspin. Blake followed it down, still firing. He didn't want any confusion over whether it was a damaged plane or a kill.

The Halberstadt disintegrated in midair as Blake continued firing his machine guns. Bits of the Halberstadt's wings and fuselage flew away, then it turned belly up, rolled over again and continued rolling, its broken struts screaming in the wind. Blake pulled his stick back and began to climb as the Halberstadt continued its last dive and crashed into the grounds Its gas tank exploded in a fiery red burst and the wreckage was covered with flames.

Blake's Spad climbed into the sky as he raised his right fist high and screamed victoriously at the setting sun.

An hour later he landed at the aerodrome near Chaudun, taxiing to a stop at the end of the rank of other escadrille planes. He unbuckled his straps, climbed out of the cockpit, dropped to the ground, removing his long-eared flying hat and the silk skullcap he wore underneath to reveal thick, wavy black hair.

He had large hazel eyes set into a lean and handsome face, and he was six feet two inches tall, long-limbed, with wide shoulders and muscles that were taut and hard. Carrying his map case and canteen, he started walking toward the headquarters building just as the mechanics and a pilot left the big hangar and headed toward his plane.

"How did you do?" asked the pilot, a skinny, mustached fellow named Pierre.

Blake held up one finger. "A Halberstadt."

The mechanics crowded around him and slapped his shoulders, offering congratulations. One of them took a flask of cognac from inside his service blouse and handed it to Blake, who unscrewed the cap and took a long swig.

Blake sucked in air through his clenched teeth to offset the Cognac burn. The mechanics laughed and continued to surround him, for he was one of the squadron's aces. Pictures of him appeared from time to time in newspapers. He handed the flask back, waved, and continued toward the headquarters of the escadrille.

The top of the sun was still visible on the horizon, and it cast long red shadows on the tarmac of the runway. Stopping, Blake took a cigarette from a gold case and lit it with a matching gold lighter. He stared for a few moments at the two elegant gold pieces. His previous cigarette case and lighter had been promised to two fellow pilots, Franklin DeWitt and Bulldog Teeter, in the event of anything happening to him during the war. But they had gone before him: he had seen them both gunned down over enemy territory — and had perhaps been partly responsible for their deaths, though he would never know for sure. As he flew over the spots where the two men had gone down, he had dropped the case and lighter in tribute to their friendship, and to what could only be described as heroism.

He shook his head and pocketed the case and lighter, closing out the uneasiness the memories brought. Inhaling deeply on his cigarette, he opened the door to headquarters and went inside.

Major Dubois looked up from his desk as Blake entered. "I know what you're going to ask me, so I might as well tell you — it has been confirmed."

Blake smiled, for now the Halberstadt was officially his. "Who reported it?"

"Our artillery observers in that sector. They said it was quite a little fight."

"It was."

"Any damage to your plane?"

"A few holes."

"The report said you continued to fire at the German aircraft as it was going down."

"I wanted to make sure. I've had too many of them get away."

"They said you fired from above. You should know by now that you never attack a two-seater from above."

"At first I attacked from beneath. It wasn't until he was going down that I fired at him from above. I came out of the sun and he didn't have much fight left in him by then anyway."

"The report said he was firing at you as he went down."

"He was."

"A few lucky shots might have got you."

"He was finished. He didn't have a prayer."

Dubois smiled thinly. "Some day you're going to push your luck too far."

"I know what I'm doing, Major."

"I hope so, Sergeant."

Blake noticed a newspaper lying on a file cabinet. Angling toward it, he read the headline: AMERICAN SOLDIERS ARRIVE IN PARIS. He picked the newspaper up and saw a photograph of American soldiers marching down the Champs-Élysées. Another photograph showed General Pershing speaking at a podium.

"Looks as though your countrymen are finally arriving in force," Dubois said.

"About time," Blake replied, scanning the rest of the newspaper article.

CHAPTER 3

General Pershing sat in his office at the new American Expeditionary Force Headquarters in Paris. On the other side of the desk sat Lieutenant Everett DeWitt, a stack of papers in his lap. Everett was neat as a pin in his tailor-made uniform, Sam Browne belt and polished boots.

"Everyone's impression," Everett was saying, "is that the Allied armies are tired and demoralized, especially the French. The huge losses sustained in their spring offensive have evidently taken the fight right out of them. Therefore, if the Germans ever mount a major full-front attack, we cannot expect our allies to hold. In view of that possibility, I think we ought to have an independent communications system that we can safeguard ourselves. We can't be certain our allies will be able to defend their own communications, never mind ours."

Pershing nodded and wrote on his pad. "Good point. Anything else?"

"One last thing, sir. If we have our own communications system, we'll need personnel to operate it. I recommend that instead of spending time to train soldiers to be telephone operators, we bring in some experienced telephone operators from the States."

Pershing raised his eyebrows. "You mean women?"

"Yes, sir," Everett replied, "and before you say no, let me point out that women perform a lot of important tasks in the British army, from chauffeuring their officers around to performing important administrative functions."

"I wasn't going to say no," Pershing replied. "If the British use women in that capacity, so can we. I'd just like to think about it a bit. Do you have anything else?"

"Not at the moment, sir."

"I'm still waiting for the report on machine gun availability."

"I'll have it for you by noon tomorrow, sir."

"Very good, Lieutenant DeWitt. You may return to your office."

"Yes, sir."

Everett rose, tucked his papers under his left arm, and saluted smartly as he marched out of General Pershing's office, continuing down a corridor in the huge mansion at 73 Rue de Varenne, which had been loaned to the AEF by a wealthy American politician named Ogden Mills. A beautiful garden had been planted at the back, and DeWitt glanced at the roses and peonies as he passed a window.

The corridors were crowded with officers of all ranks. Everett was still somewhat surprised to be among them, with direct access to General Pershing. But the American army was expanding quickly, and talented men were being brought into the general staff as rapidly as they could be found. If Everett were older they might have made him a captain or a major right off the bat.

Everett occupied a small office midway down a corridor in the basement. Several other officers occupied similar offices, and at the end of the corridor was a large open area where clerks typed and filed correspondence.

As Everett neared his door, Private Madden rose from behind his desk in the clerical area, waving his arm and dashing toward him. Everett stopped to see what he wanted.

Madden held his forefinger over his lips. "There's someone in your office, sir," he whispered. "He said he's a friend of yours. He told me his name and I wrote it down, but I lost the piece of paper."

Everett sighed in exasperation. His regular army clerks were always losing things and sending correspondence to the wrong places. It was a miracle that the army functioned at all.

"What was his rank?" Everett asked.

"He's a sergeant because I saw three stripes on his sleeve, but I don't know what kind of uniform he was wearing. I don't think it's a French uniform, and I don't think it's British. Maybe he's from Belgium?"

"I suppose I'll find out for myself in a few moments, Thanks for the information."

Everett took the final few steps to his office door, opened it up and saw a man in his mid-twenties sitting in front of his desk. The visitor was wearing the uniform of the French Foreign Legion, and when he stood, Everett could see the silver wings that were awarded to French pilots pinned to his breast pocket.

The pilot smiled, showing straight white teeth, and held out his hand. "Hi," he said, "I'm Blake Hunter. I was a friend of your brother's."

Everett shook his hand and recalled who he was. The Hunters were an old American family just like the DeWitts, and Blake was one of the famous aces with the Lafayette Escadrille, as Everett's brother Franklin had been. Franklin had been killed in action in April of that year.

"How do you do," Everett said. "Have a seat."

Everett walked behind his desk and sat, while Blake returned to the chair where he'd been sitting.

Blake smiled genially. "I hope you don't mind my barging in like this."

"Not at all," Everett replied. "What can I do for you?"

"I read your name in a newspaper article about Pershing's arrival in Paris with all his staff officers, and thought I'd come to see you about a little problem I'm having. I've decided that since America is in the war now, I'd like to enlist in one of the American air squadrons. Do you think you can help me?"

"I can introduce you to someone in the air service. I imagine they'd love to have an experienced pilot like you. We don't have much of an air arm yet."

"Air superiority will be the key to victory in this war," Blake said, reaching for his gold cigarette case. "Do you mind if I smoke?"

"Not at all. I'll have one, too."

Both men took out cigarettes and lit them up. DeWitt looked at Blake and thought him a very impressive-looking young man. He wanted to ask Blake about Franklin, but decided that might be too painful for both of them. Everett recalled his last meeting with Brooke Madigan DeWitt, Franklin's wife. Their grief over Franklin's death had been so raw that neither had been able to get beyond mere mentions of him.

"There's one other thing that I'd like you to help me with," Blake said. "I think that my older brother is over here, and I'd like to find out where he is. I haven't heard from him for a while, but I figure he's either on his way here or is here now."

"Do you know what branch of the service he's in?"

"Infantry," said Blake. "He came to France with me in 1914 and became an ambulance driver. Then he tried to get into the escadrille, but washed out of pilot school, so he joined the French Ambulance Corps. The last I heard he had returned to the States and got a commission in the army."

"What's his name?"

"Duncan W Hunter." Blake told him Duncan's serial number.

"I'll check the rosters," Everett said, rising to indicate that the meeting was over.

Blake Hunter eased his foot off the accelerator of the Renault as he neared the little village that lay ahead. He shifted down and squinted at the sign at the edge of the village. SOULAUCOURT.

This is it, he thought. He drove slowly over the cobblestoned street, seeing old men, old women and little children on the sidewalks, along with a scattering of American soldiers.

"Hey there," he said to one of the soldiers. "Where's First Battalion headquarters?"

"Take a left at the next intersection, and you'll see it straight ahead. You won't be able to miss it because it's got a big flag in front."

The soldier's shoulder patch had an Indian head on it, Blake noticed, just like the planes of the Lafayette Escadrille, and the background was a white star. Blake shifted into gear, rolled down the street, and turned left at the intersection.

It was a tiny village, with a population probably under five hundred. All its young men were either in the French army, in hospital, or killed in action. Its young women had been shipped out to reside near the munitions factories where they worked. A big pile of manure was in every front yard, and Blake knew that the farmer with the most manure was considered the richest man in town.

He saw flags flying in front of a building halfway down the street. He parked his Renault behind one of the military vehicles in front of the building and got out, placing his *kepi* on his head and walking toward the building. Climbing the steps, he opened the door and found himself in an orderly room.

A sergeant sat behind a desk on one side of the room, and a private was seated behind a desk on the other side. The sergeant looked up from a piece of correspondence that he'd been reading. He had sandy hair and wore the Indian-head patch on his right shoulder. A wooden sign on his desk said SERGEANT MAJOR WILLIAM LARRABY.

"What can I do for you?" the sergeant asked.

"I'm looking for my brother," Blake replied. "He's an officer in this battalion."

"What's his name?"

"Duncan Hunter. I don't know what his rank is, but I imagine he's a second louie."

The sergeant looked at Blake, his uniform and the wings on his breast, and his face lit with recognition. He pointed at Blake and stood up, saying, "Hey — I know who you are! You're Blake Hunter, the flier!"

Blake held out his hand. "How do you do."

"It's a real pleasure to meet you, sir."

"I'm not a sir," Blake pointed out, shaking the man's hand. "I'm only a buck sergeant."

"You're still sir to me. I've heard all about you. I'll bet Colonel Foster would love to meet you. Let me go get him."

The sergeant turned and walked through a door at the rear of the orderly room. Blake turned and looked at the private, who gawked at him shamelessly. Blake waved at him. "Hiya."

The private stood up and mumbled a greeting, still staring.

The rear door opened and the sergeant came back with a group of officers, led by a man Blake assumed was Colonel Foster.

"Blake Hunter?" the man asked.

"Yes, sir."

The colonel held out his hand. "I'm Jack Foster — pleased to meet you."

Foster introduced Blake to the other officers, and then said, "We've heard a lot about you."

Blake didn't know what to say, so he simply smiled.

"I don't mind fighting with my two feet on the ground," Foster said, "but I'd sure as hell hate to fight way up there in the sky. It must take a lot of nerve."

"I don't know," Blake replied. "I'd say it takes more nerve to charge a German trench and fight face to face."

"At least when we charge we have the ground underneath us."

"But you can't fly away from a fight, like I can."

"You haven't flown away from many fights, young man, from what I've heard."

Blake smiled in reply. It was true: he hadn't flown away from any fights.

"Care to have a drink with us?" Colonel Foster asked. "I know it's duty hours, but I'd say this is a special occasion. Wouldn't you agree, gentlemen?"

His officers nodded and said yes, but Blake looked at his watch.

"I'm afraid I don't have much time," he said. "I've got to get back to Chaudun by midnight, and I want to spend some time with my brother."

"Perhaps you can join us at mess tonight, with your brother."

"That sounds like a good idea. Where is he, anyway?"

"I'll have somebody take you out to him. He's training with his company in the field."

Blake chuckled. "Since he's an officer, I guess I'll have to salute him. Is he a second louie?"

27

"First," Foster replied. "The army is expanding rapidly, and rank is being made very quickly. You ought to think about wearing an American uniform, Hunter. They're liable to make you a general."

"I'm working on it," Blake replied.

Blake walked into the fields north of the village, accompanied by Second Lieutenant Walker, who wore the crossed cannons of the field artillery on his lapels. They came to a sign that said:

WELCOME TO VALLEY FORGE
BRING YOUR OWN POTATO

Walker smiled. "Something the men put up," he said.

In the distance, Blake could see networks of trenches facing each other across a simulated stretch of no-man's land. Massed formations of soldiers charged from one network of trenches to the other in long ragged skirmish lines, with officers behind them shouting directions. Blake could hear voices echoing across the fields.

He wondered why the doughboys were practicing that kind of massed charge, because four years of war had made the tactic obsolete. There'd been a mutiny in the French army during the spring because of charges like that. The French soldiers had refused to attack again, because the losses had been so great.

"I hope they're not going to do that when they get to the front," Blake said.

"Do what?"

"Attack like that. The German machine guns will cut them down and German artillery will rip them to shreds."

"We know, but old Black Jack believes that the only way to defeat the Germans is in aggressive open warfare."

Blake shook his head. "It doesn't work."

"Never underestimate the American soldier, sergeant."

Blake decided not to argue, but thought there'd be a bloodbath if the doughboys ever charged that way. And most of them were green troops. They'd probably break and run when the carnage began.

"I think I can make it the rest of the way by myself," Blake said. "You may return to your duty if you like, unless you'd rather get away from headquarters for a while."

"I do have a lot of work to do," Walker admitted. "I'll see you at mess?"

"Sure thing."

Walker turned and walked back to Soulaucourt, while Blake moved toward the trenches. The skirmish lines charged and the soldiers flopped down on their bellies, while other doughboys got to their feet and continued the charge. Each wave was learning how to cover the other as they advanced to the enemy trenches. Officers shouted orders, and noncoms cursed at the soldiers who'd made mistakes. Blake reached the edge of the battlefield and stood with his hands in his pockets, watching the maneuvers.

As the doughboys ran back and forth, he gave thanks that he didn't have to be among them. It seemed repetitious and boring, and they did the same thing over and over day after day — just as he had when he'd first joined the French Foreign Legion.

At night the ordinary doughboys slept in barns and attics, and when they moved to the front they'd sleep in the dirt. How nice it was, in comparison, to fight high in the clear blue sky, man to man, in a test of skill. If you were killed in the air, it happened fairly quickly, and usually you were to blame. It wasn't like those poor fellows out there, who could be sleeping peacefully in their filthy little holes in the ground and suddenly have a German artillery shell land on top of them.

The doughboys finally made it across the field to the opposite trench, and a break was ordered. Blake strolled toward the trench, his hands in his pockets, when he saw a soldier climb out and walk toward him. Blake realized the soldier was his brother. Smiling, Blake stepped over the stones and mud of the mock battlefield to meet him.

They came together on the fields, embraced awkwardly and looked into each other's faces. Duncan was older than Blake and had lighter hair, but he too was tall and lean. He wore his helmet low over his hazel eyes, and on the helmet was painted the Indian head insignia of the Second Division. Duncan's face had always had a more serious cast to it than Blake's, but when he smiled it was the full, open smile of a little boy, more winning than Blake's smile because Duncan was less conscious of its effect.

"Why didn't you tell me you were here?" Blake asked when they separated.

"We've only been here two weeks. I wrote you a note as soon as I arrived, but I guess you didn't get it."

"It's probably easier for you to get a letter through to the States than to somebody in the French Foreign Legion stationed in France. How are Mother and Father? And Allison, of course?"

"All right last time I saw them. But I haven't heard much from Allison," Duncan replied.

Their sister Allison, the most outgoing and lively of the three Hunter children, had withdrawn from the family after the death of a soldier had left her an unwed mother. It had all been hushed up, of course, with a "proper" cover story concocted to save the family reputation.

Duncan sometimes felt that Blake knew more about it than he let on — after all, he and Allison had seen a lot of each other in Paris at the time she'd met the soldier — but it seemed best to leave matters as they were, and allow Allison her privacy. Besides, Allison was nothing if not resilient. She'd be all right in time.

They walked off the battlefield to a patch of trees nearby and sat in the shade. Blake lit up a cigarette, not bothering to offer one to Duncan, who didn't smoke or drink.

"I'm trying to get into the American air service," Blake said.

"Sounds like a good idea. They'll probably make you an officer."

"But nothing will ever make me a gentleman."

They laughed, for Blake had always been the bad boy and Duncan the good one. Duncan had graduated *summa cum laude* from the University of Virginia, while Blake got through by the skin of his teeth. Duncan had been the churchgoer and teetotaler, while Blake almost never set foot inside a church and came home drunk at all hours of the night. Duncan's wife had been one of the few women in his life, while Blake had got at least two women pregnant that the family knew about, and had been involved with numerous other women.

Blake flicked some ash off the end of his cigarette. "I went to see Franklin's younger brother, Everett, who works as an aide to old Black Jack. You ever meet Everett?"

"No."

"Well, he's a rather elegant type, a bit stiff, but knows a lot of people. He sent me to see a Major Bishop in the Signal Corps, which is where the AEF aviators are right now. I think I'll be able to make the switchover without too much trouble."

"Those DeWitts usually are good at pulling strings," Duncan said.

Blake looked over his shoulder at the battlefield. "I was watching your company practice charges as I was walking across the fields. I hope you don't intend to do anything like that when you get to the front."

"We intend to do precisely that. You can't win victories sitting in a trench. We'll need to wage open warfare and capture ground if we want to beat the Fritzies."

Blake looked at him. "Do you know there was a mutiny in the French army last spring?"

"A real mutiny?"

"A real and very widespread mutiny. It happened because the French *poilus* refused to continue attacking. Their losses were so staggering it was simply too much for them. I saw some of those offensives from the air — the battlefield was literally covered with bodies for miles. If you were walking out there you couldn't put your foot down without stepping on a dead soldier. The AEF has to realize that it can't charge machine guns. Jesus, you must have seen a lot of it when you were an ambulance driver."

Duncan nodded. "I wasn't on the battlefields but I saw them come through the dressing stations. It was an endless procession of men covered with blood, and I'll never forget it. But machine-gun nests can be silenced; they're not sacred, you know. And artillery can be bombarded until it can't fire. The Americans have to win this war, Blake. The French and British are on their last legs. And if we don't attack the Germans and drive them back, we'll be fighting here in these muddy fields for the next hundred years."

Duncan's voice was steady, with a determination that surprised Blake, but he only nodded in agreement. Duncan might be the older of the two, more intellectual and serious, but that hardly meant that he belonged in the military or understood what fighting was really all about. And so far, Duncan hadn't exactly distinguished himself. Washing out of pilot school, serving as an ambulance driver and now talking about insane charges against entrenched and heavily armed Germans.

He probably won't survive the war, Blake thought unhappily. *And I probably won't either.*

CHAPTER 4

The caravan of vehicles stopped in front of the War Ministry, and French guards rushed forward to open the doors. General Pershing got out of the lead vehicle, along with several of his aides, and the rest of his staff emerged from other vehicles.

Pershing towered over most of his aides, his massive shoulders, erect posture and stern features making him appear indomitable. He climbed the steps to the War Ministry followed by guards and aides. They entered the building and traversed its wood-paneled corridors until they came to a large conference room.

The door was open, and they walked inside. Orderlies took their hats, and they proceeded to the large map table. Marshal Joffre, who had been standing in front of the table, stepped forward to greet them, followed by General Foch, General Mangin, and several other French officers.

From the other side of the table came Field Marshal Edward Haig, commander-in-chief of the British troops in France, and General Sir Julian Byng, along with a contingent of British officers and interpreters, because everyone did not speak the same language. They all shook hands, exchanged pleasantries, then gathered around the map table and got down to business.

General Haig had a thick white mustache and the sad eyes of a bloodhound. "Tell me, General Pershing — how many troops do you have in France as of today?"

"Around seventy-five thousand, with more arriving every week. I expect to have at least half a million here by the end of the year."

"You have been following the events in Russia, I take it?"

"I have."

"Then you know that Russia may conclude an armistice with the Central Powers any day now. When that happens, the Kaiser will pull all his troops from his Eastern Front and transfer them here, on the Western Front. Therefore it is imperative that you put your men into the line as soon as possible. When might we expect you to do that?"

Pershing was aware that the eyes of the leading soldiers in the world were on him, and most of them had carried far greater military responsibilities during their careers than he. Yet he stood there as representative of the United States of America, and the knowledge of that duty stiffened his resolve.

"I can't say for sure," he replied. "My troops still have a great deal more training to do. I would guess that we won't be ready until spring."

"Spring?' said Haig, aghast. "That long?"

"I'm afraid so."

Marshal Joffre cleared his throat "But that might be too late, General Pershing."

"I'm not sending my men to the front until they're ready," Pershing replied firmly. "It won't further the Allied cause to have them slaughtered. You know as well as I do that the Kaiser will take advantage of our first appearance on the line to strike a blow at American prestige and Allied morale. I want my soldiers to be prepared."

"But," said General Foch gravely, "we had expected you to help us out long before spring."

"I'm sorry," Pershing replied, "but I cannot say that my men constitute an army yet, and it would be irresponsible to send them into combat now. Only a very small percentage are combat veterans, the rest basically civilians in uniform. The

Germans, on the other hand, are a seasoned and highly effective fighting force. I repeat, I will not send my men to fight until they're ready."

Marshall Haig folded his arms and sat back to peer at the American. "But that might be a fatal delay for the Allies, General Pershing."

"I can't do more than I'm doing right now."

"I disagree. There is something you can do," said Haig. "You can funnel American soldiers into British and French units to serve as replacements. They can be trained as they're serving, and God knows we need them. Many of our divisions are down to half strength, and some are even lower than that. We're scraping the bottom of the barrel for manpower. The appearance of your husky boys in our ranks would give our men heart. And they could be trained, as I say, by combat veterans skilled in the tactics of this war."

Pershing looked Haig in the eye, then Joffre, and then Foch. "I want you gentlemen to understand something very important. American soldiers did not come here as replacements for your armies. They came here as part of the American army, and that's the only way they'll fight. I think it would be very bad for their morale to have them fight under French or British officers, just as it would be harmful to the morale of French or British soldiers to fight under American officers. My men are proud of what they are, and I will not permit them to fight under any flag but their own."

Haig gazed steadfastly at Pershing. "We are in a rather difficult situation here, General. I think our common struggle should override the concerns of individual nations."

"I do not consider this the concern of an individual nation, sir. I'm talking about maintaining the fighting effectiveness of my men, and you're talking about diminishing their fighting effectiveness. That is the long and short of it, from my point of view. My men are not here to provide replacements for your armies, and I must ask all of you to respect that point of view."

The discussion over the use of the doughboys continued throughout the afternoon, with the British and French officers raising new arguments, but General Pershing refused to budge. Finally, at five o'clock, the meeting was adjourned. Salutes and more subdued pleasantries were exchanged, and General Pershing left with his American officers, leaving the French and British commanders alone around the map table.

Marshal Haig sighed and put his hands in his pockets. "Well, he's certainly stubborn, isn't he?"

Joffre nodded in agreement. "Too stubborn, I'd say."

"Now I understand," Foch said, "why American soldiers call him the Iron Commander."

"They also call him Black Jack," Haig said. "Anybody here know why, by any chance?"

Foch and Joffre looked at each other and shook their heads. In the back of the room, a young British sublieutenant raised his hand. "They call him Black Jack because he used to command all-black cavalry regiments."

The men in the room received the explanation in silence, then slowly gathered up their papers to leave, none of them feeling encouraged by the American military presence in France.

CHAPTER 5

The band played a waltz as gentlemen danced their ladies across the floor of the British Embassy. It was a grand ball and all the leading diplomats in Paris were there, plus numerous military men and hordes of ladies. The ballroom was immense, with white columns surrounding the dance floor. Crystal chandeliers hung from the ceiling, providing support for a vast network of brightly colored ribbons.

Lieutenant Everett DeWitt, as one of General Pershing's top aides, had been invited to the gala affair. Leaning against a column, he was watching an elegant young lady dance with an equally elegant British officer. He had noticed her a half-hour before, and hadn't been able to take his eyes off her since. He'd been following her at a safe distance, watching her chat with people and accept dance after dance. She appeared to be flirtatious, high-spirited, delightful, and he couldn't take his eyes off her.

Now he was debating with himself whether to ask her for the next dance. He was sure she wouldn't refuse him — she hadn't refused anyone all evening — but he was afraid that he might do something foolish, and more than anything else he hated to behave foolishly. He was so taken with her that he knew it would be difficult to be completely self-possessed.

I might as well ask her, he thought as the dance came to an end. *Faint heart never won fair lady, and that's a terrible cliché, but happens to be true.*

He placed his glass of champagne on a nearby table, straightened his Sam Browne belt and glanced at his reflection on the nearest mirrored wall. His uniform was immaculately tailored and pressed, tie perfectly centered, not a hair on his blond head out of place. Taking a deep breath, he marched on to the dance floor. The woman and her officer were applauding the orchestra with everybody else. Everett stopped in front of her and bowed slightly.

"May I have the next dance?" he asked, trying to keep his smile from collapsing.

She looked at him as though he were a ghost. Then she became flustered, and finally forced a smile. "All right," she said brightly. She held her arms up.

"Perhaps we should wait until the music starts," Everett said, suppressing a grin.

She blushed and laughed. "Yes, of course. One can't dance without music, can one?"

Everett shrugged. "I imagine one could if one wanted to."

The British officer took a step backward. "I think I'll leave you two to your dance. Have fun." He walked away, leaving Everett alone with the woman.

"Well," she said, "I knew you would ask me to dance eventually." She looked at the ceiling, then gave an airy wave of her hand as she leveled her blue eyes on his. "Lord knows, you have been following me around all night."

Everett stood erectly, with his hands clasped behind his back. "I haven't been following you all night. It's only been half an hour. Exaggeration is the sign of the sloppy thinker."

"Well," she said huffily, "evidently I have not been watching the clock as much as you, but it has been quite a while. Even you must admit that."

Everett nodded.

"So you finally got up the courage to ask me to dance?"

"One might say that."

"Does one know how to dance?"

"One does."

"Good, because I believe the band is about to play. They are quite good, don't you think?"

"All these bands sound pretty much the same," Everett said.

"Oh? So you go to parties often?"

"Yes."

"That is strange — I have not seen you before."

"Perhaps you have seen me, but I didn't register on your mind. However, if I had seen you, I'm sure I would have remembered."

"Why?" she asked.

"You know very well why."

She pursed her lips. "I am afraid I do not."

"Yes, you do. I should think people have been telling you how pretty you are ever since you were born. Anyway, that's why I would have remembered you."

She wrinkled her forehead, but her blue eyes were sparkling. "I don't know whether that was a compliment or not. Was it?"

"Definitely." Everett saw the conductor bring down his baton, and the sound of violins filled the ballroom. He took the woman in his arms and swept her across the floor.

"My," she said. "Such drama."

He felt her strong young body against his, and smelled her perfume, which reminded him of roses. "What's your name?"

"Danielle Giraud."

"How do you do, Danielle. I'm Everett DeWitt, from New York City."

"Oh, I have been there," she said. "Filthy place. Terribly noisy."

"I love Paris," he replied, ignoring her impertinence. "Where do you live?"

"With my father and mother."

"Where's that?"

"On the Rue St Faubourg."

Everett knew that the Rue St Faubourg was the most fashionable street in Paris. This woman evidently came from the highest strata of French society; which perhaps explained why she was so impudent. But impudent or not, he was completely captivated by her. "Is your father in the French diplomatic service?"

"No, in the army. General Hercule Giraud. If you're a staff officer here in Paris you've probably never heard of him. He is a front-line commander in the Twentieth Corps."

"I've heard of the Twentieth."

"Of course you have. It is one of our most famous."

Everett knew she was not exaggerating. The Twentieth had been nicknamed the Iron Corps because it had held the Germans on the Marne.

"Your father must be an outstanding officer."

She nodded. "He is. If you ever meet him, you will know that immediately."

He held her tightly and twirled her through an opening between other dancers. "Will I be able to call on you sometime?"

"I imagine," she replied.

"How about tomorrow? Perhaps we can have lunch?"

She shook her head. "I have a dance class tomorrow."

"Are you studying to be a dancer?"

"Not a professional dancer, but I love to dance. I think it is a beautiful art form, perhaps the most beautiful. You dance very well, by the way. You probably could be very good if you studied."

He examined her face, and couldn't find one single flaw. "You're really quite beautiful," he said, the words coming out before he could stop them.

"I believe you told me that before," she said wryly, "and as you pointed out already, people have been telling me that all my life. Sometimes I get tired of it. I am just a person, after all. Have you always been a soldier?"

"No."

"I didn't think so."

"Why not?"

"You're not like most soldiers. You seem more like a very well-behaved civilian in uniform. I've been around real soldiers since I was a child, and I know what they're like."

Everett frowned. "I don't know whether to be insulted or not."

She squeezed his shoulder. "It was not intended as an insult. I have noticed that there is a huge difference between a man who has trained all his life to be a soldier, and a man who interrupts his real career to put on a uniform and fight for his country. What was your real career, by the way?"

"I didn't have one," Everett said. "I was in my last year at college when we declared war, and they graduated all of us early so we could enlist. I'd intended to go to law school and then work in my uncle's firm. He's a partner in one of the law firms on Wall Street. Do you know what Wall Street is?"

"I don't live on the moon," she replied. "Everyone knows what Wall Street is. It's the center of business life in your country, isn't it?"

"Yes."

She wrinkled her nose in thought. "I think you will make a very good lawyer. You are very persuasive."

He laughed. "I mustn't be very persuasive if I can't even convince you to have lunch with me."

"I didn't say you could *never* have lunch with me," she retorted. "I only said you can't have lunch with me tomorrow, because I have my dance lessons. But I don't have a dance lesson on Wednesday."

CHAPTER 6

It was evening in the village of Soulaucourt, and Duncan Hunter was sitting behind the desk in the small attic room where he slept, doing his paperwork. In front of him sat a wiry little private who'd arrived in the company that day and been assigned to the platoon. The private was leaning forward expectantly, waiting for Duncan to say something.

Duncan read the private's records with great interest. The private's name was Samuel William Bell. He had been a private first class only two months ago, but had jumped ship in New York, gone AWOL and finally got picked up by the MPs who threw him in the stockade. Soon afterwards PFC Bell had been court-martialed, busted, then shipped to France because experienced men were needed so badly. Bell had been in the army since 1916 and was from New Bedford, Massachusetts, where he had been a waiter.

Duncan thumbed through the pages, then looked up at Bell, who was smiling at him. "Why'd you go AWOL, Bell?"

Bell had curly black hair and his eyes twinkled amiably. He pointed at Duncan and said loudly, "I'm glad you asked me that, sir, because some people have said that I'm yeller. And although I might be a lot of bad things, I damn sure as hell ain't yeller."

Duncan nodded. "Why'd you go AWOL, Bell?"

"Well, I'm coming to that, sir. You see it was like this. They shipped us from Texas to New York City and put us right on that damn tub. We was in that damn tub, floating out in the Hudson River for ten days, and they wouldn't let us off because they were afraid we'd tell somebody where we was going, as if everybody in New York and New Jersey didn't know where the hell we was going."

"The problem wasn't where you were going," Duncan pointed out, "but *when* you were going. If German U-boat captains could find out when you were leaving, they'd intercept you in the middle of the ocean and put a few torpedoes in your boat. You wouldn't like that, would you?"

"No, sir, but I wouldn't tell anybody where — I mean when — I was going. Do you think I'm a blabbermouth? Well, I ain't. I might be a lot of things, but I ain't no goddamned blabbermouth."

"But you've got to understand," Duncan explained, "that the army can't take any chances, and that's why they wouldn't let you go ashore. Somebody might've got drunk and said something he shouldn't have said."

Bell shook his head. "I don't get that drunk, sir."

"But how's the army supposed to know?"

Bell squinched up his eyes. "You mean the army doesn't trust me? After all I've done for the army?"

Duncan sighed. It was impossible to reason with them. "Why'd you go AWOL, Bell?"

"That's what I'm trying to tell you, sir." There was frustration in Bell's voice.

Duncan looked at his watch. "Go ahead and tell me, but I don't have all night."

Bell placed the palms of his hands on his thighs and leaned forward. "Well, it was like this, sir. I was sitting down in that smelly hold of the ship, thinking about my half-sister who lives in Brooklyn. Now I love that half-sister of mine, I really do, sir. When I was little she used to give me food, because her mother was my stepmother, and her mother didn't like me, and

I usually got less than the others. I used to tell my father but he wouldn't pay no attention because he loved that bitch. And besides, everybody always thinks the worst of me anyways — that's why I'm in trouble all the time. Well anyway, sir, I just wanted to go see Tessie — that's her name, Tessie — so bad, and I thought if I got killed over here I'd never ever see her again, so I thought I'd just go and see her, and then come back to the ship and nobody'd be the wiser. But on my way back the MPs got me, sir, and put me in the hoosegow."

"Where you belonged," Duncan said sternly. "You're lucky you weren't shot for desertion in time of war."

"But I didn't desert, sir. I just went to see my half-sister Tessie, who was so good to me when I was a kid."

"How are we supposed to know that?"

Bell blinked. "Know what?"

"That you went to see your sister? And how do we know you were going to come back?"

"Because I said I would!"

"Why should we believe you? How are we supposed to know you weren't lying?"

"Because —"

Duncan held up his hand for silence. "Shut up and listen to me. This is the army, not the Boy Scouts. You should know that by now. We have rules in the army, and if you break any more of them I'm going to court-martial you. And don't you ever come in here asking me to trust you. I don't trust anyone until they've proven themselves. According to your record, you're just another AWOL. Is that clear?"

Bell looked crestfallen. "Yes, sir."

"Good. You may return to your squad now."

"Yes, sir."

Bell shot to his feet and saluted smartly. Duncan returned the salute and Bell marched out of the office, closing the door behind him. Duncan sighed with relief and closed the folder containing Bell's records, wondering if he'd been effective with him.

Duncan often found it difficult dealing with his soldiers because of the vast class and intellectual difference between them. He believed they could never understand him on his level, so he had to get down on their level and speak to them in their own language. The problem was that his words often sounded stilted when they came out of his mouth. *I'm probably not a very good infantry officer,* he thought. *For that matter, I wasn't a good aviator either — that's for sure. And I quit the ambulance corps because it wasn't enough of a challenge.*

He sighed, wondering what in hell he *was* good at. He felt as if he'd been floundering ever since getting out of college. The best he could say of his marriage to Patricia was that it had produced two beautiful children. But his relationship with Patricia had degenerated to one of tolerance at best, with her pursuing the round of social events and him pursuing ... something he hadn't yet found. Sometimes he envied his brother Blake. Life seemed so easy for him, each challenge met and conquered with a self-confidence that neared bravado. Duncan, on the other hand, seemed to move from situation to situation, never quite succeeding, never quite finding what he wanted, never really coming into his own.

Outside the building, Private Sam Bell lit a cigarette. *What a hard-ass that Lieutenant Hunter is,* he thought. *I just got here and already the son-of-a-bitch is talking about court-martials. That's no way to say hello to a new man.*

Bell walked through the dark streets of Soulaucourt toward the outskirts of town. He passed a few soldiers and civilians, but no women — at least not any young ones. He'd thought that France would be crawling with women, but hadn't seen any except elderly ones so far. *Maybe they'll let me go to Paris someday. I bet there's lots of young women in Paris.*

He came to the area where his squad was billeted. Men sat around an open fire, eating tinned beef. They looked up as Bell entered, then returned to their food and conversation. Bell rubbed the palms of his hands together and approached the fire.

"Well," he said, "anyone save some chow for me?"

Sergeant Tucker tossed him a can. "Here you go, Bell."

Bell caught it and nudged two men apart so he could sit between them. He snapped the key off the can, inserted it in the sliver of metal and peeled the top off the can. Then he took a fork out of his shirt pocket and began to eat the dry stringy meat that American soldiers called "canned willie". The faces of the men glowed in the light of the fire, rifles stacked on the floor behind them.

"I don't understand," Corporal Canfield was saying, "how they could give us a goddamn gun that don't work. The son-of-a-bitchin' thing won't be no good at all in a fight."

"Well," said Private Stewart, "it works sometimes."

"Yeah, but it's liable not to work just when you need it."

"What gun is that?" Bell asked, jabbing his fork into his canned willie.

"The Chauchat," Canfield replied. "It's supposed to be a machine gun but it's a piece of shit as far as I'm concerned."

"Well," said Bell, "we dint have no machine guns in Mexico against old Pancho Villa. It was just rifles and cavalry sabers.

General Black Jack said charge and we charged. Why, I remember the time—"

"You mean the time you deserted?" Private Murphy interrupted him.

Bell jerked his head around toward Murphy, eyeing the big burly man, who had a pug nose and dark hair cut close to his scalp. Somebody snickered, and Bell felt his face become warm.

"You say that?" Bell asked Murphy.

Murphy nodded. "Yeah, I said that."

"I ain't never been a deserter, and nobody's gonna call me one and get away with it."

Murphy shrugged. "I just did."

Bell looked him in the eye. "Then I guess you and me are gonna have to go in back of the picket line and have this out."

"It don't make a damn to me either way."

Bell stood up, hooked his thumbs in his belt, then Murphy rose, and to Bell he looked like a mountain. Murphy grinned and rolled his shoulders.

"I been wanting to put my fist in your big mouth ever since you got here, you little shit."

"Well, you're gonna get that chance right now, you fat slob." Bell tried not to betray his awe of Murphy's huge muscular bulk.

Sergeant Tucker continued eating his canned willie. "I don't know nothin' about this," he said. "I ain't heard nothin' and I ain't seen nothin'."

They put on their helmets and filed out of the barn, all except for Sergeant Tucker and Corporal Canfield. The men walked into the fields, all of them accompanying Murphy. Bell was by himself, to their right, feeling fear right down to the pit of his stomach. It would be awfully difficult to beat a big guy

49

like Murphy, and he was all alone, with no friends to offer encouragement and boost his morale.

It's always like this, he thought. Wherever he went, he had trouble making friends. He didn't understand why. He always tried to be friendly. People said he talked too much, but he only said the things that came to his mind. Life would have been different, he often thought, if he hadn't been so short. *People always make fun of the little man. They look down on him in more ways than one.*

The men walked over the crest of a hill. "This is as good a place as any," said Private White.

Bell took off his helmet and laid it on the ground, then peeled off his shirt and dropped it into his helmet. Murphy stood stripped to the waist, surrounded by his friends.

"Bust him up, Murph," one of them said.

"Kick his ass."

Murphy wiped his nose with the back of his hand. "I'll put the little loudmouth right in the hospital." He pushed through the crowd of his friends and placed his fists on his hips. "You ready — you damned deserter?"

"I'm ready," said Sam Bell.

Bell raised his fists and stalked toward Murphy. Bell had done some semi-professional boxing in Massachusetts before joining the cavalry, and was not altogether ignorant about what to do, but he'd never fought anybody as big as Murphy before. *If he hits me he'll kill me,* he thought. *I'll have to keep moving and jab, jab, jab.*

Murphy held up his fists and stomped toward Bell, who got up on his toes and started dancing.

Private Giannini guffawed. "The little shit looks like a bantam rooster."

Bell danced from side to side in front of Murphy, feinting with his left hand, as Murphy lumbered after him, holding one fist over his chest and the other several inches forward.

"Kill him, Murph," said Private Skelton, a freckle-faced boy from Georgia.

Bell darted forward and threw his jab. It went over Murphy's guard and connected with his chin. Surprised, Murphy stepped backward, and Bell followed, jabbing twice more and landing an overhead right on Murphy's nose.

Bell danced backward to see if he'd done any damage, and to his surprise he saw blood dripping from Murphy's nose. Murphy touched the back of his hand to his nose, saw the blood, and became enraged. He charged Bell, swinging with both hands. Bell tried to block his punches, but simply wasn't strong enough. Murphy battered through his defenses and slugged him again and again in the face. Bell tried to bob and weave and managed to dodge a lot of blows, but many of them got through. He heard the other soldiers cheering Murphy on, tried to jab Murphy's face again, but Murphy was coming on too strong and Bell's blows flailed uselessly against Murphy's powerful arms. Bell rushed forward and tried to clinch Murphy to give himself a chance to clear his head, but Murphy pushed him off easily and landed a haymaker on Bell's right eye.

The next thing Bell knew he was lying stomach-down on the ground. He tried to get up, but couldn't get coordinated.

"Stomp him, Murph," somebody said.

Bell opened his eyes and saw Murphy's big boot a few inches from his face. *Oh, God, no,* he thought. He saw the boot go up, then felt a terrible crunching pain against the side of his face.

"What's going on there?" yelled a voice in the distance.

Duncan lay fully clothed on his bunk, reading Carl von

Clausewitz's *On War* by the light of a kerosene lamp. Von Clausewitz had died in 1831, but was still said to be one of the guiding lights of the German army. Duncan was curious to know what his enemy was thinking.

After reading three-quarters of the book, Duncan realized that much of the strategies and tactics were out of date, but some of the philosophy was useful even to an American infantry officer like himself. Von Clausewitz stressed bold action carefully planned in advance, and had insisted that the most important quality of a good combat commander was the ability to remain calm and think clearly even in the face of the most overwhelming reversals.

There was a commotion outside his door, and then a knock.

"Who is it?" he asked.

"Military police!" said the voice on the other side of the door.

"Just a minute!" Duncan slipped his feet into his shoes, walked to the door and opened it. Two military policemen were standing on either side of Private Murphy and Private Bell, the latter of whom had been in his office only two hours ago. Murphy had blood on his upper lip and Bell looked as though he had taken a terrific beating. His nose was mashed out of shape, his lip was split, and his eyes were blackened. Blood oozed from his nose, out of his mouth and from cuts on his face. He wiped the blood with the shirt he carried in his right hand.

"Sir," said one of the MPs, "we found them fighting back of the picket line."

"We wasn't fighting, sir!" Bell piped up. "We was just talking, and then I fell down."

Duncan frowned. It was such a blatant lie that he couldn't imagine how the man could bring himself to say it. He looked at the MPs. "You may return to your rounds. I'll expect your report in the morning."

"Yes, sir," they replied, saluting and marching off.

Duncan looked at Murphy. "You go into my office," he said. Then he turned to Bell. "You wait out here until I call for you."

Duncan followed Murphy into his office. Murphy stood at attention in front of the desk, and Duncan sat heavily on the chair behind it.

"All right," Duncan said, "what happened?"

Murphy's eyes darted around frantically. "Nothin', sir."

"Don't tell me nothing! The MPs didn't bring you here for nothing!"

"We was just talkin', sir ... just walkin' and talkin', and then we tripped over a log or somethin' and fell down and hurt ourselves."

Duncan glowered at him. "Don't you lie to me, soldier!"

Murphy blanched and made no reply.

"How could you beat up a man so much smaller than you?" Duncan asked, contempt in his voice. "You ought to be ashamed of yourself. Get out of here and tell Bell to come in. Then return to your quarters and have Sergeant Tucker report to me immediately. Do you think you can remember all that?" he added sarcastically.

"Yes, sir."

"Get going."

Murphy saluted and walked out of the room, closing the door behind him. A few seconds later there was a knock on the door.

"Get in here, Bell."

The door opened and Bell marched into Duncan's office as if on parade. He stopped abruptly in front of Duncan's desk and threw a sharp salute. "Private Bell reporting, sir!"

Duncan looked at his mangled, bloody features. "What went on out there, Bell?"

"Out where, sir?"

Duncan pounded his fist on his desk. "Don't act dumb with me!"

Bell jumped at the sound. "You mean where the MPs found us?"

"You know damn well that's where I mean!"

"Well, sir, you might have meant what went on while I was out there waiting in the hall."

Duncan narrowed his eyes at Bell. "You know very well what I mean — where the MPs found you."

"It was like I said, sir. I sort of fell down."

"You can't get hurt like that from falling down. You and Private Murphy were fighting — isn't that so?"

"No, sir."

"You've been in this company less than a day, and already you're in trouble again. I ought to ship you right to the stockade."

Bell stood as still and erect as a tree, the blood drying on his face. He'd taken a very severe beating, Duncan observed, but he wasn't going to admit it. He wasn't going to point his finger at the man who'd beaten him up.

"Do you know where the dressing station is?" Duncan asked.

"No, sir."

"It's on the same street as battalion headquarters. Ask somebody there and they'll direct you to it. Get yourself looked at and then return to your quarters." He was going to tell Bell not to fight anymore, but knew that prohibition would be futile. They were all hot-headed and would fight at the drop of a hat. "You're dismissed."

"May I ask a question, sir?"

"What is it?"

"Are you gonna punish me, sir?"

"I think you've been punished enough. Get going."

"Yes, sir."

Bell saluted and marched out of the office, leaving Duncan alone. Duncan stood and paced behind his chair, wondering how he could ever be a good officer when he disliked his men. They acted like a bunch of ignorant, drunken louts, only a peg or two above apes. They were always fighting, and you had to tell them something three times before they understood. In civilian life they had held the most menial jobs, the faceless ones in the crowds on the city sidewalks, people he had ignored as he walked past. How could you win a war with such men? The German soldiers were surely of a higher quality, for they had centuries of culture behind them.

There was a knock on his door.

"Come in."

Sergeant Tucker entered the office, helmet in hand. "You wanted to see me, sir?"

"Have a seat, sergeant."

Tucker sat opposite him at the desk, a Texan with lumpy, ruddy features, in the army for fifteen years. Like most of the other veterans, he had served on the Mexican border for much of that time. Duncan didn't have a close working relationship with Tucker and considered him as incompetent as all the others.

"I guess," Duncan began, "you know why I've called you here."

"Yes, sir."

"I want to know why you didn't stop Murphy and Bell from fighting — and *don't* tell me you didn't know they were fighting, because you know everything that happens in your platoon."

Tucker smiled. "Do you mind if I have a smoke, sir?" he drawled. "I think better when I smoke."

"Go right ahead."

"Thank you, sir."

Tucker took out his dirty white bag of Bull Durham and a pack of cigarette paper. He rolled a cigarette, licked the paper with his big pink tongue, and stuck the soggy misshapen product into his mouth. Duncan waited impatiently while the man methodically replaced his makings in his shirt pocket, lit the cigarette and exhaled a cloud of smoke.

"I knew they were gonna fight," Tucker said at last, nodding slowly.

"Why didn't you stop them?"

Tucker narrowed his eyes against the acrid smoke of his cigarette. "What would've been the point of that, sir? If I stopped them they would've fought some other time when I wasn't around, and it might've been worse because they would've had to hold in their anger that much longer. I thought it was best to just get it over with."

Duncan leaned back in his chair. "I think you exercised very poor judgment, sergeant. They might have hurt each other. Private Bell looks like he's hurt pretty badly as it is."

Tucker chuckled. "He ain't hurt that bad, sir. He stood up to Murphy, and now the men will respect him. I don't think there'll be any more trouble with Bell. Sometimes a man has to do a little fighting if he wants to be accepted into a new outfit. I guess you don't know that, sir, because you really ain't been in the army that long. You can't always go by the book, sir.

These are a rough bunch of boys you got here. The army ain't no picnic in the park."

"I know that," Duncan replied testily, "but I cannot condone fighting. The men are supposed to fight the Germans, not each other."

"They ain't no Germans around yet, sir, so they have to fight each other. They like to fight, sir. That's why they're soldiers. Fighting is what they're supposed to do."

Duncan felt he should say something to reassert his authority, but couldn't think of anything appropriate. "All right, Tucker," he growled. "There'd better not be any more of this. You may return to your platoon."

Sergeant Tucker stubbed out his cigarette, stood, saluted, and left the office, a scowl on his face. *Goddamn officers,* he thought. *Wouldn't know a bull's ass from a banjo.*

CHAPTER 7

Thanks to Everett DeWitt's letter of introduction, Blake Hunter now wore the uniform of a First Lieutenant in the American air service. He sat with his luggage outside the office of Major Carl Spaatz, commander of flight training at Issoudun. Blake was reporting for duty, and listening to a loud argument going on in the office.

"What's going on in there?" Blake asked the clerk sitting behind the desk nearby.

"That's Captain Rickenbacker," the clerk said.

"What's the problem?"

"Oh, I imagine he wants a transfer again."

The door flew open and a tall, lean captain with large ears stormed out, eyes flashing with rage. He slammed the door behind him and walked past Blake down the corridor.

Blake grinned. "He sure looks mad."

"He's always mad. I'll buzz the major."

The clerk pressed a button on his desk and spoke into the telephone, then said, "You can go in now, sir. You can leave your suitcase out here if you like."

Blake opened the door and entered the office. He saw a frowning middle-aged officer sitting behind the desk. Blake saluted him. "Lieutenant Hunter reporting for duty, sir."

"I hope you're not here to argue with me, Hunter."

"Oh no, sir."

"Good. Have a seat."

Blake sat down as Spaatz opened the big brown envelope, pulling out the records. He laid them on his desk and looked them over, then suddenly looked up at Blake. "Oh, you're the Hunter who flew for the French."

"Yes, sir."

"I didn't realize that. I thought you'd just arrived from the States." He resumed his perusal of Blake's records. "A hundred and eighty-three sorties — eight confirmed kills. Well, this is quite a record you've got here, Hunter. You're just the sort of person we've been looking for to train our new pilots. Your experience will be valuable."

"I had hoped to be assigned to a pursuit squadron, sir."

"Maybe later. Right now we need you to train pilots. That fellow who was just in here wants a pursuit squadron, too, but the service needs instructors. You can understand that, can't you, Hunter?"

Blake shrugged. "I suppose so, sir."

"Good. Well, that's all for now. Report to my office at 0800 hours in the morning and I'll have something for you to do." Spaatz stood behind his desk and held out his hand. "Welcome aboard, Hunter."

"Thank you, sir."

Blake left Spaatz's and carried his suitcase to the bachelor officers' quarters, where he was assigned a private room, small but adequate. He was hungry, so he dropped his suitcases on the bed and immediately went downstairs to the officers' club.

He finally located the dining room. Paintings and photographs of airplanes decorated the walls, and ribbons of brightly colored paper hung from the ceiling. Flight officers sat at the bar and around the tables, having animated conversations.

Blake wanted a good stiff drink before ordering his meal. He found a space at the bar, but the bartender was busy pouring drinks at the other end, where some officers were singing drunkenly.

"You look familiar," said a voice to his left. Blake turned and saw the officer who'd stormed out of Major Spaatz's office. "Oh, hello there," he said with a smile.

"Where do I know you from?" the captain asked. "Were you one of my students?"

"No," Blake said. "You might have seen me outside Major Spaatz's office a little while ago. I was waiting to go in when you were coming out."

"Ah," said Rickenbacker. "So that's it. You've just arrived?"

"That's right."

"How are things in the States?"

"I wouldn't know. I haven't been there since 1914."

The captain knitted his eyebrows together. "Where the hell were you?"

"Here in France. I was flying with the French *Aéronautique*, and just switched over."

The captain sat more erectly on his stool and looked Blake up and down. "What's your name?"

"Blake Hunter."

The captain smiled. "I've heard of you, Hunter. My name's Rickenbacker. Eddie Rickenbacker."

They shook hands.

"I hope you won't regret coming here," Rickenbacker said.

"Why would I?"

"You're going to be an instructor, aren't you?"

"Yes."

"Once you become an instructor at Issoudun, it's not easy to get out."

"I told Major Spaatz I wanted to be transferred to a pursuit squadron as soon as possible."

"I've been after him to transfer me for four months, and I'm still here."

The bartender leaned toward them. "May I help you, gentlemen?"

Blake ordered whisky for himself and for Rickenbacker.

"Why won't he transfer you?" Blake asked, reaching for his glass.

"He says he needs instructors."

Blake raised his glass and took a few gulps. "I won't mind instructing for a little while, but if he doesn't let me out of here by the end of the year, I'll get out some other way."

"You must have a friend someplace."

"I do. Maybe he can do something for you."

"I got a friend someplace, too," Rickenbacker said bitterly. "I used to be Pershing's chauffeur. He let me transfer to the air service, but now I can't get in to see him anymore. I might have to do something real crazy to get out of here."

Blake raised his glass to his lips and began to feel depressed. *I hope I don't have to spend the rest of the war training other pilots to do what I want to do*, he thought.

CHAPTER 8

Kaiser Wilhelm II sat at his desk in the Imperial Palace in Berlin, studying maps of combat zones. The door opened and two elderly officers bedecked with medals entered. Side by side, they walked to the desk and saluted. The Kaiser returned their salute and asked them to be seated.

"I have important news," the Kaiser said gravely. 'I have just received word that the Bolsheviks have seized power in Moscow."

The Kaiser paused to let the information sink in. Field Marshal Paul Ludwig von Hindenburg, sitting in front of the Kaiser, rested his hands on the hilt of his sword as if it were a cane perched between his legs. He smiled faintly, for he recognized the implications of the Kaiser's remark. Colonel-General Erich Ludendorff, seated next to him, showed no reaction whatever.

Kaiser Wilhelm II continued, "I anticipate that the Bolsheviks will take Russia out of the war within the next few months. That means we shall be able to transfer the bulk of our troops on the Eastern Front to the West. Therefore, I am instructing you gentlemen to draw up plans for a major offensive in the West, to be launched as soon as Russia is eliminated as an adversary. We want to act quickly, before the Americans build up their forces in the West. The British and the French are just about finished, and the Americans hold the key to this war, as I am sure you know. Therefore we must strike with unremitting violence, and win this war once and for all!"

"Yes, Your Excellency," said Hindenburg.

"To be sure," agreed Ludendorff. "And perhaps we can start withdrawing men from the East now. The Russians probably won't be much of a factor from now on."

Hindenburg turned to Ludendorff. "We shouldn't make any dangerous assumptions. The Russian bear might still have a lot of life in him."

"I doubt it, but perhaps you are right," Ludendorff replied. "At any rate, I will direct the general staff to begin making plans, and supervise this offensive myself, of course. But with all due respect, Your Excellency, I doubt very much if the Americans will be as much of a factor as you think. From all I hear, they are just civilians in uniform. Once bullets start flying over their heads, they will break and run. Why, I'm told that they're all in training in France, and that none of them have taken a position at the front yet. They still might not be on the line when we launch this offensive. I think the Americans are the great myth of this war. Everybody thinks they are such an important factor, but I maintain my belief that they will vanish like smoke once they get a taste of German bullets and bayonets."

"That may be so," the Kaiser replied, "but at this point I do not think it prudent to underestimate them. Americans are a rough and brawling people, and it may not take much to get them ready for war."

Hindenburg leaned forward, resting his hands on his sword. "We shall know soon enough, Your Excellency. They will not be in training for ever."

CHAPTER 9

Everett Dewitt sat with Danielle Giraud in a parterre box in the Théâtre du Châtelet, watching a performance of the Ballets Russes. On stage, dancers dressed as acrobats, horses and Chinamen cavorted about with a young American ballerina. Everett was flabbergasted; he'd never seen anything like it in his life. The spectacle before him bore no resemblance whatever to classical ballet, with which he was familiar. And the music, costumes and sets were extremely bizarre. He didn't know whether he liked it or not.

Opening his program, he looked to see who was responsible for the dance. Running his finger down the page, which he could barely read in the dim light, he found that the choreography was by Léonide Massine, the music by Erik Satie, and the scenery and costumes by Pablo Picasso. He hadn't heard of any of these people before, although he had seen something in the newspapers about the Ballets Russes's impresario, Serge Diaghilev.

"Stop rustling your program," Danielle whispered.

"Sorry."

Everett placed the program on his lap and continued to watch the dance. It was the last of the evening, then he would take Danielle home. He'd been seeing her for two months, taking her to lunches, dinners and various entertainments. They had reached the point where she let him kiss her goodnight. Everett was smitten by her, and wanted very much to take her to bed. He wondered if this should be the night for him to make his main effort in that direction.

The ballet ended and the audience applauded thunderously. The curtain fell, the lights came up, and the curtain rose again, revealing the dancers standing in line to take their bows. Danielle got to her feet and clapped her hands. In the balcony, the audience was shouting, "Bravo!" Everett stood beside Danielle, smelling her apple-blossom perfume, and applauding with the rest of the audience. There were three curtain calls, and bouquets of flowers rained upon the stage. Then the curtain fell for the last time and the audience began moving to the exits.

Everett and Danielle were swept along with the ocean of people to the lobby. The women were dressed in the latest evening fashions, and many of the men wore military uniforms representing several countries, with France, England and the United States predominating. Civilian men wore tuxedos.

"Well," said Danielle as they moved outside with the crowd. "Did you like it?"

"I think I did," he said, "though it was rather ... unconventional." He looked at the throng lining the curb, jockeying for cabs. "Let's walk to the corner. It might be easier to get a cab there."

They moved through the swarms of people beneath the marquee and finally broke loose from them. Danielle adjusted her mouton jacket while Everett buttoned his trench coat and tightened the belt against the cold night air.

"Would you like a drink?" he asked.

"Where?"

"The Ritz?"

"I am so tired of the Ritz," she said. "Too much noise."

"We could go to a quiet little place — I know of several."

"I'm sure you do, but I really don't feel the need for liquid refreshment. I know! Let's take a carriage through the Bois de Boulogne!"

"Marvelous idea," Everett said, thinking of cuddling with her in that romantic setting.

He finally succeeded in hailing a cab, and told the driver to take them to the Bois de Boulogne. They rode through the darkened city, passing famous buildings and monuments. Even the Eiffel Tower was unlit, due to the fear of German bomb attacks.

They reached the Bois de Boulogne and transferred from the taxi cab to a horse-drawn carriage. It was open, with a chair of black leather, and they sat close to each other, their bodies touching, as the driver flicked his whip in the air. The horse clip-clopped on the winding road into the dark forest.

When the city streets were out of sight, Everett placed his arm around Danielle's shoulder and kissed her cheek. "I love you," he whispered.

"Be still and look at the trees."

"I can't."

He turned her face to him and kissed her lips. She touched her hand to his cheek and he felt the warmth of her breath. They kissed again, and he gazed into her eyes.

"Whenever I tell you I love you, you change the subject," he whispered. "Why is that?"

"That is not the sort of question a gentleman asks."

"It most assuredly is. We're not exactly strangers anymore, you know."

"What are we, then?"

He kissed her cheek. "I'm not sure."

"Neither am I."

"Why can't you admit that you don't love me?"

"Why are you asking me all these questions?"

"You shouldn't answer a question with a question."

"Why not?"

"You just did it again."

She pushed him away. "I shall answer questions any way I like. If you were as smart as you think, you would know that I truly am answering your questions."

He took out his cigarettes, offered her one and placed one between his lips. He lit both cigarettes and leaned back, looking at the huge old trees towering over the road.

"You're such a child sometimes," he said, annoyed.

She held her cigarette between two fingers and puffed elegantly. "You're just upset because I didn't give you the answer you want. But I did give you an answer."

"You gave me another question."

"It was my answer. You don't understand it for the same reason you don't understand the Ballets Russes. It's too abstract for you."

"Obscure would be a better word. I don't understand why some people refuse to state their views clearly."

She looked at him haughtily. "Some views are subtle, and everyone knows that subtleties are beyond the intellectual range of many people."

If she were anyone else he would have deposited her at home immediately and never seen her again. He glanced at her, seeing the moonlight glinting on her golden hair. She looked regal and utterly magnificent. He was afraid of the power she had over him.

He murmured, "Let's not argue."

"You are the one who is arguing."

He kissed her cheek. "I love you," he said, his lips brushing her ear. "Can't you see that?"

"Yes," she said distractedly.

He hesitated, then said softly, "Come home with me."

"What!"

"Come home with me,"

"What in heaven's name for?"

"You know very well what for."

"Do not be ridiculous!" She pushed him away. "The very idea!"

He looked at her morosely. "So you don't love me."

"I never said that."

"That's how you feel."

"That is your opinion."

"What's *your* opinion?"

"I am a Roman Catholic, and I may not be very religious, but I will never sleep with any man to whom I am not married. You probably do not realize it — you are, after all, an American — but your squalid proposition is an insult."

He looked at her, amazed. "Are you serious?"

She turned her head and looked him directly in the eye. "In the world I live in, when a man is in love with a woman he tells her by asking her to marry him. And *not* by asking her to come to his ridiculous little room."

"It's not that ridiculous," he said, trying to keep his tone light, to conceal his hurt.

"Apparently you are not what I thought you were. You have become just another soldier trying to have sex with a girl, and willing to say anything to get it."

He frowned. "You know that's not true, Danielle."

"How do I know that's not true?" She handed him her cigarette butt. "Put this out, please."

He stubbed it against the sole of his boot and tossed it over his shoulder. "I hadn't thought of marriage," he stammered.

"Life is so uncertain these days. I only knew that I loved you and wanted to be with you."

"I quite understand," she replied. "It's not unusual for people to be selfish. You thought you would have some fun with me and then go on to the next girl."

"It wasn't like that at all, and you know it."

"I know no such thing."

He smiled and stroked her cheek. "What must I do to change your mind? Ask you to marry me right now?"

Her eyes flashed with anger. "You don't have to do anything you don't want to do, Lieutenant DeWitt. No — I take that back. I would like you to take me home immediately!"

"But Danielle —"

"I said immediately."

Everett hesitated, then leaned forward, telling the driver to take them back to the Avenue Victor Hugo where they could get a cab.

"So soon?" asked the driver.

"Yes."

The driver turned around in the middle of the street and headed back. Everett looked sideways at Danielle, at her magnificent profile. She was sitting stiff as a statue and staring straight ahead. He wondered what to do. Had she been waiting for him to propose to her all along?

He realized with dismay that he should not have asked her to come to his room. She was a beautiful young woman from a good family, and his question had evidently been a breach of manners. You couldn't proposition American women from good families like that either, but the atmosphere of Paris and the behavior of his fellow officers were having a bad influence on him, warping his judgment.

"I'm sorry," he said. "I can see that I've made a terrible blunder."

She didn't reply.

He offered her another cigarette, but she ignored him. He lit one for himself and inhaled deeply, then blew the smoke at the trees. "I guess I'm just not sure about whether or not I want to get married."

"Don't worry about it," she said coldly. "I'm sure there are many women in Paris who will go to your room, or take you to theirs. You might have to pay them a few francs, but I don't think you will mind that."

"That's a cruel thing to say."

"It's nothing compared to what you have said to me." He sighed. "Regardless of what you think, I really do love you, Danielle."

"Who needs your kind of love?"

"I don't think you're being fair. You've put the worst possible interpretation on my intentions, but I apologize anyway. I'm afraid I can't do more than that."

"You don't have to do more than that," she said. "In fact, you don't have to do anything at all, Everett, because we are not going to see each other anymore."

CHAPTER 10

In November, the Twenty-third Regiment of the Second Division was moved up to a quiet section of the line in the Lorraine area to get some experience of actual conditions at the front. The French Fifty-eighth Regiment, whom they relieved, were resentful of the Americans' arrival; the sector was considered by the French to be a rest area, and to leave it meant going to a more active area. Grumbling and fearful, they left their elaborate network of trenches, and the doughboys piled in.

It was a cold, cloudy day. Lieutenant Duncan Hunter stood on the edge of a trench, watching his men moving back and forth inside it, inspecting the fortifications and poking their heads inside the dugouts and pillboxes. They were in high spirits, eager to start fighting the Germans, who were around five hundred yards away across no-man's land.

"I think I can see the Hun bastards!" said Private Gianinni.

"Where?" asked Private Hughes.

Gianinni pointed. "Over there."

"Well, if you can see them, they can see you. We'd better keep our heads down."

Duncan jumped into the trench and walked through it, his helmet slanted over his eyes and his forty-five dangling in its holster from his waist. He wore boots, leggings and his Sam Browne belt. His jacket had become loose on him because he'd lost weight during the past few months, but his lean body had lost none of its strength.

The trench was wickered and sandbagged, constructed with turns every several yards to limit the damage a direct hit from an artillery shell would make. It smelled of earth and urine, and was muddy at the bottom. It was the forward trench, and behind it were secondary and reserve trenches, so that the doughboys could fall back to shelter in the event of a strong German attack.

A group of men in front of him began to jump and shout.

"It's a rat!" yelled Private Skelton.

"Kill the son-of-a-bitch!" shouted Private White.

Private Stewart swung his rifle at the ground, and Duncan saw a furry gray rat scramble up the side of the trench and run into no-man's land.

"That's it!" said Skelton. "Go bite the goddamn Huns!"

Duncan approached the group of men. "Stewart!" he said.

Stewart came to attention. "Yes, sir?"

Duncan walked up to him. "Do you think your rifle is a baseball bat, Stewart?"

"No, sir."

"Then why are you using it as a baseball bat?"

"I don't know, sir."

"What if you'd broken the stock? What would you use to fight with then?"

"The stock's made of awful strong wood, sir. It'd take more than that to break it."

Duncan could see the man was nervous, just as all of them were whenever he criticized them. Stewart had a pimply face and a nose like a carrot. He couldn't be much more than eighteen. Duncan leaned closer toward him and made his voice hard.

"I don't ever want to see you using your weapon for anything other than what it was intended. Is that clear, Stewart?"

"Yes, sir."

"Carry on."

"Yes, sir."

Duncan walked past him and the others, who stood silently and looked at him with respect born of fear. He knew they didn't like him, but he didn't care. He spotted Sergeant Tucker.

"May I have a few words with you, Sergeant?"

"Yes, sir." Tucker sighed, knowing what was coming.

They walked several paces away from the other men. Duncan eyed Tucker, who looked back unflinchingly. Duncan knew that Tucker was the only man in the platoon who wasn't afraid of him, and often wondered whether that was good or bad.

"Did you see what Private Stewart was just doing with his rifle, Sergeant?"

"Yes, sir."

"Why didn't you stop him?"

"You stopped him before I had a chance to, sir."

"It seems to me that the men should know better than that by now. We're at the front and we should all behave in a soldierly manner."

"Well," Tucker said with a smile, "they're a playful bunch, sir."

"They're going to have to grow up, Sergeant. We can't tolerate any foolishness in this combat zone. I expect you to make sure there are no repetitions of that sorry spectacle. Is that clear?"

"I'll do my best, sir."

"Come with me. I want to show you where you'll deploy the machine guns."

"Yes, sir."

A shot rang out. Duncan and Sergeant Tucker spun around.

"I got him!" shouted the unmistakable voice of Private Sam Bell.

"That fool," Duncan muttered.

Duncan and Tucker charged through the trench toward Bell's voice. Other men followed them. They turned a corner and saw Bell surrounded by three other soldiers. Bell held his rifle in the air and danced around in the trench. "I got him — I got him!"

Duncan charged toward Bell. "What the hell do you think you're doing?"

Bell snapped to attention. "Me, sir?"

"Did you just fire your weapon?"

"Yes, sir!" Bell replied proudly, puffing out his chest. "And I hit the son-of-a-bitch, too."

Duncan planted his fists on his hips and leaned toward Bell. "Who told you to fire your rifle?"

"Nobody, sir."

"Then why in the hell did you fire it?"

"Because I saw a German, sir, and I shot the son-of-a-bitch."

Duncan s face turned red with rage. "You don't fire a goddamn thing unless you get permission. Do you hear me?"

"Yes, sir!" Bell replied, glancing uncertainly at Tucker.

"You probably didn't hit a damn thing anyway!" Duncan growled.

"But I saw him fall, sir!"

Corporal Canfield, standing nearby, shuffled his feet. "I saw him go down too, sir."

Duncan blinked, feeling the tide turning against him.

"You saw who go down?"

"The German, sir. I spotted him too and was looking at him when Private Bell fired. The German's whole head and part of his shoulders were showing. As soon as Private Bell fired, the German dropped out of sight."

There were footsteps and a commotion on the other side of the trench. Captain Harrington, the company commander, appeared with his executive officer, Lieutenant Dufford.

"What the hell's going on here?" demanded Harrington, a craggy-faced officer who'd risen from the ranks.

Duncan snapped to attention. "This man fired his rifle without permission, sir," he said, indicating Private Bell.

"I killed the son-of-a-bitch," Bell said weakly.

Harrington raised his bushy eyebrows. "You killed what son-of-a-bitch?"

"The German son-of-a-bitch, sir." Bell pointed toward the German lines. "I saw him over there and I shot him."

"How do you know you shot him?"

"I saw him go down."

Corporal Canfield cleared his throat. "I saw him go down too, sir."

"He might've ducked," Captain Harrington said, "but good work anyway." He patted Bell on the shoulder. "Shows you were keeping your eyes open. All men on duty should keep their eyes open at all times. This may be a quiet sector, but it might get hot — you never know."

Duncan felt all his men looking at him. "But, sir," he said, "I thought the men weren't to fire their weapons unless ordered to do so."

"That's right, Lieutenant Hunter, but the situation is a little different now that we're at the front. I didn't think the men would have anything to shoot at in this particular sector, but evidently targets can present themselves, and the men should take advantage of them." He turned to the men standing nearby. "But I don't want anybody shooting just for the hell of it, understand?"

They all nodded.

"Carry on. Lieutenant Hunter — I'd like to speak with you alone for a moment."

"Yes, sir."

Duncan followed Captain Harrington and Lieutenant Dufford back to the other side of the trench, where Harrington stopped and examined Duncan's face.

"I take it that you chewed that man out?"

"I did, sir."

"I don't think you should have, but I suppose it was my fault, since my orders weren't explicit. Still, you shouldn't discourage your men from being aggressive, and you shouldn't make a mountain out of a molehill."

"Sir," said Duncan, "I thought your orders were very explicit. You said that the men weren't supposed to fire their weapons unless ordered to do so. What could be clearer than that?"

Harrington scowled. "You're not very flexible, Lieutenant. I don't know how you can learn to be flexible, but you've got to learn somehow. I hope you'll try."

"I'll do my best, sir," Duncan replied, "but I've always believed that to make my platoon an efficient combat unit, it should function as smoothly and unequivocally as a machine."

"Men aren't machines, Lieutenant Hunter," Harrington said gravely. "And that includes you and me. That is all. Carry on."

"Yes, sir."

Captain Harrington turned and walked away, followed by Lieutenant Dufford. Duncan watched them go, taking off his helmet and wiping his forehead with the back of his sleeve. *I'm getting off to a bad start at the front,* he thought. *The men think I made a fool of myself and I probably did. Somehow I'll have to try to turn this situation around.*

"Sergeant Tucker!" he shouted.

"Yes, sir!"

"Let's go check those machine guns!"

On the other side of no-man's land, the German soldiers huddled over the body of their comrade.

"Right between the eyes," said Corporal Schneidhuber, shaking his head.

"I told him to keep his head down, but he would not listen," said Private Bosch. "He always wants to see what's going on."

"Let that be a lesson to all of you rookies," said Schneidhuber. "Keep your damned heads down."

They heard the rapid approach of footsteps and looked up. A private with a thin black mustache and burning eyes was moving swiftly through the trench. He carried a leather dispatch pouch and wore a soft pancake-styled cap.

The private slowed down and looked at the fallen soldier. "What happened to him?"

"Couldn't keep his head down," replied Schneidhuber. "Got it right between the eyes."

The private frowned. "If he couldn't keep his head down, he got what he deserved." He quickened his pace and passed them by, continuing through the trench and turning right at the corner.

"Cold-blooded one, isn't he?" asked Private Haushofer, kneeling over the body.

Schneidhuber nodded. "He's been around for a long time. He's one of the original regimental runners." He stood up and stretched. "Bosch, get a medical orderly."

77

"Yes, Corporal Schneidhuber."

In the trench perpendicular to the one in which the dead soldier lay, the private with the dispatches dodged around other soldiers as he made his way to the headquarters of the Third Company.

He was Private Adolf Hitler. He had enlisted in the army on the day Germany declared war, and participated in many of the biggest battles, so dead soldiers no longer affected him. He had been awarded the Iron Cross Second Class for bravery under fire.

He reached the dugout that served as the Third Sturm Company's headquarters, and went inside. A corporal sat behind a makeshift desk.

"I have an important dispatch for the captain," the private said.

"Go right in."

The private walked around the desk and pushed aside the curtain to the captain's office. Walking inside, he marched to the captain's desk and saluted.

"Private Adolf Hitler, reporting with a dispatch from Colonel Engelhardt, sir."

Captain Karl Ritter von Beck held out his hand. "Give it here. Were you ordered to wait for a reply?"

"No, sir." Private Hitler took the envelope from his dispatch case and handed it to Captain Beck.

"Wait anyway. I might have something to send back. You may stand at ease."

"Thank you, sir."

Hitler placed his arms behind his back and relaxed as Captain Beck read the message. It stated that a German spy had reported seeing an American military unit move into the line opposite the List Regiment, of which the Third Sturm Company was part. The message ordered the Third Sturm Company to attack the Americans opposite them that night to find out what kind of soldiers they were, and take as many prisoners as possible. Captain Beck was to report to regimental headquarters at 1300 hours to receive his orders in greater detail. He was to make certain his men would be especially quiet, so as not to alert the Americans that the attack was imminent. Beck took a piece of paper and wrote that he would be at regimental headquarters at 1300 hours, along with his adjutant.

"Take this back with you," he said, handing the note to Hitler.

"Yes, sir. Anything else, sir?"

"That will be all."

"Yes, sir." Hitler saluted and walked quickly out of the orderly room.

By ten o'clock in the morning, Lieutenant Duncan Hunter had his platoon deployed with textbook precision. His two machine guns were in bunkers and had overlapping fields of fire. His two trench mortars were set up in the secondary trench and had all available targets zeroed in. Half the platoon was manning trenches, the rest improving fortifications or performing other types of work on the position.

Soldiers from the Signal Corps checked the communication wires and installed telephones. An order had come down from battalion headquarters directing all companies to reinforce their positions with additional barbed wire. Duncan planned to lead his men out to perform that task at night. All in all, things were going pretty well. He hoped it would stay quiet until he and his men learned the ropes.

He had selected a centrally located bunker for his platoon's command post, wooden cots built into its walls by the French. Now seated at his desk, he heard the clink of shovel against earth nearby. Opening his knapsack, he took out some paper and an envelope to write his mother a letter. He wanted to tell her he was all right because he knew that she worried, but he wouldn't mention that he'd moved to the front. There was always the danger that the Germans might capture the letter and use it to help determine troop dispositions behind the Allied lines.

Outside, Private Bell proudly and happily walked to the latrine while singing:

'Won't you pick up your dress for a soldier,
For a poor old soldier boooyyy...'

Bell felt marvelous. He was the first man in the company, and maybe in the whole regiment, to kill a German, and that had made him the center of attraction, which he loved. Soldiers waved to him and said hello. They were already calling him Eagle-Eye Bell.

He'd been accepted into the platoon since his fight with Murphy, and now was one of the most popular men. He'd even gained additional status because Lieutenant Hunter had been made to look foolish because of him. The lieutenant wasn't very popular in the platoon.

He walked into the latrine, a smelly cavern with a roof of dirt and stones. A big hole, with a pole stretched over it, was the toilet. The pole was perched on Y-shaped posts, and you pulled down your pants and sat on the pole with your rear end hanging over it.

'Won't you pick up your dress for a soldier,
For a poor old soldier boy.'

Along the far wall were urinals consisting of funnels with the Kaiser's face painted on them. Bell took out a cigarette and lit up while emptying his bowels. The room stank horribly, but Bell had been using outside latrines for so long he was used to them.

When finished, he buttoned up his pants and left the latrine. Looking around, he felt great to be alive, even though it was a cold, gloomy day. He loved the rough and ready life of soldiering and the camaraderie of the front lines. He also liked the country he was in, the rolling hills and fields with their patches of forests and small villages with red-tiled roofs. The scuttlebutt said there was a whorehouse in one of the towns nearby, and Bell was trying to figure a way to get there with a few of the guys.

He jumped back into the main trench and made his way back to his position, passing soldiers lined up, smoking cigarettes and joking around. They were all in high spirits and happy to be up on the line at last.

Bell reached his position in the second platoon, between Private Bailey and Private White. "Everything come out all right?" asked White, a cigarette dangling from the corner of his mouth.

Bell laughed. "See any Fritzies?"

"Nope. They've been real quiet over there."

"Figures," Bell said. "This is supposed to be a rest area — for us and them."

Private Bailey spat into the mud. "Maybe they'll let us do one of them attacks that we been practicing so much."

Bell shook his head. "Not yet they won't. They don't think we're ready."

"We're ready."

"I know we're ready, but they don't think so. Shit, when we go after them Fritzies, they won't know what hit 'em."

White held up his rifle. "I'm gonna stick this right up the Kaiser's ass."

"He'd probably like it," Bell said.

"Here comes the padre."

Bell saw Father Donahue turn the corner and walk into the trench. He was a roly-poly man with a red nose and was always smiling.

"How're we doing, boys?" he asked with a wave of his hand. He was dressed like any other officer, except that he had crosses on his lapels and wore no pistol.

"Just fine, Father," White replied.

Father Donahue looked at the sky. "Looks like rain."

"Sure does."

"Keep dry, boys."

"Hey, Father," said White. "You hear the news?"

Father Donahue stopped. "What news?"

"Bell here killed a German."

Father Donahue's mouth opened, and he appeared confused for a few seconds. Then he held out his hand to Bell. "Congratulations, soldier."

"Thank you, sir."

"Keep up the good work, boys." Father Donahue waved at them and proceeded to the next trench.

Bell shook his head. "That guy always gets me."

White chuckled. "I knew it'd shake his tree when I told him you shot a German. He didn't know whether to shit or go blind for a while there."

"Sometimes I feel sorry for him," Bailey said. "He don't belong here."

The men ate canned beans for lunch, then began their first afternoon at the front. At three o'clock it began to rain, so they congregated in bunkers where they smoked cigarettes, played cards and swapped stories. Dinner was more canned willie. As dusk fell, trucks arrived with the barbed wire that was supposed to be laid in no-man's land that night, to back up the barbed wire that was already there. The doughboys unloaded the stiff coils of barbed wire and stacked them behind the trenches. Many fingers were cut and uniforms torn.

When the work was finished, the men returned to their dugouts. At eight o'clock guards were posted, and men not on duty were permitted to sleep.

Sam Bell was one of the guards standing alone in a section of the trench, shivering miserably as rain dropped on to his helmet. His rifle with bayonet attached leaned against the wall of the trench within grabbing distance. His teeth chattered, and he moved his soaked feet around in the mud in an effort to keep them warm. Occasionally he raised his head and peered into no-man's land. He couldn't see farther than ten yards in front of him, and it reminded him of nights of guard duty in Mexico, where he'd had to worry about some *bandito* suddenly appearing out of the darkness and sticking a shiv into his gut.

If he hadn't pulled so much guard duty already in his military career, he would have been frightened. Perhaps that was why he'd been put on guard this first night: he was experienced. But despite his experience, he was never able to rid himself of the night's uncertainties. Sometimes his eyes played tricks on him and he thought he saw German spiked helmets out there, although the Germans hadn't worn spiked helmets since 1915.

He thought he heard footsteps and quickly brought his rifle to his shoulder, but no one appeared.

His helmet was heavy on his head. Sometimes his neck muscles ached from wearing the damn thing. And it magnified the ping of raindrops falling on to it.

He ducked in the trench, took off the helmet and ran his fingers through his curly hair, wondering if the helmet really would stop a bullet. He doubted it, but put it back on his head nonetheless.

What would the women back in New Bedford think if they could see him at the front? They'd probably admire him, he thought, as they never had when he was a waiter in that old hash house down on the docks. Hell, they'd probably even let him into their beds. Looking over the top of the trench again, he parted his lips and sang softly:

'Won't you pick up your dress for a soldier,
For a poor old soldier boy…'

Lieutenant Hunter heard a sound and sat upright in bed. Evidently the sound was footsteps outside his bunker, probably just the changing of the guard. He glanced at his watch to make sure: midnight exactly. The guards changed every two hours, so that was who he had heard. *Nothing to worry about. Go back to sleep.*

He lay back on the hard wood, resting his head on his pack and listening to the rain pattering on the roof. In two and a half hours he'd have to get up and prepare to lead the men into no-man's land with additional barbed wire. He was a little nervous about the first time in his life that he'd be exposed to real danger.

He was apprehensive, not just for himself but also for his men. If an ordinary soldier became scared, that was his own business. But if an officer was scared, it undermined the efforts of all the men under him.

After Duncan had washed out of flight school, he'd thought about becoming an ordinary foot soldier, but his parents would never have stood for that, and his friends would have considered him a freak, so he had become an officer and felt like even more of a freak. *I might have made a decent soldier,* he thought, *but I'm not such a good officer.*

Nervous, he swung around and planted his feet on the floor, wishing there was something he could do. Now he understood why most of the men smoked. Maybe he should start smoking. A drink might not be so bad, either.

I've got to calm down, he told himself. *The men are relying on me and I can't let them down.* He looked at his watch and wondered what he would do with himself until it was time to get to work.

Five hundred yards away in the German trenches, the soldiers of *Sturm* Company Three prepared for their foray into the American trenches. They sat in their bunkers and dugouts nearly identical to those in which the doughboys were sleeping, and sharpened trench knives with pocket whetstones. Some blew sand from the wires that activated their potato-masher grenades. The officers oiled their Lugers and the armorer passed out ammunition. It would be a quick attack, calculated to surprise the Americans. The Sturm soldiers would kill as many as possible, capture several for questioning, destroy everything in sight, then speed back to their trenches.

Outside in the open trenches, the mortar squads huddled around their weapons, which looked like narrow stovepipes on legs. Beside them were stacked boxes of mortar rounds which they would pour into the American position when the signal was given. Farther back were the howitzers and artillery pieces which would also help launch the attack. The Kaiser's soldiers waiting in the trenches were anxious to inflict a defeat upon the Americans. Minutes seemed to crawl by.

In his bunker, Captain Beck strapped on his Luger. His eyes glittered underneath the brim of his helmet and he smiled faintly, for he was confident of the outcome of the raid into the American position.

Lieutenant Strauss, his adjutant, stood in the corner. "I wish I could go with you."

"Don't be a fool," Beck replied.

Beck left the office and entered the room occupied by his orderly, Corporal Weber, who sat behind a desk. Private Hitler, the regimental orderly, sat on a chair nearby, his soft cap in his lap. He was to report the results of the raid to regimental headquarters. The light of a kerosene lamp shone on his gaunt features as he gazed at Captain Beck with undisguised admiration.

Beck nodded to him and went outside to the trench, deserted except for a lone guard who stood on a boulder and stared out through glassy eyes at no-man's land. Beck passed him. The rain was moderately heavy now, but Beck wore no trench coat because it would slow him down. Speed was of the essence on an operation like this.

He entered the dugout on the other side of the trench and saw a group of men huddled around a kerosene lamp, their hair matted and dirty faces unshaven, preparing their equipment for the raid.

"Sergeant Feldheimer?" asked Beck.

The lanky sergeant stood up. "Yes, sir?"

"Have the men fall out into the trench."

Beck turned and walked back to the middle of the trench, followed by the men who'd been in the dugout. They lined up against the parapets, carrying rifles and bayonets, some lugging Bangalore torpedoes. Beck could feel their tension and anxiety, or maybe it was his own; he wasn't sure. No matter how easy the raid, a few men would always be lost. Would he, after numerous major and minor battles spanning nearly four years, meet his own end tonight in the muddy fields of France?

The trench filled with men, and from nearby trenches he could hear the stomp of boots and clatter of equipment. He looked at his watch. It was nearly one o'clock in the morning.

"Just a few more minutes, boys," he said.

His men looked at one another. Most were battle-seasoned veterans like himself, and had fought on the Marne, at Ypres and on the Somme. They were confident that they were members of the finest army in the world. Tonight they would have the honor of bloodying the Americans for the first time.

Private Hitler came out of the bunker and looked at them, his heart swelling with pride in the Fatherland. They were such fine men, so noble and magnificent. He wished he could go with them, but he'd volunteered for battle duty many times and had been told he was too valuable as a runner.

Suddenly the air was rent with the booming sound of artillery explosions. The bombardment was beginning, and they could hear the shells whistling over their heads on their way to the American lines. Private Hitler ran to the parapet and peered over it as the shells rained down in orange and red explosions on the American positions.

Duncan Hunter was lacing his boots when the first shell landed a few hundred yards away. Surprised, he raised his head. Then a shell landed near his bunker, the explosion nearly bursting his eardrums. The wall and ceiling caved in and he fell to the floor. The air was filled with smoke and dirt. He blacked out for a few seconds, and when consciousness returned he lay in a tiny space with dirt covering his legs and timbers slanting in all directions. He looked up and saw a huge jagged hole in the roof. The door flew open and Sergeant Tucker charged in.

"Are you all right, sir?"

"I think so…"

"Let me help you up, sir."

Sergeant Tucker grabbed Duncan under the arm and pulled him to his feet. Duncan moved his limbs and took a few steps.

"I'm all right," he said, still slightly dazed.

"You're bleeding from your ears, sir."

Duncan touched his fingers to his ears and they came back smeared with blood. Tucker picked up Duncan's helmet and handed it to him. Duncan put the helmet on and picked up the telephone off the floor, touching it to his ear.

"It's dead," he muttered.

The earth shook with the violence of more explosions. Duncan felt for his pistol to make certain he still had it. He heard men shouting outside in the trenches as he resumed tying his bootlaces.

"I don't know whether this is just a bombardment or they're going to attack us," he said to Tucker. "Tell the men to stay in their dugouts until I order them out. They'll be safer there, and the Germans will stop shelling before they attack, if they attack."

"Yes, sir."

Tucker pushed aside the door and stepped into the trench. Duncan found his binoculars, hung them around his neck, dug his map case out of the debris and draped it over his shoulders. He felt as though he had everything under control.

Then another shell slammed to earth near the bunker. A terrible roaring sound filled his ears and the ground shook like an earthquake. He lost his balance and toppled to the ground as the strap on his helmet felt like it would tear his head off. The sound died away, to be replaced by shell bursts nearby. Duncan was terrified at the sudden thought of being crushed by earth and timbers. Scrambling to his feet, he dashed into the trench outside.

There was a huge hole in the middle of the trench. He dived inside it. At the bottom was the torso of a man lying face down, his arms and legs gone. Duncan, his lips trembling, stared at this gruesome apparition in the flashes of explosions. Fascination overcame fear, and he reached to the mangled body to see who it was. He pushed it over and then dropped back, pressing his spine against the wall of the trench.

His eyes bulged in horror as he gazed at the distorted features of Private Giannini.

Captain Beck stood with his men in the German trenches. He looked at his watch — one o'clock, time to move forward. He took his Luger out of its holster, raised it high in the air and gestured toward the American lines.

"Forward!"

He scrambled up the side of the trench and advanced into no-man's land, his men following him. Private Hitler watched them go and called out: "Good luck!" His body tingled with excitement at the thought of the mission they were on. He'd give anything to go with them, but orders were orders and he had to wait where he was until they came back.

Duncan crawled out of the hole and stood up. Explosions were thundering everywhere. He looked around, and could only liken what he saw to being in the middle of hell. Sheets of flame rose into the sky and shock waves from shell bursts blew gales of dirt and debris in all directions. He looked down into the hole and again saw Private Giannini, who had been alive only a few minutes before.

The men are depending on me for leadership, Duncan thought. *I can't let them down.* Holding his hand against the trench for support, he made his way to the bunker at the end, pushed the door open and stepped inside. The men, huddled around their kerosene lamp, glanced up at him, and he saw from the expressions on their faces that he must look a mess, with blood running out his ears and his uniform covered with dirt. *I have to be calm and in control of the situation,* he told himself. *This is their first shelling and they mustn't think they're going through it without a leader.*

"Anybody got a cigarette?" he asked.

Every one of the men in the bunker reached into his shirt and came up with a pack. Private Murphy was closest and Duncan picked a cigarette out of his pack.

Sergeant Tucker stepped forward with a lighter. "I didn't know you smoked, sir."

"I don't," Duncan said with a grin, "but I think it's time I started."

The men chuckled as Duncan sucked on the cigarette, Tucker holding the match under it. He inhaled and suddenly his lungs were on fire. Coughing, he fanned the air and looked at the cigarette. "How do you fellows smoke these things?"

"They're real good once you get used to them, sir," Murphy said helpfully.

Duncan puffed again, and this time the tobacco actually didn't taste so bad. "I'll have to stay with you men for a while," he said. "My bunker's just about finished."

The men looked at one another and he could see they were uneasy; they didn't feel comfortable around him. A good officer, he realized should have better rapport with his men.

A mortar round landed nearby, clumps of dirt falling on to them from the ceiling. They ducked their heads and held their helmets as the light in the kerosene lamp wavered.

Duncan sat on the floor with his men and inhaled the cigarette again. It burned, but not as much as before. "Sounds like those Fritzies over there are mad at us."

"Well," said Private Bell, "if they don't stop this damned shelling, I'm gonna get mad at them!"

"It won't go on forever," Duncan told them, "and when it stops they might attack. So we'd better be ready to pour out into those trenches and fight the bastards. If it gets to that, remember your training, do as Sergeant Tucker and I tell you, and don't give up an inch of ground unless ordered to do so. Any questions?"

"Anyone see old Giannini?" asked Private Bailey.

Duncan didn't know how to say it, but Sergeant Tucker saved him the trouble.

"He's dead," Tucker grunted. "Shell landed on him out there. School days are over, kiddies. You're in a real war now."

Captain Beck led his men across the shell holes and barbed wire of no-man's land. The area had been fought over fiercely for two years and now resembled drawings he'd seen of the moon's surface. A few dead trees still were standing, stripped of bark and bereft of leaves. He looked to his left and right and saw his men forming a skirmish line, faces determined and hands carrying weapons high.

Turning ahead, he saw shells falling on the American positions. It was a classic box barrage: nothing could get through to the American trenches and nothing could get out. At exactly quarter to two the barrage would suddenly end, then Sturm Company Three would go in and massacre the surviving Americans. The poor rookies wouldn't know what had hit them.

The Germans continued moving forward, hunched over, watching their box barrage. The first coils of American barbed wire loomed up ahead. Beck held out both his arms and his men stopped. He motioned with his hands to the ground, and they all flopped on to their stomachs. Dropping to one knee, he pointed with his left hand toward the barbed wire.

Six men carrying Bangalore torpedoes leaped to their feet and ran toward the barbed wire, led by Sergeant Franck. He gave them the signal, a motion with his right hand. They activated the fuses and then ran back to where the others were, getting down on their stomachs again.

Captain Beck also lay on his stomach and gazed at his watch, seconds ticking away. Then the Bangalore torpedoes exploded in brilliant yellow flashes. The men ducked their heads, and when they looked up saw six huge holes blasted in the barbed wire.

Beck looked through the hole directly in front of him and saw shells still falling on the American trenches. The barrage had only a few minutes more to go.

Duncan and his men huddled together on the floor of their bunker as bone-shattering devastation ruptured the earth all around them. Timbers dropped from the roof and clods of dirt fell upon them. One of the timbers landed on the kerosene lamp, mangling it beyond repair and snuffing out the light.

"This can't go on forever, men," Duncan said, trying to make his voice sound confident.

Somebody screamed and sobbed in a corner.

"Get a hold of yourself!" said the deep drawling voice of Sergeant Tucker.

The man continued to whine. Duncan made his way through the frightened doughboys. He wanted to calm the man down so that he wouldn't panic the others. Something told him the man was Private Bell, but when he drew close he saw it was Private Skelton, the kid from Georgia.

"Take it easy," Duncan said, putting his arm around the man's shoulder. "It'll end pretty soon."

Skelton trembled and sobbed, and Duncan thought that if he hadn't been in charge he might be tempted to fall apart, too. The continual explosions, and the fear each one generated, would grind down anyone's courage. Each time a shell landed he could feel the impact in his teeth.

"Anyone got another cigarette?" he asked.

Private Kincaid held out a pack. Duncan took a cigarette and Private Bell lit it for him. Inhaling, Duncan thought the smoke calmed him a little.

The door was flung open and Captain Harrington walked into the bunker, followed by his runner, Private Shumsky. Harrington planted his fists on his hips and looked down at his men. He looked like a bulldog wearing a Second Division helmet.

"What the hell's going on in here?" he roared.

Sergeant Tucker turned toward him. "We're just having a little party, sir."

Duncan let go of Skelton and got to his feet. He didn't know whether to salute or not. Somehow it didn't seem the thing to do. He wished Captain Harrington would get down.

"Is that you, Hunter?" Harrington asked.

"Yes, sir."

"You-all look like a bunch of goddamn trench rats."

The men looked at one another, noticing for the first time that they were all covered with dirt. A few of them snickered.

"You-all ain't afraid in here, are you?"

"Hell, no!" said Private Bell.

"That's what I thought." Harrington looked at Duncan again. "Any casualties?"

"Only Private Giannini, sir."

"That's who's in the hole outside?"

"Yes, sir."

"We'll take care of him later. Our observers have reported seeing Germans out there in no-man's land. We think they're gonna pay us a little visit, so you'd better fix bayonets as soon as the shelling stops, and go out there and give them a warm welcome."

Private Murphy took his bayonet out of its scabbard and prepared to hook it to his rifle.

Harrington held out his hand. "Not yet. You damn clowns are liable to stab each other going out the door. Do it when you get outside."

Sheepishly, Murphy returned the bayonet to his scabbard.

"Well," Harrington said, "pretty soon you're all gonna be doing what you've been training for these past few months. I know you'll give a good account of yourselves, because you're American soldiers. I've got to run along now, but I'll be with you in the trenches when the time comes. Carry on."

Harrington turned and walked out of the bunker, Private Shumsky behind him. Duncan sat on the floor again and thought of Harrington striding through the trenches with shells falling all around. *That old son-of-a-bitch really has got guts,* he admitted to himself.

Suddenly the shelling stopped.

Duncan drew his forty-five. "Everybody out!"

Captain Beck jumped to his feet and pointed his Luger at the American lines. "Forward!" he screamed.

He ran toward the American trenches, and his men leaped up and followed him. They raced through holes in the barbed wire, holding their bayonets straight ahead. Jumping over shell holes, running around dead trees, they made their way toward the green American soldiers.

They came to another coil of barbed wire. Men with Bangalore torpedoes ran forward, pushed them under the barbed wire, set the detonators and ran back. The explosives blew the wire apart, and they all charged forward again through the holes in the barbed wire. Beck was out in front, holding the barrel of his Luger pointed in the air. He heard the crackle of rifle fire ahead of him; the Americans were getting into position.

"Faster! Follow me!"

In two skirmish lines, Sturm Company Three closed the distance between them and the first American trench. More Americans fired their rifles, and one German stumbled and fell to the ground, a bullet through his chest. Beck heard the pop of a Very pistol and saw a flare streak into the sky, then burst, and suddenly no-man's land became illuminated. Beck felt naked but he pointed his Luger straight ahead and bellowed: "Follow me!"

The American trenches came closer. The battle-hardened Germans lowered their bayonets and prepared to jump in.

"Here they come!" yelled Private Bell.

He took careful aim with his rifle and squeezed off a round. The German in his sights pitched forward on to his face.

"I got another one!"

A second flare was shot into the air, and the battlefield became brighter. Duncan stood in the trench with his men, holding his forty-five with both hands and aiming at a German, who was still a little too far away. In a few seconds he'd be closer, and Duncan would shoot the son-of-a-bitch. He pulled the trigger, his pistol blasted — but the German kept coming. Duncan and his doughboys fired a few quick volleys, but before they could do more the Germans were on top of them.

The Germans jumped into the trench, and vicious hand-to-hand fighting began. Bell, gritting his teeth, lunged forward and rammed his bayonet into a German's stomach before the German's feet even hit the ground. Bell yanked his bayonet out, turned, and saw another German standing in front of him. The German shouted something and streaked his bayonet toward Bell's heart, but Bell was nimble and managed to dodge out of the way. He danced on the balls of his feet and feinted with his bayonet as the German followed him. The German lunged at Bell again, but Bell sidestepped, feinted, and then made his own lunge. The German was off balance, and watched with horror as the bayonet sped toward his heart. It pierced his tunic and smashed through his ribs. Bell heaved backward yanking the bayonet out, and blood gushed after it.

Someone fell against Bell and he sagged against the side of the trench. As he tried to rise, he saw a German raise his rifle butt to bash him in the head. Bell leaped to the side. A shot rang out at the same time, and the German closed his eyes as he fell forward, a bullet in his back.

The trench filled with grunting, cursing men, their rifles clashing against each other. Men fought shoulder to shoulder and sometimes the press became so great they could barely move their arms.

Duncan held his forty-five with two hands and shot Germans at point-blank range, while counting off rounds in his mind. When he had only three left in the pistol he reached to his belt with his left hand and pulled out another clip as fighting raged all around him. He fired three more times at close range, hit three more Germans, then ejected the empty clip from the forty-five and slammed in the new one, but before he could load the chamber a German saw him and tried to attack him with his bayonet. Duncan raised his arm to protect himself and deflected the bayonet to the side, but it cut through his jacket and ripped open his arm.

Nearly fainting from the sudden blazing pain, Duncan aimed wildly at the German and pulled the trigger. The forty-five kicked into the air and belched smoke, the big slug hitting the German in the shoulder, spinning him around. Duncan fired again, and this time the slug hit the German in the back, smashing into his rib cavity and killing him.

"Push them back!" Duncan yelled. "Kill them all!"

The doughboys fought in a wild fury. Although outnumbered by more experienced soldiers, they were rough men, and had been eager to fight the Germans ever since they had arrived in France. They parried bayonet thrusts with their rifles and slammed their butt plates against German skulls. Some swung their rifles like baseball bats, clobbering Germans on all sides, while others removed the bayonets from their rifles and fought close in.

In another section of the trench, Captain Beck was aiming his Luger at a doughboy when out of nowhere a rifle stock came down and whacked him on the wrist, knocking the Luger out of his hands. For a split second he didn't know whether to bend down and retrieve the Luger or attack the doughboy who'd swung at him.

He decided to attack. realizing he wouldn't have time to pick up the Luger. The doughboy swung his rifle again, and Beck caught it in midair, kicking the doughboy in the groin. The doughboy's eyes rolled into his head and he sagged to his knees. Beck kicked him in the face, bent down, picked up his Luger, and shot the groaning doughboy in the stomach.

Beck looked around. He'd thought his Sturm soldiers would have overwhelmed the Americans by now, but the Americans were holding them off. An American charged with a bayonet and Beck shot him in the face. Another American took a step backward and fired his rifle from the waist at Beck. The muzzle of his rifle flashed, illuminating the long bayonet, and Beck felt as though a truck had crashed into his stomach. Dropping his Luger, he fell to the ground, trying to cover the wound with his hands.

Captain Harrington had taken a rifle and bayonet from a fallen doughboy and was slashing Germans with it. "We've got them, boys!" he yelled. "Press on!" A few yards away, a German fired his rifle at Harrington, blowing off one of his epaulettes. Harrington flinched, then pulled the trigger of the rifle he was carrying. The bullet hit the German in the chest, and down he went.

Harrington jumped over the German's body and lunged at the German behind him, breaking through his guard and stabbing him in the belly. He yanked his bayonet downward, shouted victoriously, and smashed another German in the face with his rifle butt. The German fell backward as Harrington held the rifle in the slashing position, then brought it down diagonally. It caught the German in the neck and ripped across his torso to his waist. The German screamed horribly and dropped to his knees. Harrington bashed him in the head and attacked the next German he saw, who charged with rifle and bayonet at the same moment. Their rifles clashed in mid-air as they pushed against each other, trying to knock each other off balance.

Their faces only inches apart, Harrington could see that his adversary was around twenty-five years old, unshaven, an expression of fierce determination on his face. He tried to kick Harrington in the groin, but Harrington sidestepped and heaved with all his strength at the German. The German cursed and gritted his teeth, straining against Captain Harrington. Suddenly, the German's eyes and mouth opened in surprise. Harrington saw the point of a bayonet sticking through the German's stomach. The German went limp and fell to the ground as a mountainous-looking doughboy behind him pulled out his bayonet and turned to find his next victim.

The brawny doughboy was Private Ambrose Murphy, the biggest soldier in the trench, who loved a good fight and was having the time of his life. He thrust his rifle and bayonet at a German who didn't have the strength to parry, and the bayonet broke through the German's ribs and sank to the hilt in his chest. Blood foamed out of the German's mouth and his legs sagged, but Murphy held him stuck in the air, looking at him for a few moments with morbid fascination, then pulling back suddenly and letting the German fall to the ground.

"Get the bastards!" he yelled.

Murphy jumped in front of another German, feinted with his bayonet and bashed him in the face with his rifle stock. The blow broke the German's jaw and he went flying unconscious against the wall of the trench. Murphy saw a German pistol lying on the ground and picked it up with his left hand. In front of him was a German facing the opposite direction. Murphy pulled the trigger, shooting him in the back and sending him pitching forward on to the doughboy he was fighting with. Murphy drew a bead on another German, shooting him in the rear. The German grabbed the seat of his pants and yelped pathetically as another doughboy thrust his bayonet through his innards.

Something zinged against Murphy s head, and his helmet flew off. Dropping to one knee, he blinked and saw a German pointing a rifle at him. Murphy dodged to the side as the mud beside him exploded with the impact of the German's bullet. Murphy threw his rifle at the German, and as the German ducked, Murphy leaped at him, grabbing him by the throat. He squeezed with all his strength, and the German's eyes and tongue bulged out. Something went snap in Murphy's hands and the German went limp. Murphy let him fall, snatched the rifle and bayonet from his hands, and charged bareheaded through the trench, battering every German who got in his way.

The flares grew dimmer and it became difficult to see who was friend or foe in the trenches. Duncan, fighting with a rifle and bayonet he'd picked up, felt himself becoming weaker from loss of blood. A German attacked him, and Duncan tried to fend him off. He parried the German's first thrust but didn't have the strength to parry the next one. The German's rifle pushed Duncan's rifle to the side and the German's bayonet ripped into Duncan's face. He felt fierce pain and the sensation of a steel blade against his skull.

Everything went black as he fell into unconsciousness and dropped to the mud.

Someone shot up another flare, and night became day again. Corporal Schneidhuber of Sturm Company Three looked around and saw the trench filled with bodies. He was splattered with American blood, but so far unharmed himself.

There were no Americans near him, and he paused to catch his breath.

Somebody moved a few feet away, and he readied his rifle and bayonet to run him through if was an American. He jumped toward the writhing figure and was shocked to see Captain Beck moaning and trying to hold his guts in. It suddenly dawned on Schneidhuber that the raid had not gone as planned, and they'd better get the hell out of there. He didn't know who was in charge now, but decided to take the responsibility on himself.

"Retreat!" he screamed. "Fall back!"

He lifted Captain Beck, slung him over his shoulder, and picked Beck's Luger off the ground. "Fall back!" he bellowed again.

He was turning to climb the side of the trench when he heard footsteps running toward him. It was an American soldier. Schneidhuber took quick aim and pulled the trigger. The Luger fired but the shot missed. The American soldier kept coming, his helmet low over his eyes and his bayonet pointed at Schneidhuber, who took more careful aim and fired again. The American tripped and stumbled on to the other bodies lying in the trench.

"Back!" yelled Schneidhuber as he climbed the wall of the trench. "Retreat!"

Many of the Germans were too heavily engaged to break away, but some vaulted up the sides of the trenches and proceeded to run back to their lines. Private Hencke, dueling with a small American soldier and unable to fell him, saw Private Grunwald climbing the wall of the trench.

"Grunwald!" Hencke called out. "Help me take this one prisoner!"

Grunwald dropped to the bottom of the trench and crept up on the American soldier while Hencke kept his attention. At the last moment Private Bell heard somebody behind him and turned around to see who it was. Hencke shot the butt of his rifle forward and slammed Bell on the back of his head. Stunned, Bell dropped his rifle. Grunwald punched Bell in the face with the butt of his own rifle, and Bell flew backward to the bottom of the trench where he lay motionless.

Hencke scooped Bell up in his arms like a baby and looked at Grunwald. "Let's get the hell out of here!"

Hencke and Grunwald climbed up the side of the trench and ran into no-man's land, heading toward their own lines. They saw small groups of other Germans out there, going in the same direction. Behind them they heard the crackle of rifle fire and shouts of victory from the American trench.

CHAPTER 11

Duncan heard a low, rumbling sound and felt himself being bounced around. He didn't know who or where he was, and struggled to become fully conscious. He felt as though he were floating in space, surrounded by an infinity of darkness. He wondered if he was dead.

He was sick and nauseous, and his head was aflame. Groaning, he opened his eyes and made out dark, angular shapes. His mouth was dry and the pain in his head was almost too much to bear. He heard moans around him, and the sound of an engine. Something was making him rock from side to side. He took a deep breath, his ears pounding, then tried to raise his head and saw men stacked three high. Something was dripping on to his face, and he tried to wipe it away with his sleeve.

He realized he was in an ambulance moving along at high speed. Whenever it hit a bump he bounced in the air and hit the bottom of the canvas cot above him. The soldier up there was bleeding profusely, and his blood was dripping on to Duncan, but Duncan couldn't move out of the way. All he could do was brace himself with his legs, and remember how he used to drive an ambulance in the French army, with the back of the ambulance stacked with broken, bleeding men. Now he was a broken, bleeding man in the back of an ambulance, and somebody else was driving.

"Doctor..." moaned one of the men.

A woman s voice spoke from the front of the ambulance. "We'll be at the dressing station soon. Try to hang on."

She spoke with an English accent. Duncan knew that many English women drove ambulances for the Allied armies. He'd known some of them when he drove an ambulance himself.

"How far to the dressing station?" he asked weakly.

"A few more miles," the woman said.

Duncan smiled wryly. He'd driven many men back from the front, and when they asked how far they had to go he always told them not much farther even if the dressing station was ten miles off. He knew the woman in front was probably doing the same.

Blood continued to drip on to him, but he didn't have the strength to wipe it away. It splattered on to his face and the bandage wrapped around his head. His skull felt as though hot coals were heaped on top of it.

The man above him was delirious. "They just keep coming!" he muttered. "They just keep coming!"

Duncan closed his eyes and drifted into unconsciousness.

Private Adolf Hitler sat in *Sturm* Company Three's forward trench, waiting for the shock troops to return so he could report the results of the mission to Colonel Engelhardt.

"What time is it now, sir?" Hitler asked Lieutenant Strauss, who was Company Three's adjutant.

Strauss looked at his watch. "Two-thirty."

"Should they not be back by now?"

"Yes."

The rain fell lightly and Hitler shivered in the trench. He hoped the shock troops from Company Three would return soon so he could go back to his warm, comfortable bunker at regimental headquarters. Being out in the rain like this reminded him of his days in Vienna, when he was destitute and often went without food, sometimes sleeping in parks and railroad stations.

"I think they are coming," Lieutenant Strauss said, peering over the top of the trench.

Hitler looked and saw small, dark shapes in no-man's land, dimly illuminated by flares. "Where are the rest of them?" he muttered.

Strauss didn't reply; he was counting the men as they came closer. There were only forty-six, whereas ninety-eight had gone on the raid. Some carried wounded comrades, and many had left their weapons behind. Lieutenant Strauss felt a sinking sensation in his stomach. Evidently the raid had failed.

Hitler came to the same realization. He felt dizzy, his mind unable to digest the conclusion he was forced to draw. *It is impossible,* he thought. *How could such a thing happen?*

Soldiers tumbled into the trench, bleeding and carrying their wounded. Corporal Schneidhuber laid Captain Beck down in the mud and felt his pulse. "Still alive," he muttered.

Strauss saw Captain Beck and came rushing over, followed by Hitler. "What happened to him?"

"Stomach wound," Schneidhuber replied. "He's still alive, though. Call the medics."

Strauss turned to Hitler. "Tell Sergeant Feldheimer to call the medics."

Hitler rushed off toward the Third Company command post bunker but paused momentarily when he saw a friend, Private Falkenstein, slide down the wall of the trench in front of him. "What happened over there, Falkenstein?"

Falkenstein looked exhausted. "They stopped us."

Hitler blinked. "How could they stop you?" he asked, amazed.

"I don't know…"

Hitler wanted to ask more questions, but he had to notify Sergeant Feldheimer about calling the medics. He sped through the bays and finally came to the command post bunker. Sergeant Feldheimer was sitting at the front desk, speaking on the field telephone. He cupped his hand over the mouthpiece and said, "What is it, Hitler?"

"The men are back, Sergeant, and some are badly wounded. Call the medics. Captain Beck was one of the casualties."

Feldheimer cut off the conversation he was having and called the medics. Hitler left the bunker and returned outside, where he saw a group of Sturm soldiers standing around a short man wearing a strange uniform, an American prisoner.

"He is awfully small," Hitler said.

"The others were much bigger," said Grunwald. "They were a tough bunch."

Hitler looked at the American soldier standing defiantly with hands tied behind his back, uniform torn, bleeding from a cut on his cheek. Hitler could sense the fighting spirit of the short soldier and was surprised. He'd thought the Americans would be cowards when they got into battle.

Lieutenant Strauss walked up to the group. "Come with me, Hitler," he said. "I'll give you the dispatch to take back to Colonel Engelhardt."

Hitler followed Lieutenant Strauss back to the command post bunker, and tried to dispel the feelings of dread that curdled in his breast.

The ambulance stopped and the rear door opened. "Take it easy with 'em, boys," somebody said.

Duncan opened his eyes. His face was covered with blood that was coagulating around his eyes.

Medics came into the ambulance and transferred the men to stretchers. "This one's dead," one of them said when he came to the man above Duncan.

"Leave him for last," said another voice. "Get the one beneath him."

The medics bent down and looked at Duncan, who tried to smile. "I'm alive."

"I can see that, sir."

Two medics lifted him, laid him on a stretcher, and carried the stretcher to the door of the ambulance, where two more men took hold of it. Duncan emerged into the cool night. Something prompted him to glance to the side. He saw a woman wearing a brown coat and beret standing there.

"Thanks for the lift," he said.

"Good luck, soldier," she replied."

Duncan was carried to a building and laid on the floor among other wounded men. The pain in his head was so fierce he felt like crying out. He gritted his teeth and tried to tolerate it, but when a soldier with a red cross on his sleeve walked by Duncan feebly held up his hand. "Can you give me something to stop the pain?"

The soldier stopped and looked down at him. "Only the doctors can give out medicine like that, sir."

"Can you get a doctor?"

"There'll be one here shortly, sir," the soldier said wearily, automatically, as he turned and walked off.

Duncan knew how the soldier felt; he had been in many dressing stations like this back when he'd driven ambulances. All the wounded men wanted to be looked at right away, but never enough doctors. Sometimes men's lives could have been saved if they could have seen a doctor sooner. He had often reflected on this, and on the capriciousness of fate, but it didn't seem so abstract now he was wounded himself.

He might die here while a doctor was treating someone in another part of the building. His mother would be devastated, as would his sister, Allison, but his father would show no emotion because his father was tough as leather and nails. His father would probably say something like, "Well, at least he did his duty."

Duncan wondered how his brother Blake would take it. Probably it wouldn't bother him so much. Many of Blake's closest friends had died, and Blake had caused much death himself. No doubt he was immune to it by now. Blake, the younger brother ... the stronger brother...

He heard footsteps nearby and opened his eyes. He realized he must have been dreaming, and wondered how long he'd been asleep. His head hurt as though somebody had hit it with a hatchet. He looked out of the corner of his eye to see a doctor and two nurses leaning over a man. Duncan wanted to ask the doctor for morphine to kill his pain, but he knew he should wait his turn with the rest of them. He felt terribly weak, and was having difficulty thinking clearly. He kept seeing images of the fight in the trenches, men grunting as they clashed with one another. Duncan was glad he'd stood his ground and fought like a soldier. He hadn't broken and run, as he'd feared he might. *I don't have anything to be ashamed of,* he thought. *I did my duty as best I could.*

"How do you feel, Lieutenant?" asked a voice above him.

Duncan opened his eyes and saw the doctor leaning over him, with two nurses standing in the background. "It hurts pretty bad, doctor. Could you give me some morphine?"

"Where does it hurt?"

"My head."

"What about your arm?"

"It's not nearly as bad as my head."

The doctor turned to a nurse. "Give him a shot."

"Yes, doctor."

Duncan closed his eyes. He felt something cold against his arm, and then the prick of the needle.

"You'll feel better in just a few moments," the nurse said.

Duncan felt them removing the bandage from his head. He opened his eyes and saw hands. Fingers touched his scalp. "He may have a concussion," the doctor said.

"The blood on my face isn't all mine," Duncan said, his voice no more than a whisper. "The soldier above me on the ambulance was bleeding on me."

"Don't try to talk."

Duncan closed his eyes and suddenly felt floaty. He took a deep breath and saw mists swirling against his eyelids. The pain in his head diminished. In the mists he saw the German soldier coming at him with the bayonet, and he raised his arm to deflect the blow.

"Take it easy, Lieutenant," the doctor said.

Duncan heard the nurse whisper: "He should be knocked out any moment now."

There was a roaring in Duncan's ears, then the black night rose up and engulfed him.

Sam Bell stood with his hands tied behind him as the German officers looked him over. They were in a large office in a building about ten miles behind the German lines. A portrait of the Kaiser hung behind the desk. Bell thought the German officers' uniforms were ridiculous, with all their medals and gold braid, but he was too scared to laugh. He stood erectly and jutted out his jaw as they chatted among themselves in

German.

"He is rather small," said Colonel Engelhardt, twirling his blond, Kaiser-like mustache.

"They say most of them were much larger than this one," replied Major Holstein.

"Perhaps they're lying," Colonel Engelhardt said. "Perhaps they're just saying that because they were beaten by the Americans and want to make excuses. But there can be no excuses for a defeat like this. Evidently Sturm Company Three is not the hard-fighting unit we thought they were."

"Or," said Captain Eulenburg, "the Americans are tougher than we thought they were."

Engelhardt waved his hand. "Nonsense. What can they know of war?" He looked at Bell. "Ask him his name."

Eulenburg, an officer in his early twenties, turned to Bell and said in English: "What is your name, soldier?"

"Bell."

"Ask him the name of his unit."

Eulenburg translated the question.

Bell stood ever straighter. "I ain't telling you the name of my unit."

The colonel smiled. "Tough little bird, is he not?" He gazed at Bell, whose uniform was torn in several places. The American had evidently been in the thick of the fighting. "Ask him where he is from in America."

When Eulenburg repeated the question Bell wondered whether or not to answer. He realized that his answer would have no military significance whatever, but on the other hand, he and the other doughboys had been ordered to give only their names, ranks and serial numbers if captured.

"I ain't talking," Bell said.

The colonel looked annoyed as Eulenburg translated. "Take him away and see if you can get some information out of him."

Eulenburg called the guards and ordered them to escort Bell to his office, then Eulenburg followed them into the hall, passing Private Hitler, who sat beside the door to make himself available in case Engelhardt wanted to send him on a mission.

Eulenburg entered his office and spoke to the guards standing in front of his desk with Bell. "Untie him."

As the guards untied the ropes, Eulenburg sat behind his desk and sat down. He opened his silver cigarette case and took out a cigarette, lighting it with a wooden match. When the guards were finished untying Bell, Eulenburg told them to leave the room and wait outside the door.

Alone now, Eulenburg smiled at Bell. "Have a seat." His English had a British inflection, Bell noticed, in addition to his German accent.

Bell knew he should remain standing but he felt tired, so he sat down, glancing around quickly as he settled into the chair. There was a window behind the German officer's desk and another window to Bell's right. Bell had already calculated that he was on the second floor of the building.

"Have a cigarette," said Eulenburg, holding out his cigarette case.

Bell knew he should refuse the cigarette. He and the other doughboys had received lectures about how the Germans would try to soften them up if they were captured: if they relaxed, they were more likely to give away information that could get their buddies killed.

"Go ahead," said Eulenburg with a friendly smile. "You never know when you might get a chance to smoke again."

Why not? Bell thought. If he had accepted the chair he might as well take a cigarette, too. He leaned forward and took one out of the case. Eulenburg tossed him a wooden match. Bell lit his German cigarette, inhaled, and noticed that it tasted much different from American cigarettes.

"What unit did you say you were in?" asked Eulenburg.

"I ain't talking," Bell replied defiantly. "I'm gonna smoke the cigarette but I ain't gonna tell you nothin', so you might as well save your breath."

Eulenburg shrugged good-naturedly. "What harm would it do for you to tell me the name of your unit?"

"I don't know nothin' about nothin'."

"Where are you from?"

"Nowhere."

"I mean what city or town in the United States?"

"I ain't telling."

"I visited America once," Eulenburg said. "I was in New York, Boston and Washington, D.C. I liked it there very much. Are you from any of those three cities?"

"No."

"Are you from a city on the east coast of the United States?"

"I ain't talking."

Eulenburg smiled. "Come, now. You must not be so stubborn. If you talk with me a little you will be sent to a very nice prisoner camp. If you do not, we will have to put you someplace that you will not like very much."

"I don't give a shit."

"You will when you get into that little jail cell. You will wish you had been friendlier to me, and then it will be too late. I would talk if I were you."

"You ain't me," Bell said, his eyes on the cigarette between his thumb and the nail of his forefinger.

"I will give you one last chance," Eulenburg said, the evenness of his tone becoming forced now.

Bell raised his hand and flicked the cigarette into Eulenburg's face. Startled, Eulenburg shouted as sparks fell off his nose. Bell was already halfway across the room, covering his face with his arms as he leaped toward the window, his knees and elbows hitting first.

He crashed through the window and sailed into the air along with shards of glass and pieces of wood from the frame. Opening his eyes, he saw the ground coming up fast. He braced himself, landed hard, and rolled immediately to cushion the shock. He glanced around quickly; he was in an alley behind the building. His left foot hurt, but he hobbled quickly out of the alley. Behind him he could hear shouts and whistles.

He came to the street behind the building. He didn't know which way to turn, but decided to bear right and keep going straight until he was out of town. He limped along swiftly as possible in the cover of darkness. The streetlights were out in the town to save fuel and make it difficult for Allied observers to spot it at night. The sidewalks and streets were deserted; it was four in the morning. He knew that sooner or later he'd run into German soldiers, but he'd worry about that when it happened.

He heard the sound of an automobile engine, and headlights flashed into the street behind him. Making a sharp right turn, Sam Bell ran toward the back yard of a house, where he dived under some bushes. He lay still for a while; he was unable to see the street, but he heard no unusual sounds and saw no German soldiers.

Peering about, he tried to get his bearings. The back of the house was in front of him, and nearby was a whitewashed shed. He decided the shed might be a better hiding place. There might also be a tool in there that he could use for a weapon. Crawling from underneath the bush, he tiptoed toward the shed, turned the handle of the door, and quickly stepped inside.

It smelled like kerosene and dead leaves. In the dim light he saw that there were some tools lying upon the workbench. On a hanger at the side of the workbench were some clothes. Bell examined them: workpants, a jacket and a black beret. *Hot dog,* he thought, unbuttoning his tunic. *I might get out of this mess after all.*

CHAPTER 12

Lieutenant Everett Dewitt walked quickly down the Avenue de la Republique, on his way from the French War Ministry to General Pershing's headquarters. It was eleven o'clock in the morning and he carried a briefcase bulging with papers. He turned a corner and nearly dropped the briefcase in surprise, for walking toward him, no more than ten feet away, was Danielle Giraud, whom he hadn't seen since their night at the ballet. He didn't know whether or not to say hello, considering the argument they'd had before parting.

Danielle smiled when she recognized him. "Well, hello," she said. Her manner, he noted, was not at all unfriendly.

"Hello, Danielle," he replied, tipping his hat and still unsure of himself.

"How have you been, Everett?" she asked, as if they'd never even had an argument.

"Rather well. And you?"

"Fine, thank you."

There were a few moments of awkward silence. He should hurry back to his office, but she looked lovely in her navy-blue coat.

"I've missed you," he blurted.

She laughed gaily. "Don't be silly. I'm sure you have plenty of other girls to keep you occupied."

"I miss you, anyway," he said. "I'm very sorry about my behavior the last time we were together. It really was unpardonable. Do you ... do you think we could see each other some time?"

She looked away. "I don't know," she said vaguely. "I suppose I really don't have any serious objection."

He glanced at his watch. "Are you doing anything for lunch?"

"It's rather early for lunch."

"We could have a glass of wine first."

"You appeared to be in a hurry, Everett. Weren't you going someplace?"

He frowned. "As a matter of fact, I was. I must get back to my office."

"Then we can't very well have lunch, can we?"

"I guess not," he admitted.

"Everett!" shouted a male voice.

Everett turned in the direction of the voice, and was surprised to see Blake Hunter striding toward him out of the crowd of pedestrians. Blake held out his hand. "How are you, old man?"

Everett was surprised by the heartiness of Blake's greeting. They'd met only once, and Everett had received no reply after he'd sent Blake a written introduction to a friend in the American air service. Still, Blake had been a friend of Everett's brother Franklin, and Everett was no more immune to Blake's charm and vitality than anyone else. Blake looked magnificent, like an officer on a recruiting poster. He wore an American uniform now, the result of Everett's introduction.

"Hello, Blake. What brings you to Paris?"

Blake was nearly a head taller than Everett, with his visored cap worn low over his eyes. "My brother is in the hospital here. He was wounded at the front."

"Not seriously, I hope."

"Fortunately not."

Everett turned to Danielle. "Danielle, this is a friend of mine, Blake Hunter. Blake, this is Danielle Giraud."

Danielle looked up at Blake and smiled. "How do you do."

He grinned, showing his dazzling white teeth. "Hi."

She noticed his eyes scrutinizing her face, then her figure. Her smile grew broader and she gave a light laugh.

Blake appeared amused. "Did I do something funny?"

"Never mind." She glanced away, but the smile still lit her face.

Everett could perceive that they liked each other, and felt a stab of jealousy. "What hospital is Duncan in?"

"The one on the Rue D'Orsay. I'm sure he'd enjoy a visit from time to time. He's taken up smoking and would probably appreciate cigarettes. I won't be able to attend to his personal needs very well, because I must return to Issoudun tomorrow."

"How do you like it there?"

"Hate it, but I'm trying to get a transfer to a pursuit squadron. You couldn't help me with something like that, could you?"

"I don't have any influence in the air service beyond the introduction I arranged for you."

Blake shrugged. "Then I guess I'll have to do what a friend of mine did. They wouldn't give him a transfer, so he took up his plane and terrorized some folks at a soccer game for about a half-hour, diving toward the grandstands and all. When he returned to base, the C.O. was so anxious to get rid of him that he was transferred out right away."

Everett wrinkled his brow. "That doesn't seem like the best way to go about it. They might throw you out of the service."

"Then I'll fly for the French again."

"You flew for France?" Danielle exclaimed.

"Yes," Blake admitted.

117

"You were in the Lafayette Escadrille?"

"Yes."

She gazed at him with new interest.

Everett looked at his watch. "I really must go back to my office. Can I put you in a cab, Danielle?"

"I can get along by myself, thank you."

"Where were you headed, Blake?"

"I was going to the Crillon for a drink."

"Wish I could join you." He turned to Danielle. "Well, goodbye."

"Goodbye," she replied.

He hesitated for a moment, wanting to say more, but Danielle's earlier friendliness had vanished and her manner was not encouraging.

He looked at Blake and shook his hand. "Nice seeing you again."

"Likewise."

"I'll stop by to see your brother sometime."

"That would be kind of you."

"If you're ever in Paris and have nothing to do, give me a call."

"I'll do that."

Everett turned and walked away swiftly. He wanted to look back over his shoulder to see what Blake and Danielle were doing, but that would be bad form. *She'll probably fall in love with him,* Everett thought. *I imagine women find him irresistible.*

They stood on the street corner, their eyes twinkling at each other. She knew she really should be going. It wouldn't do to have him think she was attracted to him, even if that happened to be the truth.

"Are you doing anything important right now?" he asked in his smooth baritone.

"No."

"Why don't you come to the Crillon with me and have a drink?"

"Isn't that the dreadful place where all the pilots go and get drunk?"

"As a matter of fact it is."

"I've always wanted to go there."

"Then let's go."

"Very well. But I don't like rowdiness, and if it gets that way I hope you won't mind if I leave."

"Of course not." He stepped toward the curb. "I'll get a cab."

"Why don't we walk? It's not far."

"Are you sure you won't mind walking? I've noticed that women generally don't like to walk very far. I think it has something to do with the strange shoes they wear."

She raised one of her feet. "These shoes are not strange, and moreover they are very comfortable. I could walk miles in them. In fact I often have."

"You've convinced me," he replied, linking his arm with hers.

They turned and headed toward the Crillon. It was a cool day, the wind whipping their coats and making their complexions rosy. They passed other pedestrians ambling by the gaily decorated windows of the Parisian shops.

Duncan cleared his throat. "Do you know Everett very well?"

She glanced sideways at him. "What do you mean by very well?"

"Are you lovers or something like that?"

"Don't be ridiculous!"

"Why am I being ridiculous? You two look very well together."

She wanted to say that she thought she looked much better with Blake. But instead she told him, "Everett is a very nice person, but we are not lovers by any means. However," she quickly added, "we have been out together on several dates in the past."

"I got the impression, while we all were standing together back there, that he liked you quite a lot."

"I believe that is so."

"I also had the impression that you didn't like him a lot. Is that so, too?"

She looked at him-reproachfully. "Don't you think that's rather a personal question?"

"I suppose it is, but so what?"

"I don't like personal questions. They spoil everything. Are you and Everett close friends?"

"I hardly know him at all. Our families have had dealings with each other over the years, and I was sort of friendly with his brother Franklin, who was killed in action not long ago. He was in the escadrille also."

"Everett mentioned him to me. He thought quite a lot of Franklin. Evidently Franklin's death was quite a blow to Everett and his whole family. There was a wife too, I understand."

"Yes. Her name is Brooke. It was quite a tragedy for their family, but tragedies happens all the time. The same thing probably will happen to me. What can one do?"

"Nothing. My brother was killed in the war also. He was an infantry officer."

"Like my brother."

"Yes. I hope your brother isn't hurt badly."

"He's not, but he's got a scar on his face that he'll probably wear for the rest of his life."

"Not necessarily," she said. "I understand that some skilled doctors can do wonders in erasing scars. Oh — look at that!"

He followed her eyes and saw a store window that displayed women's clothes. She walked to the window and looked inside like a greedy child. "What a beautiful dress!"

He stood beside her and looked at the clothes. "Which one?"

"The silk one with the pretty colors and black shoulder straps. Do you like it?"

"It's all right, I suppose."

"You don't like it," she pouted.

He shrugged. "I don't like it and don't dislike it. As far as I'm concerned, fashion is the ultimate pettiness."

She looked at him sharply. "Are you saying that I'm a petty person?"

"No, I didn't say that."

"But you implied it."

He smiled. "Perhaps I did."

She wanted to turn around and walk briskly away from him, but couldn't bring herself to do so. She thought him awfully good-looking, and she'd always wanted to see exactly what transpired at the notorious Crillon.

"I can't help it if I like pretty clothes," she said finally. "I'm no different from any other woman in that respect."

He laughed. "No, I don't suppose you are."

"Are you laughing at me?"

"I'm laughing at the world."

"Now you are being dishonest. You *are* laughing at me."

"Okay, so I'm laughing at you. You're a child, but you're an awfully pretty child." He gazed at her face. "Too pretty for your own good, I suppose."

She pursed her lips and gave him a sidelong glance. "No one can be too pretty for her own good."

"Yes they can, because they can be spoiled."

"Then you must be spoiled too, because you are a handsome man, of your type."

"Of my *type*?" he asked. "I had no idea that I was a type. What type am I?"

She placed her forefinger against her chin and considered him. "The cold-blooded, vicious type."

He laughed.

"It's not funny," she said.

"That's because you don't have a sense of humor." He glanced at his watch. "We'd better get going." He took her arm and began walking.

"Do you have an appointment?"

"No."

"Why the hurry?"

"Because I want to start drinking."

"Are you a drunkard?"

"Probably."

"I've heard that all you pilots are drunkards."

"We are."

"Why?"

"How should I know? For the same reason you like pretty clothes, I imagine."

"I fail to see the connection."

"It may be too subtle for you."

She wrinkled her nose. That was the same argument she had given Everett on the night of the ballet. She realized now that it was an insult. But if Blake insulted her, why was she so attracted to him? She examined him again.

He seemed strong and sure of himself, and he really was an exceptionally good-looking man. The fact that he was a pilot added to his glamour. Something told her she ought to leave him and go home, but she was like a fish that had been hooked and was now being reeled in.

They continued to quibble during their walk through the streets of Paris. Upon arriving at the Crillon Hotel, they found the lobby filled with pilots and women. Everyone seemed to know Blake, who shook hands, slapped shoulders and exchanged wisecracks, introducing Danielle to everyone they encountered as they made their way to the lounge.

At the hat-check room just outside the entrance to the lounge, Danielle removed her navy-blue coat, revealing a white sweater and a gray skirt underneath. Blake noted the simplicity of her clothes and their flawless cut, setting off her small, neat figure and letting her beauty speak for itself. He had no doubt that it was a calculated feminine effect.

He took Danielle's arm and led her into the lounge, a noisy, smoky hall. A gigantic propellor was suspended above the bar mirror, and paintings of airplanes hung on the walls.

The bar and tables were crowded with pilots and women, everybody laughing and talking, singing songs, calling out to people on the other side of the room. Blake was recognized immediately, and the scene in the lobby was repeated, with men rising to shake his hand and ask how he was. Danielle saw pilots passed out cold with their faces lying on tables as other people talked over their heads. She thought the women were dressed too flashily and their behavior seemed cheap. Some kissed men shamelessly. *So this is the Crillon,* Danielle thought. *It looks like Sodom and Gomorrah to me.*

"We might as well sit here," Blake said, pulling back a chair at a large table where a party was already in progress.

"Where'd you find the pretty little bird?" asked a drunken pilot at the table.

"I picked her up on the street," Blake replied, dropping into a chair. "Danielle, this is Raoul Lufberry."

Danielle smiled and nodded at the man, blushing because of what Blake had said.

"He really didn't pick me up on the street," she said softly.

Lufberry laughed uproariously.

"And this," said Blake, "is one of my illustrious countrymen, the irrepressible Lieutenant Elliott Springs."

Springs winked at her. "Nice to meet you."

"Hello," she said.

"Introduce yourself to the women," Blake said. "I don't remember their names." He raised his hand in the air. *"Garçon!"*

While Blake spoke with the waiter, Danielle introduced herself to the two women sitting at the table. One was a Briton named Peggy, and the other a Frenchwoman named Marie. Both were older than Danielle, who thought they wore too much make-up and appeared half drunk.

Lufberry raised a glass of whisky to his lips. "How do you like the American air service?" he asked Blake.

"They won't let me fly."

"Why not?"

"They need me as an instructor, but I'll break away from that duty pretty soon." He looked at Springs. "How are you doing these days?"

"Not too well. We don't have any good planes."

"No Spads yet?"

"No. Sometimes I think I should have stayed with the British air force."

Danielle was confused. "You were with the British air force?"

"Yes," Springs replied. "I flew with the British just the way Blake flew with the French. What did you say your name was?"

"Danielle."

"Danielle what?"

"Daniele Giraud."

Lufberry leaned forward drunkenly. "You wouldn't be related to General Giraud, would you?"

"He's my father," Danielle replied.

Blake looked at Danielle in surprise. "You didn't tell me your father was a general."

"You didn't ask."

The band started to play a fast tune, and Lufberry and Springs took their women to the dance floor. The waiter came with a bottle of champagne and two glasses and began to open the bottle, but Blake snatched it out of his hands and popped the cork himself. The cork hit the ceiling and people at surrounding tables cheered. Blake filled Danielle's glass as the waiter receded into the smoke and noise. Then he filled his own glass and raised it in the air.

"To your very substantial beauty," he said.

She raised her glass to her lips and sipped. The noise in the lounge was incredible. She looked about the murky room, feeling out of place among the tipsy crowd of revelers.

"You don't like champagne?" Blake asked, refilling his glass.

"No, it is fine."

"Then why do you look so unhappy?"

"I'm not unhappy."

"Sure you are. You don't like it here. I didn't think you would. I'll get you a cab if you like."

"I'll stay," she replied, "unless you really want me to leave…"

He shook his head. "No, I don't want you to leave. Whatever gave you that idea?"

"I'm afraid I might be spoiling your fun. I'm not accustomed to this sort of place, you know."

"You're not spoiling my fun. I like to look at you. You make me realize that the world can be a very nice place, despite everything."

Her eyes softened. "That was a very sweet thing to say, Blake."

He appeared embarrassed for a few seconds, then brightened again. "You want to dance?"

"All right."

They stood and threaded their way through the tables. Blake walked behind her, admiring the curves of her body. *But she's just a child,* he thought. *Maybe I shouldn't have brought her here.*

They sidestepped on to the crowded dance floor, and he placed his arm around her waist and took her hand. They could only take small steps, and the other dancers kept bumping into them.

"I don't dance very well," he said, "but I wanted to touch you anyway."

She looked into his eyes and felt a chill go through her.

"It wasn't fair of me to bring you here," he confessed. "You really don't belong here."

"Well," she replied, looking around, "I've always been curious about the Crillon. I've heard so much about it. It certainly lives up to its reputation."

"Pilots are a little wild because the war drives us crazy. Gee, you smell good."

He held her closer and she let him because she liked the way he felt. There was something gallant and fine about him, combined with a bit of the naughty little boy.

"The daughter of a general," he whispered. "I should have known."

"Why should you have known?"

"Please don't get mad at me for saying so, but you're somewhat arrogant, my dear."

"Perhaps you confuse self-respect with arrogance."

"Perhaps. Do you do anything besides being pretty?"

"I study dancing."

"Ballet?"

"Exactly."

"I'd love to see you in your tights."

She didn't know how to respond to his remark, and he noticed her consternation.

"I shouldn't have said that," he told her. "I'd better put you in a cab before I say something worse."

Again she didn't know what to say, but didn't want to leave. She thought she'd make a joke of it. "I'm the daughter of a soldier," she said gaily. "You couldn't say anything that could shock me."

"Oh yes I could. Come on."

He pulled her off the crowded dance floor and toward the crowded tables.

"Where are we going?" she asked.

"You're going home."

"But I don't want to go home!"

"You're going home anyway!"

"Let me go, Blake!"

"No."

"You're hurting me!"

127

He spun around suddenly and let her hand go. Stepping toward her, he grabbed her shoulders and brought his face close to hers.

"Please go before I behave badly," he said earnestly. "You're a sweet kid and I don't want to behave badly with you."

"Then why must you?" she asked above the chatter and laughter around her.

"I can't explain it."

She looked down at the wings on his jacket. "You want to go to bed with me, don't you?"

He nodded. "Yes."

"That's all you soldiers want to do."

He smiled sadly. "Yes."

"I guess you are right. Perhaps I had better leave. Then you can find somebody to go to bed with."

"I'm sorry," he said. "I shouldn't have invited you here."

"You keep saying that."

"It's the truth. I don't want you on my conscience. Come on."

She followed him out of the noisy room, and the hat-check girl got her coat. Blake helped her on with it and walked her out of the lobby to the sidewalk in front of the hotel. The wind was blowing, and she held the collar of her coat closed. As Blake raised his hand in the air, she remembered something her father had told her about the high death rate among pilots. Blake was handsome and vigorous, yet she had the sudden conviction that he was going to die.

"Gee," he said, "you look like you're going to cry. Don't take it so hard, kid. I'm doing this for your own good."

"I know," she replied. "I'll be all right."

"It isn't because I don't like you or anything. The problem is that I do like you, and ... well ... you deserve someone better." He laughed and shook his head. "Listen to me! I don't think my friends would believe I just said that."

She smiled sadly. "I don't think there is anyone better than you, Blake."

A taxi cab stopped at the curb. They stood staring at each other for a few moments. Then his eyes flashed and he reached for her, clasping her in his arms. She raised her face and he kissed her lips passionately. She opened her mouth and tasted his tongue, feeling the stubble of his beard against her cheek, and smelling his fragrance, so like a meadow in the sun.

He moved away from her suddenly, his eyes wild, and opened the door of the taxi cab.

"Go," he said, pushing her toward the cab.

She lowered her head and stepped inside. He did not follow her in. Instead he closed the door behind her. As the driver steered the cab into the street, she turned around, looking out of the rear window to see Blake rushing up the steps of the Crillon Hotel.

CHAPTER 13

The French soldier's name was Raoul Fleury and he'd been on guard in the trench for a half hour. It was night and he peered over the top of the parapet into no-man's land looking for signs of a raid. A heavy cloud layer obscured the moon; it was pitch-black out there. Fleury wouldn't be able to see the Germans until they were ten yards away.

"Don't shoot!" shouted a voice in English.

Fleury was shocked by the voice, but he didn't speak English. It was coming from no-man's land, but he couldn't see anybody. "Who goes there!" he yelled in French.

"Américain!" replied the voice. *"Américain!"*

Fleury saw a white handkerchief being waved at him. If this was a German trick, he'd better get help.

"Sergeant of the guard!" he shouted. "Sergeant of the guard!"

Out there in no-man's land, a short man in civilian clothes stood up, still waving the handkerchief and walking forward in a crouch. Fleury took aim at him, eyes darting around to make sure the man was alone. Apparently no one else was there.

"Américain!" the man said again.

The man approached the side of the trench, holding both his hands in the air. He smiled and slid down just as footsteps could be heard running inside the trench. The sergeant of the guard arrived with two privates. They looked suspiciously at the man and pointed their rifles at him.

The man smiled. "No speak French," he said.

The sergeant of the guard scowled and looked at Fleury. "What did he say?"

"I don't know," said Fleury.

"Américain," the man said, smiling but evidently worried.

"I think," said Private Fleury, "that he's saying he's an American. Maybe we should get Lieutenant Langlois. He speaks English."

The sergeant of the guard nodded. "You men stay here and make sure nobody else is out there. I'll take this one to Langlois." He pointed the bayonet of his rifle in the direction of Lieutenant Langlois's dugout. "Start moving, you."

"Américain," the man said weakly as he held his hands high and walked toward the dugout.

Inside, Lieutenant Langlois looked up from the letter he was writing to his wife. He had a long, sad face and close-cropped blond hair. "What the hell is this supposed to be?" he asked as the contingent descended upon him. He looked at the man in civilian clothes. "Who is he?"

"He just showed up from no-man's land, sir," said the sergeant of the guard. "He says he's an American but we can't get much out of him because he doesn't speak French. That's why we brought him to you, sir."

"He was alone?"

"Yes, sir."

"Are you sure?"

"We didn't see anyone else out there, sir. Would you like me to take a patrol into no-man's land to see if anyone else is out there?"

"Maybe you'd better, just to be on the safe side."

"Yes, sir." The sergeant of the guard saluted and left the dugout.

Langlois looked at the little man in the civilian clothes. "You are American?" he asked in heavily accented English.

"Yes, sir," said the man, obviously relieved that he'd found someone who spoke some English. "The Germans took me prisoner, but I broke away."

Langlois picked up a pencil calmly, as though American prisoners were commonplace in his trenches. "Your name?"

"Private Samuel William Bell, sir. Company B, Twenty-third Infantry Regiment, Second Division. Could I possibly get something to eat, sir? I ain't et nothin' for two days."

Langlois looked at one of the soldiers guarding Bell. "Has he been searched yet?"

"I don't know, sir."

Langlois pointed to Bell and spoke to him in accented English again. "Take off all your clothes."

Bell grimaced. "But it's cold in here!"

"Do it next to the stove."

Grumbling, Bell stood next to the small, pot-bellied stove and unbuttoned his jacket. Langlois looked down at the letter he'd been writing to his wife, smiled, and put pen to paper again.

You will never believe what just happened. My guards brought in a man dressed in civilian clothes who claims to be an American soldier escaped from the Germans. He is a nasty little fellow and smells to high heaven, as do all of us do down here. If he is who he says he is, he'll be back in his unit by tomorrow. We never know what will happen next in this war.

Danielle Giraud stepped out of her bathtub into the huge, fluffy white towel held in the air by Georgette, her maid. She wrapped herself in the towel as Georgette rubbed her hair. She could see her reflection even through the foggy condensation that covered the mirror, and she smiled at her rosy complexion and the twisted strands of blonde hair that lay on her forehead.

She put on her slippers and languorously walked out of the bathroom, leaving Georgette to drain the tub and tidy up the room. Danielle sat before her make-up table and looked at herself in the large mirror. She knew it was difficult to be objective about oneself, but could see that she was beautiful, which gave her great pleasure. It would have given her more pleasure if she'd done something to achieve her beauty, but it had been a gift from God, and she accepted it as gracefully as her years would allow.

There were dangers connected to her beauty, and she was aware of many of them. One of the foremost was narcissism, of which she was quite unaware. Looking over her shoulder, she saw that the bathroom door was closed and heard Georgette working away. Danielle stood in front of the mirror and let the towel fall from her shoulders, uncovering her body.

She was always amazed at how perfect she was. Not too heavy, nor too light. Nothing out of proportion. Skin like strawberries and cream. Her father was a rather unattractive man, though she loved him dearly, and her mother was quite plain also. She considered herself as a kind of miracle.

The bathroom door was flung open and Georgette marched in on her matchstick legs. "Shall I help with your clothes, mademoiselle?"

Danielle returned to her seat. "I can manage."

"If mademoiselle should need me for anything, I shall be right down the hall."

Georgette left the room and closed the door behind her. Danielle picked up her hairbrush and began to stroke it through her shoulder-length golden hair. The towel dropped off her shoulders, uncovering the tops of her breasts. The effect was very fetching, she thought, but she could never wear a gown that fit like that. It would be too vulgar, and if there was anything in the world that she thoroughly detested it was vulgarity.

Human beings cannot control their destinies, she thought, *but they can at least control their vulgarity.* She simply refused to behave like other women her age, who went from one squalid love affair to another with an endless procession of buffoons and imbeciles. And although she wasn't especially happy, she believed other young women weren't, either. At least she had her dignity, and if she ever met a man to whom she could give herself totally, he would not get a body that had been kissed by every pair of drunken lips in Paris.

Danielle had begun to think she'd never find a man who could meet her high standards — but then she had met Blake Hunter. Until him, the men she'd known had either been awkward and silly, like Everett DeWitt, or loud and obnoxious, like older men who wanted to appear knowledgeable about everything but who were really no different from younger men.

Blake had been different from any man she'd ever known. As a general's daughter, she'd met war heroes before, but they'd all seemed rather shy and embarrassed about what they'd done. Blake was so normal and natural, yet a heroic quality radiated from his being. She'd only been with him a few short hours, but considered herself a good judge of character.

She could almost see him as one of the great knights of the Crusades, like Stephen de Blois or Raymond de Toulouse. Blake wasn't ashamed of what he was, but not excessively proud, either. And he suffered, like all the great knights — she was sure of it. Danielle knew, just as certainly as she knew the address of her house, that Blake was lonely, that he needed her, and that only he — or a man like him — would be worthy of her.

Danielle chuckled at her thoughts, realizing that sometimes she was a little absurd. Yet, as she brushed her hair, she couldn't help thinking that on the deepest levels of life, everything was exactly as she imagined. Blake certainly wasn't Stephen de Blois, and could never hope to be. But on the other hand, wasn't he the twentieth-century equivalent of that great knight, riding an airplane instead of a horse, wielding machine guns instead of a sword?

Danielle wanted to write Blake a letter to invite him to tea when next he came to Paris, but believed a young lady shouldn't throw oneself at men. If they wanted you badly enough, they'd come for you, and if they didn't, then they shouldn't have you anyway.

I can wait forever, she thought as she threw the towel on to her bed. Then she walked naked to the dresser, opened a drawer and selected the silk underthings that she intended to wear that evening.

Duncan spotted the lady ambulance driver at the officers' mess in the hospital, a large, poorly lit room with high ceilings and paint peeling everywhere. She wore her brown wool coat and matching beret, and sat alone at a table alongside a wall, sipping a cup of something.

He thought he'd say hello and thank her for driving him to the dressing station, realizing all the while that he was a hypocrite, because if he hadn't found her attractive, he probably wouldn't make the effort.

He lifted his cup and saucer with his good arm and carried them toward her table. His face was still bandaged, and the pain from the bullet that had been removed from his leg was making him limp. He knew he must look a mess, but he felt himself attracted to this young woman, and couldn't stop himself. After fighting for his life in that trench, walking up to a woman and talking with her didn't seem quite as hazardous as it might have done before.

"Hello there," he said, stopping at her table.

She looked up and smiled sleepily. "Hello."

"I don't suppose you recognize me in this get-up." He pointed to the bandage on his face.

"Have we met?"

"Yes, but we haven't been introduced. You took me for a ride a few weeks ago in your lovely ambulance. I'm Duncan Hunter."

"I'm Catherine Hawkins," she replied. "Well, it's nice to see you up and around. Care to sit down?"

"Love to."

He sat opposite her and gazed at her face, thinking she was even prettier close up. There was something about her that he thought marvelously exciting, something besides the shining auburn hair, the eyes that were so dark against the pale skin of her face, the firm fullness of her figure.

"Where did I pick you up?" she asked.

"In Lorraine. Night of November 15."

"I recall that an American unit was raided around then, and we brought back quite a few loads. I imagine it must have been pretty terrible."

"Strangely enough, it really wasn't. Everything was happening so quickly that I didn't have time to think about it. I suppose it's more terrible now in my memory, than it was when it was happening."

"I never thought of it that way, but of course it would have to be, from a psychological point of view."

Duncan nodded. "How long have you been driving an ambulance?"

"Seven months."

"I drove an ambulance for the French, too. I was thinking of that the night you drove me to the dressing station — how I'd been the driver so many times, and suddenly I was in back with the wounded."

She looked at him searchingly, and he noticed that her eyes were vaguely oriental. "I don't remember," she said. "Perhaps another driver brought you back. A number of us were in that sector then."

"I'm sure it was you."

She shrugged and pushed her teacup aside. "Anything is possible. You say you drove an ambulance for the French?"

"Yes."

"Which unit?"

"289th."

"Was the 289th in the Somme?"

"We sure were."

She looked down at the table, where she was toying with the handle of the teacup. "My husband died on the Somme. He was with the Thirty-sixth Ulster." She raised her eyes. "Do you remember driving back any men from the Thirty-sixth Ulster?"

He shook his head. "No."

She reached into the pocket of her coat. "I have a picture of him here. Would you take a look at it — just on the off chance?"

"Sure."

She took out a leather wallet, extracting a photograph which she handed to him. He held it up to the light and saw a hale and jolly-looking fellow, exactly the kind of man she would have married. They'd have grand old time eating fabulous meals and raising children, but instead he had fallen in the mud of the Somme River, and she was driving ambulances in Lorraine.

"I don't remember him," he said, handing the photo back.

She tried to smile. "Just thought I'd try."

"It's hard to keep track of all the faces. I'm sure you know that."

"Yes — it was silly of me." She tucked the photograph into the wallet and laid the wallet beside the ashtray, then glanced down at his wedding ring. "I see that you're married."

"That I am," Duncan sighed.

"It's decent of you to wear your ring. Many soldiers come to France and put their rings in their pockets because they don't want the French girls to know they're married."

"I don't blame them. The war has turned everything upside down. When people are facing death and destruction at every turn, they shouldn't be criticized for taking whatever little pleasure comes their way."

She shrugged. "I don't know what to think about that. The war is beastly and everyone is beastly. I don't hate the Germans and I'm sure they don't hate me. Sometimes I think that this war is the beginning of the end of the world." She touched her hand to her cheek, aware that she'd become more emotional than she liked to be with people whom she barely knew. "I think it's time I left."

"Can I see you again?" Duncan asked.

"What for?" she asked, surprised.

"To talk like this, have a drink or two, perhaps go to the theater."

She hesitated. "I don't really know how you could get in touch with me. My unit moves around a lot. We're the 349th Ambulance. Right now we're in Saint-Etienne, but who knows where we'll be next week?"

"I'll find you."

She smiled. "I wonder what you'll look like without all those bandages?"

"Probably worse than you can imagine."

"I doubt that. Well ... I hope you get well quickly. And if I don't see you again, good luck."

He stood as she did. "I hope to see you again."

She smoothed the front of her coat and adjusted the beret on her head. "Goodbye, Duncan. Godspeed."

"Same to you, Catherine."

She and walked away, her head half covered by the fur collar of her coat. He sat and watched as she left the dining room. Then there were just the heads of the officers and nurses, the buzz of their voices, and the long, gray afternoon.

CHAPTER 14

Captain Joseph Harrington sat behind the desk in his command post bunker, smoking a cigar his wife had sent him from Milwaukee, and reading a directive from headquarters about the dangers of venereal disease. Harrington didn't understand why venereal disease was such a big problem, considering no women were around. He wished headquarters would spend their time figuring out a way to do something about the cooties, which were driving him crazy.

He reached down and scratched his groin, then suddenly heard a great hullabaloo in the trench outside. Putting on his helmet and drawing his forty-five, he went out into the trench and saw half the company cheering and jumping up and down.

"What the hell's going on here?" he boomed.

They all stopped and looked at him, suddenly self-conscious. Parting ranks, they let a short soldier pass between them. Harrington's eyes lit up when he saw who it was.

"It's Sam Bell!" Harrington said. "Sam Bell is back!"

Bell stopped in front of him and saluted smartly. They'd given him a new uniform at division headquarters, and he looked ready to go on parade.

"Private Sam Bell reporting back for regular duty, sir."

Harrington returned his salute. "Well, good for you, Bell! Glad to have you back! Come on into my office for a bit, and then you can get back to your platoon."

"Yes, sir."

Harrington entered first, and Bell followed.

"Have a seat, Bell."

Bell sat on the rickety wood chair in front of the desk as Harrington lowered himself into his own chair.

"What the hell happened to you out there?"

"They took me prisoner, sir," Bell replied, grinning.

"How'd they do that?"

"Don't ask me. One minute I was here, and the next thing I was over there with the Fritzies. Boy, what a bunch of silly bastards they turned out to be. They put me in a room all alone with an officer, so I just jumped out the window and never stopped running until I crossed into the French lines day before yesterday. I spent all day yesterday telling the fellers up at division about it and they're gonna put it in a little book of some kind. So you can read all about it if you want to — I don't think I could go through the whole rigmarole again so soon."

"There's just one thing I wanna know," Harrington said. "How'd you make it across no-man's land?"

"Weren't difficult at all. First of all, I stole some civilian clothes, so I didn't look like no soldier. Then I went over at night when visibility was piss poor. I spent most of the time crawlin' on my belly, so no one could see anything." He paused and smiled. "Sir, you gotta get up pretty early in the morning to catch Sam Bell."

Harrington scratched his craggy nose. "Bell, I think I'm gonna make you a private, first class."

Bell beamed. "That's real kind of you, sir."

"I'll have the orders cut in the morning. You'd better have the stripes on your sleeves by 1200 hours tomorrow, or else. Glad to have you back. You may report to your platoon."

"Yes, sir."

Bell stood, saluted, left the bunker, and was greeted by his pals in the trench outside.

"I'm gonna be a PFC," Bell said, elated. "Anybody got any whisky?"

Murphy draped his arm over Bell's shoulder. "We got a new man name of Stearns, and he's making some."

"Out of what?"

"Potato peels and other shit."

Bell spat. "Yuk."

"Well, what you think whisky is? It's only garbage juice that's been fermented and distilled."

"I guess so," Bell said. "I suppose the first thing I should do is report in to Lieutenant Hunter."

Private White piped up, "Oh — he ain't here."

"Where's he at?"

"In a hospital someplace. He got cut up in the raid. We lost about a third of the company."

"Did Tucker make it?"

"Shit," said Private Conroy, "you can't kill Tucker. That son-of-a-bitch is too mean to die. I saw him a-fightin' and a-pitchin' in that trench — I tell you it was a sight that would strike fear into the heart of the devil himself."

"Where's he at?" Bell asked.

Murphy chuckled. "With Private Stearns — where else?"

The Spad engine purred smoothly as Blake Hunter looked over the side at the Third Aviation Instruction Center at Issoudun, France. It was early in the morning and he'd just taken the plane up. He'd told them he just wanted to get a little practice above the field — and boy, were they going be surprised.

He'd eaten nothing for breakfast, preferring to sip only water. He'd planned this flight for days, adding and rejecting new elements, and now had it memorized completely and was ready to go. If Eddie Rickenbacker could get a transfer for buzzing a French soccer game, Blake thought he should get one even faster for buzzing the Aviation Instruction Center itself.

Well, here goes, Blake thought, pushing the stick forward. The engine howled, the Spad began its dive, Blake pulled out the throttle all the way and balanced the wings. The cold December wind took an end of his white silk scarf out of his leather jacket and made it trail a few feet behind him as the wings strained against the struts and wires.

Directly below him was the headquarters building, where the staff members were sitting down to begin their morning's work. He saw a few people come out of buildings and look up into the sky, pointing at him, no doubt wondering what in the hell he thought he was doing.

The headquarters building came closer, and he pulled the stick back at the last moment, certain that if he'd waited two more seconds he would have put one of his wheels through the roof.

The Hispano-Suiza engine whined as the Spad climbed into the sky. Blake glanced behind him, seeing people pouring out of the headquarters building and buildings nearby. He continued to rise, performed a slow back flip, then pushed the stick forward again, diving down at the building for his second pass.

The people in front of the building crowded around and looked up at him. In the final moments of the dive he saw panic on their faces as they scattered. He nearly touched the ground in front of the building, then pulled back the stick and climbed again, his wing struts screaming, the Hispano-Suiza engine snarling like an angry lion. Upward he soared, chuckling to himself at the memory of the men's faces.

Looking down at the road, he saw a truck convoy. That hadn't been part of his plan, but he thought he'd take advantage of it anyway. Easing the stick forward, he dived down at the convoy, thinking how easy it would be to strafe it if it had been an enemy convoy.

On the road, the driver of the first truck blew his horn, but Blake kept diving. The first truck drove off the road into a ditch, the second followed, and the third stopped cold. Blake pulled out of the dive, skimming the tops of the other trucks, then banking to the side, dipping dangerously low over the gas tanks where the aviation fuel was stored. He zoomed toward the racks where new planes were stored, their noses down and tails high in the air.

He zipped over the tops of the stacked planes on the ground as pilots and mechanics ducked underneath them, shaking fists and cursing. Blake laughed as he pulled back his stick and took the Spad into the sky once more. This would be his last pass, the final for good measure. Then he'd land and report to Major Spaatz, telling him there was something wrong with the plane he'd taken up. He was sure Spaatz would take the hint.

Banking to the side, he looped down out of the clouds, aiming for the headquarters building again. The grounds and runway were covered with men, running in all directions, probably unsure whether they would be safer in buildings or out in the open. "You're safe no matter where you go," Blake muttered. "I won't hit you."

He swung toward the headquarters building again and saw the men flattening themselves on the ground nearby. Then he aimed the Spad as close to the roof as possible, soared over it, pulled back the stick and climbed into the blue sky again. At five thousand feet he leveled off, circled a few times, then began his descent.

The wind was steady as he brought the Spad down with textbook precision. His left wheel touched, and a split second later his right wheel also hit the ground. Pushing down his flaps, he coasted along the runway and felt marvelous. The Spad had done just what he'd wanted it to do, and he hadn't made one mistake. Sometimes he even impressed himself with his flying skill.

The Spad came to a stop, and he switched off the engine and unbuckled himself from the seat. Crowds of men from all parts of the aviation center ran toward him. He climbed out of the Spad and jumped to the ground.

The mechanics arrived first, and looked at him as though he were crazy, but they didn't say anything because he was an officer and they were enlisted men. Lieutenant Donald Hudson, a young ace who was skinny as a sparrow, was the first officer to arrive.

"What happened up there?" he asked, greatly agitated.

"Something wrong with the Spad," Blake said. "Nearly killed myself. Lost complete control for a while. Scary as hell."

Hudson climbed into the cockpit as the others crowded around with their questions. Blake told them the same story, that he'd had trouble with the Spad.

Hudson popped his head out of the cockpit. "I can't find anything wrong in here."

A corporal from the orderly room pushed his way through the crowd. "Major Spaatz wants to see you right away, sir!"

"That's where I'm heading."

The pilots and students followed Blake across the runway, chattering about how the Spad had nearly taken the roof off a building, or how they'd almost been crowned by one of the wheels.

"The plane's in bad shape," Blake said to them.

Blake entered the orderly room, and the sergeant pointed to Major Spaatz's office. When Blake opened the door Spaatz was sitting behind his desk, writing furiously. Spaatz stopped when he saw Blake and held up his hand. "Don't say a word!" he commanded.

"But, sir, I —"

"I said don't say a word!"

"Yes, sir."

Blake stood at attention. Spaatz continued to write, looking down at his desk. "I'm going to give you the transfer you've been asking for. You can pick it up at Sergeant Murray's desk at 1200 hours today. By 1230 hours I want you off this aviation center, lock, stock, and barrel. If you're still here after that time, I'm going to have you court martialed. That's all. Get out of here, and don't ever let me see your face again."

"Yes, sir."

Blake did an about-face and marched out of the office, his expression sober. But outside on the runway, he threw his long-eared flying hat into the air and laughed in triumph.

At five o'clock that evening Blake was in the lounge of the Crillon Hotel, moderately drunk. He was talking to a woman named Peggy, who evidently knew everyone who'd ever left the ground, and gradually he began to feel maudlin, realizing that throughout his brief adulthood he'd spent most of his days risking his life, and most of his nights trying to lure tarts like Peggy into bed.

"What's wrong with you, Blake?" she asked, grabbing his shoulder and shaking it, nearly tearing off his lieutenant bar. "I've never seen you like this. If you don't get happy I'm going to leave."

He shrugged. "Go ahead and leave. Who gives a damn?"

"Well!" she said, widening her eyes. "I never!" She stood, picked up her drink, and staggered to the next table, where she collapsed on a young captain's lap. "Hello there," she said. "I don't believe I know your name."

He pinched her behind. "If you can't remember my name, Peggy dear, then I suppose I should be greatly insulted."

She squinted at him and looked puzzled. "First of all, stop pinching me, and second, have you ever worn a mustache?"

"Never."

"Are you sure we know each other that well?"

"If I mentioned the Trafalgar Hotel in London, would that help?"

She touched her finger to her nose. "The Trafalgar Hotel in London?" Then her jaw dropped. "Oh my goodness!"

He smiled. "I knew that would jog your memory."

"Oh my word!"

"Would you like a drink?"

"I think I'd better have one, yes, thank you. Do you mind if I sit on a chair?"

"No, of course not."

She slid off his lap and wheezed as she dropped on to a nearby chair. By now she had forgotten all about Blake, who sat only a few feet away, drinking a glass of dark rum and feeling sorry for himself.

He was in one of those moods where he thought nobody cared about him. These moods overtook him at the most unlikely times, such as today when he'd finally obtained the transfer he'd wanted for months. Normally he was confident that he was liked and admired, but when the black clouds gathered over his soul he felt isolated and miserable.

He wasn't even sure of Duncan's loyalty; he'd seduced one of Duncan's girlfriends a long time ago. And his "best friend,"

Franklin DeWitt? Not only was Franklin dead, but their friendship had ended badly. It was a memory he rarely allowed into his consciousness, but now he was too drunk and depressed to close it out.

He had vied with Franklin for Brooke Madigan, although he hadn't really been in love with her. No, it was more a matter of not being able to believe that someone like Franklin, who was a writer, hardly a dashing figure — or that anyone, for that matter — could successfully woo a woman away from him. But Franklin had not only been successful with Brooke but had also turned out to be a damned good pilot, which had earned him a share of the limelight that Blake had always enjoyed.

Then, when Blake's sister Allison had turned up pregnant — probably, although not necessarily, by Franklin — Blake had gone berserk. Allison was one of the most decent-hearted people Blake knew, but wasn't exactly a prude, and had initiated an affair with Franklin at a time when Blake had been carrying on with Franklin's wife Brooke. When Allison told Blake about her unwanted pregnancy, Blake demanded that Franklin divorce Brooke and marry Allison. Blake even goaded Franklin into an air fight, one-on-one, which ended tragically when Germans spotted them and zoomed in for the kill, shooting down Franklin and Bulldog Teeter. Blake had managed to escape the ambush, but had felt guilt-ridden ever since.

Franklin and Teeter died because of my vanity, Blake admitted to himself. *I didn't shoot Franklin down, but I'm responsible for his death anyway. What a selfish vain swine I am. Someone ought to shoot me down. It's exactly what I deserve. The only person I ever think about is myself. Deep down I'm either a stupid killer or a bloody fool. Life is a bottomless pit of misery, and we have no hope of climbing out.*

Suddenly the memory of Danielle Giraud invaded his mind, and the bottomless pit of despair became imbued with a golden glow. *She's a special person,* Blake thought, *not like the tramps who hang around here. She's like the morning of a summer day, and these women here are like winter nights in the Arctic.*

He wondered what she was doing. It was around six thirty in the afternoon. *She's probably at home, preparing to have dinner. Should I call her?*

Now the great internal wrestling match began. One part of him said to call her, because the worst thing she could do was hang up on him, which would be regrettable but not fatal. The other part of him said to stop, that she was too fine for him, that he shouldn't meddle with such a person.

As always, his selfishness won out. Rising from the table, he smoothed the front of his jacket, adjusted his Sam Browne belt, and ambled unsteadily toward the lobby, where he would make the call.

Danielle was sitting in her room, looking at an illustrated society magazine, when Georgette knocked lightly on the door and entered.

"Telephone call for you, mademoiselle. A Lieutenant Hunter."

Danielle put down her magazine. "Lieutenant Hunter you say?"

"Yes, mademoiselle."

"I'll take the call in here."

Georgette closed the door. Danielle sat still for a moment, looking at the telephone on the table nearby. *So he's finally calling,* she thought. She'd known that sooner or later he would. She picked up the phone. "Blake?"

"Danielle? Hello."

"Hello."

"I'm drunk."

"I can discern that."

"How are you?"

"All right. What about you, other than the fact that you're drunk?"

There was a long pause. "I shouldn't have called."

"Why not?"

The phone went dead in her ear. She tapped the bar and got the operator, who said she had no idea what had happened to the call or where it had originated. Danielle hung up the phone and in two seconds figured out that he must have called from the Crillon — where else? Evidently he had called her because he needed her, but had passed out or been cut off.

I'll go to the Crillon, she thought, heading toward her closet. *Blake needs me.*

Blake staggered back to the lounge, feeling worse than ever. He knew now that he shouldn't have called. He was a drunken lout, a known womanizer, and he should leave Danielle alone. She was special. Besides, she was the daughter of a French general, and French generals had notoriously bad tempers. Calling her had been a major miscalculation, especially when drunk. *I should just go to bed and sleep it off,* he thought.

He crossed the lounge, bumping into some friends on their way out. Officers shook his hand and women kissed his cheek. The band was playing a lively tune and a bunch of drunks were trying to dance to it. He spotted a vacant table for two in a corner and collapsed on to one of the chairs.

"It's really too ridiculous," he mumbled as he looked around him, sinking lower in gloom every moment. He reached into his jacket pocket, took out a cigarette and lit it up.

"What's wrong, Blake?" The voice was that of a drinking pal who noticed Blake's long face as he passed by.

"It's all too ridiculous."

"You take life too seriously, Blake. It's just whisky and girls and the dawn patrol — what the hell."

The officer slapped him on the back and staggered off. Blake knew he was right, but sometimes it was difficult not to take life seriously. When you called a woman like Danielle Giraud and acted like a drunken fool, it was embarrassing. Blake hated doing anything that would make him look bad. He wanted to be splendid and perfect and gallant, like the young men in cigarette ads who didn't get drunk and call society women for the hell of it.

Blake saw a waiter and flagged him down to order a glass of rum. While waiting for it to arrive, he realized that he should have visited his brother today at the hospital, but had felt a greater need for the gang at the Crillon, these rowdy, drunken men and giddy, promiscuous ladies. *This war has ruined me. I was a decent man before I came to France, wasn't I?* But he knew deep down that he'd never been a decent man.

The waiter brought his drink, and he gulped down half of it. He felt very tired. He stubbed out his cigarette and was tempted to loosen his tie … but no, that wouldn't look very nice, so he just cradled his head in his arms and closed his eyes.

She entered the noisy lounge and couldn't see him anywhere. As she advanced farther into the room, someone grabbed her arm.

"Siddown and have a drink, sweetheart!"

"Take your hand off me, please."

"Sorry about that, sweetheart."

She shook loose and then spotted Blake passed out at a table in a dark corner. She nearly burst into tears at the sight of him, sprawled over the table, a war hero like that, all alone. Well, he wouldn't be alone anymore. She pushed determinedly through the crowds and sat on the chair opposite him, placing her hand over his.

He cocked open an eye. Then, seeing her, he raised his head. "Danielle!"

"How do you feel?" she asked him.

"Um…" He rubbed his face and smoothed down his hair. "I'm not sure. What are you doing here?"

"I was worried about you."

"I don't think it was such a great idea for you to come here…"

"I think it's a good thing I did come. Have you any idea what time it is?"

"Sometime in the afternoon, I imagine."

"That's correct," she said, "and in case you've forgotten, it's a beautiful day. All the stores have Christmas decorations up and the sky is blue. I think you need some fresh air. Besides, I cannot stand this place."

He groaned. "Actually I don't think I can stand this place much longer, either."

"I have a marvelous idea," she said. "Let's take a carriage through the Bois de Boulogne like last time."

"Isn't it too cold?"

"It'll clear your head, which I'm sure is just what you need."

He stared at her. "Have you really come here just to see me?"

"Of course." She narrowed her eyes. "Listen, Blake — we both know that our meeting was no random occurrence. We also know that one day you would have called and I would have come to you. We are not ordinary people, Blake, and that is why we are together."

Blake pondered that as he rose unsteadily to his feet. She took his arm, and together they walked toward the door.

Their carriage ride in the Bois de Boulogne included many warm embraces, sweet kisses, and murmurings of deepest feelings and fondest dreams. Afterwards they rode a cab to the nearest, most luxurious hotel they could find, where they spent the night in each other's arms.

PART 2

CHAPTER 15

It was the first of March, 1918. The bootsteps of Field Marshal Hindenburg and General Ludendorff echoed along the marbled corridors of the Imperial Palace in Berlin. The two old warlords were in perfect step, as though on parade. They said nothing and looked straight ahead as they moved along. Guards lining the corridors gazed with admiration and wonder at the two foremost commanders in the Imperial German army.

Hindenburg and Ludendorff halted in front of Kaiser Wilhelm's door. Ludendorff bowed slightly from the waist, indicating that Hindenburg, the senior officer, should go first. Hindenburg opened the door and entered the office. Ludendorff followed and took his place at Hindenburg's side again. Together they marched toward the desk and saluted.

The Kaiser returned their salute and told them to sit down. He looked gravely at them, his chest shining with medals and decorations, although he'd never fired a shot in anger. "Gentlemen," he said, "our hour is at hand." He paused for dramatic effect, while Ludendorff and Hindenburg looked significantly at each other. "Gentlemen," the Kaiser continued, "the Bolshevik government of Russia and my government have finally, after much negotiation, reached agreement over an armistice. It will be signed formally during the next two or three days. That means the time we have been waiting for has at last arrived. Now we can transfer troops from east to west and smash the Allies into the sea. It has been a long, cold winter, gentlemen. We and the enemy have been at a stalemate.

These have been difficult months for soldiers such as ourselves. But now God is smiling on us. I will give you four weeks to prepare, then I want you to launch our major offensive in the West. The three of us have labored over the details of this operation throughout the winter, and as far as I'm concerned, there is nothing further to discuss. Put the plan in motion, and win the war for Germany. That is all. You may go."

It was night at the AEF Headquarters at Chaumont. General Pershing sat behind his antique wooden desk, his glasses low over his nose, plowing through paperwork, when there was a knock on the door.

"Come in!"

The door opened and First Lieutenant Everett DeWitt entered. "You wished to see me, sir?"

Pershing took off his glasses and rubbed his eyes. "Have a seat, Everett."

"Yes, sir."

Pershing pushed his glasses back up his nose and set his paperwork aside. His office was large and sparsely furnished, with a six-foot map of Europe tacked to one of the walls. One electric light bulb illuminated the map, another lit the top of Pershing's desk.

"I'm having another of those little problems that you're so good with," Pershing said. "This time it's a legal problem. You were studying to be a lawyer when we declared war — that's why I want to talk to you. Here's the problem. Some of our soldiers are getting into trouble with the French civilian authorities, and no one in the Judge Advocate's Corps can say for sure who has jurisdiction, us or the French. I guess you probably realize that our people in the Judge Advocate's Corps aren't up to this kind of thing. It's way the hell over their heads, the legal precedents and all, and I think we should get some professional civilian help. Do you think you can find somebody?"

"Sure," said Everett. "My uncle is a partner in a Wall Street law firm. I'm sure he can recommend somebody. He might even come himself."

"I'll make him a colonel if he does," Pershing said smilingly.

There was a knock on the door.

"Come in."

The door opened and Major Redford entered the office. "Something just came up, sir, and I thought I'd better tell you right away." He glanced at Everett. "Am I interrupting anything important?"

"Not at all," said Pershing. "Pull up a chair and have a seat."

Redford, a tall rangy intelligence officer, leaned forward and said: "Sir — the Germans have just changed all their codes."

"When did you find this out?"

"Shortly after midnight, sir."

Pershing frowned and looked at his watch. It was nearly half past midnight. "I wonder what they're up to."

"Well, if we piece this together with information we've received about troop movements behind their lines, and the fact that the British have seen an unusual number of German officers observing British troop movements, and we know they're transferring their divisions from the Russian front to here, it would seem that the Germans are preparing the major offensive that we've been expecting, probably in the British sector."

"The French sector is weaker," said Everett. "I think that when they come, it'll be through the French sector."

"My guess," said Pershing, "is that they'll try to split the French and British apart and drive through to the channel ports. We'll know for sure soon enough. Well, Everett, I think I'm finished with what I had for you. Ralph, would you stay for a few minutes, please?"

Redford remained in his chair as Everett rose, gathered up his papers and walked out of the office. He didn't bother to salute, because he was in and out of there so often that it didn't make sense anymore.

CHAPTER 16

First Lieutenant Duncan Hunter of the Second Division was finally discharged from the hospital and returned to his unit, where he and his doughboys intensified their training for the major German attack everyone was expecting. But no one knew when and where it would commence, so he was able to wangle a few days' leave in Paris.

He was sitting in the first-class compartment of a train and looking out of the window as it pulled into the Gare de l'Est. He intended to spend his time relaxing, and trying to track down the ambulance driver Catherine Hawkins. He hadn't had any opportunities to search for her since he'd been discharged from the hospital. Women ambulance drivers sometimes showed up near the trenches, but she was never among them. None of the ambulance drivers Duncan had spoken with knew her. Sometimes he thought she must have returned to England.

He looked out of the window at people rushing alongside the train, noticing at least half of them in uniform. *Just about everyone's a soldier now,* he thought.

The train finally jolted to a halt. He took his canvas knapsack from the overhead webbing and waited until two elderly gentlemen left the compartment. Then he followed them out, made his way down the aisle and debarked from the train.

The station was noisy and filled with people hurrying about. He walked swiftly away from the platform and into the main station, looking forward to possibly seeing Blake, who was supposed to be getting a short leave around this time, too. Everyone was trying to get some time off, because they all knew that something big was in the air, and once it got under way no one would be going anywhere for a long time.

Suddenly he thought he saw her. Freezing in his tracks, he stared through the mass of humanity at a woman in a dark-brown coat across the vast floor. Duncan blinked and his heart began to race. Was that her or was he imagining things? A path cleared in the crowd and he was able to see her again. He was astounded — the woman looked just like Catherine Hawkins.

"Catherine!" he shouted, waving his hand in the air.

But many people were shouting and waving, and the woman didn't turn around. Duncan moved toward her, threading his way through the crowd. *I hope that's her,* he thought. *What an extraordinary coincidence if it is.*

As Duncan made his way across the railway station, he could not possibly know that the Germans had launched their huge attack that morning, pouring sixty-two divisions into the British sector on a forty-three-mile front between Arras and La Fère. The attack had been preceded by the most extensive artillery barrage in the history of the world, and the fog and mist were so terrible that the British couldn't see the Germans until the Germans were right on top of them.

The German offensive was making brilliant progress, and the Kaiser had every right to be elated as he stepped from his Mercedes-Benz in a wooded area near the town of Laon. In front of him, wreathed with camouflage netting, was the famous Krupp siege cannon, monstrously long, with an effective range of eighty miles. The Kaiser had come to Laon to watch the gun fire a few shells at Paris.

Everything was in readiness for the Kaiser's visit. The major in charge of the gun saluted, then the Krupp factory officials shook his hand. The Kaiser, followed by his entourage, inspected the cannon and its crew, asking numerous technical questions.

The Krupp siege cannon had no sophisticated targeting mechanisms, its aim based primarily on complex calculations involving weight of the projectile, wind velocity, humidity, likely trajectory, and power of the explosive charge that would launch the projectile. No one could predict exactly where the projectile would land. There were too many variables. It might not even land on Paris.

When the Kaiser's curiosity was satisfied, he was escorted to a wooden bunker a few hundred yards away, in case the cannon blew up. The Krupp siege cannon was a temperamental new invention and no one was completely sure what might happen when it was fired, its muzzle blast ear-splitting. The Kaiser and his entourage huddled in the bunker, gazing through narrow slits at the immense cannon.

The crew loaded the massive explosive charge that would launch the deadly projectile into the sky. Then they loaded the gigantic projectile itself, which contained a huge quantity of explosives designed to detonate on contact with the target, whatever that target happened to be. Then the crew closed the breech. The Krupp siege cannon was ready to fire.

The major held the string in his hand, closed his eyes and pulled the string. The shell exploded thunderously, wreathing the gun in clouds of smoke. The shell rose twenty-five miles into the sky, then plummeted downward toward peaceful, unsuspecting Paris.

Inside the Gare de l'Est, Duncan pushed through the crowd toward the woman he thought to be Catherine Hawkins. She was struggling toward an exit, carrying two suitcases, and the closer he came the more certain he was that she was Catherine.

Only around twenty yards away now, he called out her name again. He saw her stop and look around. Now he could see her full face.

"Catherine!" he shouted.

Her eyes suddenly shone with recognition. He saw the beginning of a smile on her face as she took a step toward him. Elated, he surged toward her through the crowd.

At that moment the German artillery shell crashed into the Gare de l'Est and exploded. Huge columns came crashing to the floor, segments of the roof following them down. Duncan saw Catherine's smiling face become a mask of terror.

He charged through the shrieking throngs and jumped on top of her as debris fell throughout the train station. Shielding her body with his, he buried his face in her hair and covered his head with his hands. People screamed hysterically and the floor trembled as immense chunks of concrete and marble slammed into it. Duncan and Catherine shivered against each other for several seconds, then Duncan realized there were no more explosions and no more debris falling. He opened his eyes and looked around.

All the electric lights were out and a thick fog of dust was everywhere. Broken columns and walls leaned in all directions, and people staggered in a daze among them. The only light came in long shafts through the holes in the roof. People wailed and screamed in every corner of the station.

"I think we're safe now," he said, getting off her.

She slowly sat up, astounded by the devastation around them. "What happened?"

"Must have been a German bomb of some kind."

"My God! We must help these people."

And they did, until the ambulances and medical personnel arrived.

A Supreme Allied War Council was scheduled that morning in the town of Beauvais, about forty-five miles north of Paris. General Pershing arrived early, accompanied by his staff. First he visited the local cathedral, a fine specimen of thirteenth-century Gothic architecture, then continued to the nearby Hôtel de Ville, where the meeting would take place.

Marshal Haig, General Foch, General Pétain and Sir Henry Wilson were already there. They had to wait an hour before the arrival of Georges Clemenceau, the new premier of France, who was accompanied by Lloyd George, prime minister of England. Interpreters were present as usual.

A platform made from banquet tables was set up in the middle of the room, and on it were spread the appropriate maps. The meeting began with a discussion of the latest military situation. From all indications, it appeared that the German army was making great gains against the British.

After the British generals finished explaining their situation, Clemenceau, the famed Lion of France, placed one hand on the map table and the other on his lapel.

"Gentlemen," he said, "I fear that at this moment we face the gravest crisis of this war, and all the blood we have spilled will be for nothing if we fail to respond successfully. We are gathered here today to settle one very simple problem regarding the appointment of an overall commander for our military forces in Europe. It has been suggested that General Foch be given this appointment, providing we can all reach an understanding as to the nature of his authority and its legal basis. I believe it is crucial that we appoint one overall commander right here and now, so that we can begin fighting as a unified force. Gentlemen, I need not remind you that the duty of the foot soldier is to fight for his country, and the duty of his country's leaders is to make difficult decisions wisely and expeditiously. Does anyone care to comment on this matter?"

Lloyd George stepped forward. "We have had more than three years of this war," he said, "and we have not had unity of action during any of that time. During this last year we've had two kinds of strategy, one by Haig and another by Pétain, both different, and nothing was gained. Now recent events have stirred up the British people. The Germans must be stopped. History hangs in the balance here — make no mistake about it. It is not too late to reap the benefits of unified action under one supreme commander. And now I should like to hear General Pershing's views on this matter."

All eyes turned to old Black Jack as he stood and faced them. Placing both his hands behind his back and squaring his shoulders, he said: "The principle of unity of command is undoubtedly the correct one for the Allies to follow. I do not believe it is possible to have unity of action without a supreme commander. I think the necessary action should be taken by this council at once. I am in favor of conferring the supreme command upon General Foch."

Everyone appeared to be in agreement, so the necessary resolution was drawn up. The leaders of each nation signed it, and as of that hour General Foch became Field Marshal Foch and commander-in-chief of Allied forces in Europe.

The next topic of discussion was the deployment of American troops in the present crisis. This time General Pershing made no objections, because he was aware that the situation had become critical. He agreed to make himself and his men available to Foch, but with the proviso that American divisions be permitted to serve intact.

The meeting adjourned and the men returned to their respective military units or governments.

Meanwhile, in Paris, the first exodus of citizens began. People were beginning to believe that nothing could stop the Germans from capturing their city.

In a hotel room off the Place Des Vosges, Duncan Hunter of the Second Division Infantry and Catherine Hawkins of the Ambulance Service lay in each other's arms. In the distance they could hear the faint sounds of artillery barrages. The war was coming closer to Paris, and many citizens were fleeing, but lovers live in their own little universe, and Duncan held Catherine tightly against him, relishing the firm curvaceous warmth of her body.

"You know," she said, 'you remind me of my husband. He was built very much like you."

He sighed and rolled off her. Reaching over to the night table, he picked up his pack of cigarettes.

"Did I just make you angry?" she asked.

He scowled. "What's the point of talking about your husband now?"

"Because I'm thinking of him now. I'm not supposed to think about him when you're around?"

"If you must," he replied, lighting a cigarette and then passing the cigarettes and matches to her.

"I get so sick of men," she said wearily.

"You talk as though you know so many of them."

"No, but I'm sick of them anyway. You're all fine when you're being people, but when you're being men you're disgusting."

"Men aren't people?"

"Men are men. They're childish, selfish, and they grab you."

"You don't like to be grabbed?"

165

"I don't like to be told that I shouldn't talk about my husband. I'll talk about him whenever I like. And if you don't like it, leave."

She took a cigarette, lit it, and handed the pack and matches back to him. He lay back and stared up at the dark ceiling, wondering what his platoon was doing. A major German offensive was evidently under way. He should cut his leave short and get back to them.

"I wish this war would go away," he said, blowing smoke at the ceiling. "It's getting to be so grim."

"Yes," she agreed. "It's strange how much the world has changed. When the war started everybody was so happy. It was all glory and parades. Now it's all horror and funeral processions. Everyone feels so hopeless. If I didn't feel so hopeless myself, I would never have gone to bed with you, Duncan. But I can't say no to myself anymore. I don't care about anything."

Duncan was stung by the remark, but reminded himself that Catherine was every bit a lady — one of the characteristics that he liked in her — and under other circumstances she indeed would not have gone to bed with him on such short acquaintance.

He said, "You must care about something if you keep driving for the French."

"I just do it — I really don't think about it that much. But you still care about things, Duncan. I like that about you. You're actually optimistic. Of course, your country hasn't been through what my country has in this war. When America starts losing a half million men in a few days of fighting, I don't think any of you will be so optimistic, not even you."

Duncan shook his head in the darkness. "We're aware of the mistakes that other countries have made, and we're not going to repeat them. All the other countries are tired and demoralized. Even the Germans are tired and demoralized, although evidently they're making good progress now. But the doughboys are raring to go. You should see my men, Catherine. They can't wait to get out there and fight the Germans. And they're tough boys, crack shots with rifles. They follow orders usually, and they have a strong sense of camaraderie. God help the Germans when they run up against those crazy doughboys."

Catherine smiled. "You really like your men, don't you?"

"They're a helluva bunch. I didn't like them so much at first, but they're starting to grow on me."

"Edward used to like his men very much, too. He always wrote about them in his letters to me. Do you write about your men to your wife?"

"I don't write to her that often."

"Why?"

"We really don't have much of a marriage. We married when we were too young to realize what we were doing, and our parents really pushed us into it. It was a very advantageous marriage from our families' viewpoint. I have two little children, so the family name will live on."

"Tell me what she's like, Duncan. Does she look like me?"

"No."

"That's strange. I thought she might look like me, since you look so much like Edward. Sometimes, while you were making love to me there, I thought you were Edward. It was so strange."

'I have a theory," Duncan said, "and maybe it's derived from something I read once about the Hindu religion — that people really aren't the distinct entities they think they are, and that once you look beneath their superficial characteristics, their personalities all melt together into one fundamental being."

"God?"

"I'm not that religious. I don't think much about God."

"Look, Duncan — it's getting light."

He too had noticed that the room had lightened while they'd been talking. "We'll have to leave pretty soon," he said, stubbing out his cigarette in the ashtray.

She rolled toward him, touched her body to his, and put out her own cigarette. "I'm going to miss you," she said, kissing his neck.

He wrapped his arms around her. "I'll miss you, too."

They kissed, squirming against each other. He was amazed at how magnificent her body felt. She was firm and strong, her stomach flat, her bottom all muscle. He rolled her on to her back and they made love wistfully, knowing that soon they'd be parted.

CHAPTER 17

In a wooded area not far from the front, General Ludendorff stood over his map table, trying to figure out what to do next. He looked like a small walrus wearing a helmet and a droopy mustache, but was considered the greatest military mind of the war. It was widely believed among the upper strata of German society that he was the power behind the throne, the *Reichstag*, and the army.

Although Hindenburg was nominally commander-in-chief of the army, in reality its commander was Ludendorff. Hindenburg was merely the figurehead. Ludendorff signed Hindenburg's name to orders without asking permission.

Now Ludendorff had to figure out how to maintain the force of his offensive, which was clearly running out of steam. The British were falling back, but they weren't broken yet by any means. His strategic objectives in the offensive were to separate the British army from the French army, then destroy the British. He'd accomplished neither, and was forced to admit that thus far his great offensive was a failure, despite impressive gains on the map.

And there were other problems. His infantry couldn't advance rapidly through the destruction in front of them, and his artillery was even slower than the infantry. His transport was having great difficulty re-supplying the front over nonexistent roads.

Ludendorff gazed thoughtfully at the map. His aides watched him respectfully, careful not to make any noise that might distract his great strategic mind. Among the aides was Major

Karl Ritter von Beck, who'd recently joined Ludendorff's staff after being released from the hospital. Often he visited the front lines for Ludendorff, and was among the few who realized that the great offensive had failed to attain its strategic objectives.

On the map Ludendorff saw a move that he thought might win him a victory. If he turned his armies around and headed for Paris, he might be able to capture it in two or three days. Then the French would probably surrender, and if they didn't, at least their army would be greatly demoralized. He would ride into Paris on a white horse, and historians would inscribe his name on the page with all the great conquerors of history. Then he could wheel his army north and deal with the British once and for all.

As for the Americans, he didn't think they'd amount to much in the war. They'd declared war almost a year ago, and were still unable to field an army. Ludendorff was inclined to believe they were a big hoax.

He studied the map to determine how to move on Paris. His eyes fell on the names of many obscure and unheard-of villages. Soon those sleepy villages, which had managed to stay free from harm for so long, would be ripped apart by the German war machine.

One of those villages was nothing more than a whistle-stop on the Paris-Nancy railroad line. It was located near the banks of the Marne River, and was called Château-Thierry.

Blake sat in the cockpit of a new Spad as it droned steadily through the morning sky. His goggles tight around his eyes, white silk scarf fluttering in the air behind him, he held the stick tightly, glancing quickly around at the seven other planes from his squadron. They were on the dawn patrol, the Marne

River below them.

Eddie Rickenbacker, in a plane up ahead, pointed to the ground. Blake glanced down and saw dots moving on the landscape, indicating heavy traffic. The Germans obviously were up to something, perhaps preparing an attack through this sector. The pilots would report these peculiar enemy movements as soon as they returned to base. The people in Intelligence would know how to evaluate the information.

The dawn patrol continued to fly in a northwesterly direction. Visibility was good, with no clouds. Blake felt tired and bored. He hoped they wouldn't run into German planes; his attitude toward fighting having changed since he'd fallen in love with Danielle Giraud. He had a gold locket with her picture hanging from his neck by a gold chain. They were planning to get engaged. He envisioned a happy life with her, which wouldn't happen if he got killed before it began.

The sky disappeared as he thought of Danielle, so lovely, like a dream come true. And she loved him back, had even given him her virginity, and sworn to stand by him forever. Never had love been so sweet to him. Never had he known that he, a rowdy and a wastrel, could fall so deeply in love. But it had happened, as miracles sometimes do.

He became aware that the formation in front of him was changing. Arms waved out of cockpits and a faint roaring sound could be heard above. Duncan snapped to his senses and looked toward the sun. Small dark forms were there, evidently German planes.

Blake pushed his stick to the side and begin evasion tactics. His Spad veered away from his squadron and the German attackers. He wondered how many German planes were there. *They surprised us,* he told himself. *Maybe if I'd had my eyes open I would have seen them sooner.*

He did a barrel roll through the air, then another, straightened out the Spad, pulled back the stick, climbed into the morning sky, and heard the first bursts of machine-gun fire. Glancing up, he saw German planes swarming all around him and the other Spads from the 94th. Bullets whistled through the air as Blake positioned his flaps so that he spun as he climbed. A spray of bullets hit the engine cowling and he identified its source: a white German Fokker bearing down at him from above.

A white Fokker, Blake thought. *Who's that?* He pulled back his stick and did a back flip in the sky, diving down to earth again, but the white Fokker followed him like a bloodhound. As Blake tried to get away he remembered that a famous German aviator flew a white Fokker, but couldn't recall his name.

Bullets slipped through the fabric of his fuselage as he tried to out-maneuver the white Fokker. Pulling back his stick, he sent the Spad climbing again, but the Fokker stayed on his tail. Glancing around quickly, Blake saw that he and the other doughboy pilots were outnumbered by two or three to one. They had fallen into a trap like a bunch of rookies and might never make it back to their lines with information about suspicious German movements. This big German patrol was probably in the air to prevent Allied planes from seeing or reporting what was taking place down there.

Blake climbed and dived repeatedly in an ever-diminishing circle, but the white Fokker stayed on his tail, firing machine guns. Blake twisted and turned, trying every escape tactic he knew, but still the German stayed after him. The most he could do was prevent the German from getting a straight, clear shot at him, but he couldn't get away.

He's very good, whoever he is, Blake thought as he gritted his teeth and worked his controls frantically. Another Fokker dove directly in front of him so Blake gave him a burst from his machine guns, shooting away sections of the Fokker's propellor and engine compartment.

There was wild confusion in the air, planes diving all around each other. Two Fokkers crashed into each other and exploded into an orange ball of fire. The debris dropped to earth, then an American plane was shot out of the sky.

The white Fokker stayed after him. *How relentless he is,* Blake thought, climbing into the sky once more. *That German son-of-a-bitch hasn't thought of anything except me since this fight began. He must have spotted me from above, noticed that I wasn't paying attention, and thought I'd be easy prey.*

Then all at once he remembered who flew a white Fokker, the flamboyant Captain Hermann Goering, one of Germany's top aces and a winner of the Pour le Mérite, Germany's highest award for valor. *Goering is after me,* Blake thought, a chill passing through him. *How can I ever get away from a pilot like that?*

He realized he had only one chance: to lure Goering into the path of an American plane that might be able to shoot him down. Goering was paying so much attention to him that he might not notice. The ruse might work.

Blake performed another loop through the air, while trying to lure Goering into the path of another Spad, but everyone was heavily engaged. Another American plane disintegrated in midair, the victim of a Fokker attack from behind. *They're going to get us all,* Blake thought. *If I had been paying attention we might have avoided this.*

He glanced back and saw Goering still behind him, trying to swing into position. Blake's stomach ached with nervous cramps as he struggled to get away. He knew he didn't have much time. Once a few of those Fokkers ganged up on him it would be all over.

Then he heard a new sound. Glancing up into the sky, he saw more planes. *Oh, my God,* he thought. *Now we're finished for sure.* There were about a dozen of them in V formation, and they peeled off one by one as they began to dive. Goering's Fokker suddenly snarled. Blake turned around and was astonished to see Goering breaking off the fight and climbing into the sky. Blake looked at the new group of attacking planes again, and realized they were Nieuports — French planes. The French were coming to the rescue!

The French pilots swooped down out of the sky as Fokkers scattered in front of them. Goering was already heading back to Germany and the other Fokkers would try to follow him. Blake scanned the sky and saw no more Fokkers menacing him. Heaving a sigh of relief, he pulled back his stick and began to climb, resolving to stay awake in the future.

It was evening when the Second Division arrived in the vicinity of Château-Thierry. Word had been passed down that a German offensive would likely smash into their sector soon, so the doughboys were ordered to construct a solid defensive position, with the American Third Division on their left and a brigade of French soldiers on their right.

The doughboys had no trench mortars or hand grenades, and were plagued with critical ammunition shortages. But Field Marshall Foch hadn't expected the green Americans to do much fighting. He was confident that the French soldiers ahead would stop the German drive, then the doughboys could move up quickly to plug any holes in the line. There was plenty of everything closer to the front where it was needed.

The doughboys had bacon sandwiches for dinner and slept on the ground without benefit of shelters. Fresh buds could be smelled on that pleasant spring night. By this time tomorrow there'd be trenches and latrines all over the place, but tonight they slept in untouched meadows and woods, beneath a half moon, and it made the farm boys among them wish they were home.

They were awakened at three o'clock in the morning by a thunderous artillery barrage in the distance. Sitting up on the ground, they saw the eastern horizon glow with light. Earth tremors could be felt in the seats of their pants, and they realized that only an incredibly massive bombardment could be felt at such a great distance. Unable to sleep anymore, they stood and watched the bombardment, glad it wasn't the Second Division that was receiving the shelling.

A half hour later the Twenty-third Regiment was ordered to move out. They formed double columns and marched off into the night. Their new mission was to fortify a forest area near the Marne River called Belleau Wood.

At four o'clock in the morning, General Pershing and his staff surrounded the map table in the AEF conference room at Chaumont. Lieutenant Everett DeWitt was reading a communication from Field Marshal Foch. The French army in the south had been subjected to a fierce enemy bombardment beginning at 0300 hours, followed by a ground attack that tore the French front apart. The French were falling back in disarray, and the Germans were in hot pursuit. The only organized military units left to stop the Germans were the American Second and Third Divisions and the French brigade. Foch ordered Pershing to hold the Germans until French reinforcements could be brought to bear against the Germans.

DeWitt finished reading the communiqué, and the officers stared down at the map. They could see the line of German advance and the pins that indicated the positions of the Second and Third Divisions.

"We won't give them an inch," General Pershing said, his jaw set angrily. "I want the word passed to all commands in the Château-Thierry sector that they are not to fall back no matter what. They're under orders to stop the Germans and throw them back. All other echelons throughout the AEF will focus on giving the men of the Second and Third everything they need in the way of ammunition and equipment. We're finally going into action as an army in this war, and we are not going to lose our first battle. That would be unthinkable."

As Pershing continued his impromptu speech, Everett looked down at the map, trying to imagine how he'd react if a few thousand Germans came running directly at him. Would he stand and fight, or become a coward? At times like this, Everett wondered what he was made of. Sometimes he thought he ought to transfer to the front, so he could find out who he was, one way or the other.

In the dawn light, the sound of picks and shovels working the ground could be heard in Belleau Wood. The Second Division doughboys were in high spirits, stripped naked to their waists, their helmets hanging from branches as they wielded their tools and sang a song.

"The Second Division was digging a ditch, parlez-vous;
The Second Division was digging a ditch, parlez-vous;
The Second Division was digging a ditch
To bury the Kaiser, that son-of-a-bitch,
Inky dinky parlez-vous."

Duncan thought his men were amazing. They'd been told that the Germans were coming soon in force, and they had cheered like a bunch of kids going to a baseball game. They couldn't wait to get their hands on the Germans and pay them back for that sneak attack in November.

Duncan checked his platoon perimeter, feeling pride in his unit and men. They worked hard and happily for their few pennies a day and the lousy food they were given. All of them were crack shots and understood open warfare. If his men ever received an order to attack, the Germans would be in for a big surprise. Duncan's big farm boys and city hoodlums would be awfully hard to stop once they got rolling.

A field kitchen showed up at six o'clock in the morning, so the men paused for a breakfast of scrambled eggs, bread and coffee. Then they went back to work and continued to build fortifications. Duncan set up his four machine guns at the edge of the woods, facing the fields ahead. If the Germans attacked, those machine guns would mean everything. A British officer had told him that two German machine guns had held up a British regiment for a day, British bodies heaped six feet high all over the field, and the German machine guns were overwhelmed only when they ran out of ammunition.

After digging the machine guns into their emplacements, the doughboys felled trees and sawed logs to make roofs for the dugouts. They covered the roofs with alternating layers of dirt and stone. When they finished, a long narrow opening was all that could be seen in front of the bunkers. If Germans entered the field, the machine guns would slice them down.

Captain Harrington came by to inspect the positions and pronounced them superb. He joked with the men and slapped them on their backs.

"Hey, Bell!" he thundered, looking into a freshly dug trench. "What the hell are you doing down there?"

Bell, naked to the waist and covered with dirt, was digging at the bottom of his trench. "I'm digging a hole for grenades, sir."

"But we don't have any grenades, Bell."

"I'm talking about German grenades, sir."

"You're gonna let a German get close enough to throw grenades at you, Bell?"

Bell straightened up and grinned. "No, sir!"

"Then what the hell are you digging the hole for?"

"Well, sir, maybe somebody else might let a German get that close."

"What!" Harrington thundered. "Are you trying to tell me that another good Second Division man would let a German through?"

"No, sir!"

"Then what the hell are you talking about, Bell?"

Bell wiped the top of his head with his hand. "I don't know exactly how it's gonna happen, sir, but if a hand grenade ever happens to fall into this trench, I'm gonna kick it right down this goddamn hole where it won't be able to hurt nobody."

"Hey, that isn't a bad idea, Bell."

"I thought you'd think so once you knew what it was for, sir."

Suddenly shouting could be heard on the enemy side of the line. The doughboys were pointing at a road leading to the front. Harrington raised his binoculars and focused on the road, where men wearing the blue uniforms of the French army were headed toward American lines, evidently in headlong retreat from the Germans, who were doubtless hot on their heels.

"Lieutenant Hunter!"

Duncan jumped over the trench and ran toward Harrington.

"You'd better tell your men to get a move on. French soldiers are coming yonder, and the Krauts won't be far behind them."

Duncan and his men watched solemnly as the battered French soldiers moved through their position to the rear. The French were bleeding and tattered, with haunted eyes.

Bell, ever the comedian, pointed toward the German lines. "Hey — the Germans are that way!"

The French soldiers couldn't speak English, but it wasn't hard for them to figure out what he was saying. One gnarled old French sergeant looked down into the trenches and said in his language, "We have waited so long for you Americans, and now you have got here too late!"

The French and Americans talked back and forth to each other, although neither could speak the other's language. But Duncan could speak both languages and knew what was going on. The French were angry at the Americans for staying out of the fight for so long, and the Americans were criticizing the French for retreating.

Processions of French soldiers continued throughout the morning, as the doughboys worked to improve their fortifications. Then, around noon, the last French soldiers passed by, and the fields ahead became ominously quiet. Everyone figured that the Germans must be moving their artillery closer so they could go to work on the new American positions.

A rolling kitchen arrived at the trenches and the men were served beef stew with thick slices of French bread for lunch. Many of the doughboys wondered if this would be their last meal. When they finished they put their mess kits away and took their positions in the trenches.

They looked at the field ahead, watching and waiting for the Germans to come.

On the French front, Catherine Hawkins stood behind her ambulance and smoked a cigarette as the wounded were carried in. Shells were bursting close by and people kept telling her to get down, but she didn't think a bomb would dare fall on an ambulance woman.

She was no military strategist, but she knew the French had been falling back steadily for three days. Men rushed about, carrying rifles and bayonets in the fields all around her. The front trenches were about a thousand yards from when she was, but the front trenches kept moving backward.

The medical corpsmen handed her the roster and she put it in her pocket.

"I'll be back in about an hour," she said.

"We probably will not be here in another hour."

"I'll find you wherever you are. Good luck."

"You too. We'll need all the luck we can get today. From what I have heard, the Germans have broken through our frontlines. I have even heard that they are attacking the Americans farther south."

"The Americans, you say?"

"That is what I have heard. We finally will find out what those big-mouthed bastards are all about." Suddenly the corpsman became embarrassed. "Sorry," he said, "I forgot you were an American."

"I'm not American — I'm British."

"Sorry anyway."

The corpsman walked away. Catherine got into her ambulance and started it up. "Hang on back there," she said. "The ride might be a little bumpy."

She shifted into gear and drove away, thinking about Duncan and his Second Division on the southern end of the line. Deep in her heart, Catherine didn't think the American soldiers could hold. They didn't have enough experience to stop the Germans. No one could stop the Germans now. Even Paris was being evacuated.

She feared that the war was coming to an end, and Imperial Germany would be the victor. But more than that, she was afraid that Duncan would be killed. *Oh, Lord,* she thought, *don't let him die. I don't think I could bear to lose another one.*

"You okay, ma'am?" asked a voice from the rear of the ambulance.

"I'm fine," she replied above the roar of the engine, wiping her eye with her knuckle. "How are you feeling?"

"I'm not sure."

"Try to get some rest. We'll be at the dressing station in a little while."

Catherine held the wheel with both hands as she sped toward the field hospital. Columns of marching soldiers moved to the side of the road to make way for her, their faces suddenly lit as a defective shell burst high in the sky. It looked like a gigantic red rose for a few moments, then it disappeared.

How like a human life, she thought.

CHAPTER 18

Duncan watched the field ahead for signs of advancing Germans. It had been quiet too long, and the Germans were long overdue. It wasn't like them to dawdle. They attacked like a hurricane and didn't let up unless you kicked their teeth down their throats. His eyeballs stung as he lowered the binoculars.

"See anything, sir?" asked Sergeant Tucker.

"Nothing."

"Somebody ought to send a fucking patrol down there to find out where the Fritzies are."

"I imagine quite a few patrols are out already."

"How come they didn't send us out on patrol?"

"I don't know."

"We deserved the chance, didn't we?"

"Yes, but there'll be lots more patrols. As soon as this platoon is called to furnish one, you'll be the first to go."

"That'd be real nice of you, sir."

Duncan smiled inwardly as he raised his binoculars to his eyes. The childish antics of his men used to distress him, now amused him, like a bunch of overgrown children with all the exuberance and decency of children but none of the deviousness of adults. That was how they were when they were sober, anyway. When they were drunk, they were quite another matter.

"Look, sir!" said Private Sinclair.

"What is it?"

"At the edge of the woods…"

Duncan scanned the edge of the woods with his binoculars and saw a few dozen Germans. They were about eight hundred yards away, probably the vanguard of an attacking force. Duncan wondered how many of them would charge. Would they just come pouring across the field or try tricky tactical maneuvers? More of them came out of the woods, then formed into long ranks. *They'll try to rush us,* Duncan decided. *They think they can run right over us.*

"Man your posts!" shouted Captain Harrington.

There was bustling and rushing as men who'd been working and shoveling in the trench grabbed their rifles and took their positions. Machine gunners positioned themselves behind their guns, and the crews prepared to feed in ammunition. They all wore their steel helmets low over their eyes, all certain they could stop the Krauts.

Duncan walked through the trench, adjusting the deployment of his men, then crawled into one of the machine-gun dugouts. It was commanded by Corporal Davidson, who sat behind the gun, working it from side to side on its transverse mechanism, his potential field of fire enfilading most of the area before him, Davidson licking his lips in anticipation of some action. The other men fidgeted with the belts of ammunition. One of them wiped the breech with a cloth that had a few drops of oil on it. Duncan checked the gun's field of fire and worked the bolt a few times. The machine gun was brand new and had never been fired in warfare.

"Make every shot count," Duncan said. "Kill 'em all."

"Yes, sir."

Duncan crawled out of the dugout. As he was raising himself to his full height, he heard Captain Harrington's voice shouting: "Open fire!"

Duncan dashed to the side of the trench and looked over the parapets. Germans were advancing across the field in long gray ranks, and the Americans opened fire with all they had. The well-trained German troops, instead of hesitating, began to double-time forward with their rifles and bayonets held high. Their lines remained straight but many of them were falling to the ground.

"Keep firing!" Duncan yelled. "Keep firing!"

Halfway down the trench, Bell stood behind his Springfield rifle and slowly squeezed off rounds. He held one German in his sights, shot him, worked the bolt action, sighted another German, and shot him, too. He was amazed at how simple it was. *How can they charge like this?* he wondered. *I wouldn't do it.*

The machine-gun dugouts were filling with gunsmoke as guns were fired in rapid bursts. Belts of ammo zipped through the breeches, and when the last bullet fired off, a new belt was fed in. The gunners swung their weapons back and forth, not bothering to aim because their transverse mechanisms had been set to the correct height.

Then suddenly the Germans ranks stopped. They picked up their wounded, turned, and ran back to the shelter of the woods. Soon they were gone, and the field looked exactly as it had when the sun had dawned upon it that morning.

The men from Company B looked at one another in surprise.

"Gee," said Corporal Murphy, "I didn't think it'd be that easy."

"It's not over yet," Duncan said. He figured it was a probing attack to determine where doughboys were and how many of them. He expected an artillery barrage to commence soon.

Sure enough, he heard booming sounds in the distance. Moments later came the whistle of incoming shells. Huddling in the bottom of trenches, the doughboys knew what would happen next. Big German 155 shells began crashing to earth, debris and smoke exploding into the air, the ground heaving and men holding on to their helmets.

A direct hit in one of the trenches blew half of the Fourth Platoon into the air. Captain Harrington's voice could be heard above the explosions, shouting orders. The men hadn't had time to build an extensive network of bunkers, so all they could do was crowd beneath their unfinished fortifications and hope a shell wouldn't fall on them.

"Goddamned Heinie bastards!" Bell shouted. "I hope they'll try to come up here again. Oh, boy, do I hope they'll just goddamn try it."

Like most of the doughboys, Bell was itching for a fight. They'd been in France so long and trained so hard, but the only action they'd seen had been that cold night in November. Most of the doughboys hadn't even had that. It was getting to be embarrassing as well as frustrating.

Duncan cautiously crawled up the side of the trench, peered through his binoculars over the top, but couldn't see anything through the smoke and haze. An explosion nearby made him duck.

"See anything, sir?" asked Private White.

"Not a thing."

Duncan got down in the trench with the rest of them. The Germans were pouring on the artillery and would unquestionably follow with a major attack. Duncan suddenly became aware that there was something peculiar in the sky.

"Gas!" he yelled.

"Gas!" somebody repeated.

They ripped open their canvas bags and pulled out their gas masks. Draping them over their faces, they placed the big rubber clips over their nostrils and took the air tubes into their mouths. Their vision was restricted and the masks were awkward, but at least the doughboys could breathe without having gas eat holes in their lungs.

Artillery shells continued to fall. One landed near the parapet of the Second Platoon trench and caved in part of the wall, burying three soldiers. The others came to their aid and dug them out, as the trenches became covered by yellowish-green mist.

Duncan climbed to the top of the trench again and looked through his binoculars. He thought he saw movement in the field, but couldn't be certain because the lenses of his gas mask obscured his vision. Then he heard a machine-gun volley from his left, followed by random rifle shots. Straining his eyes, he was certain now that the Germans were advancing through the field, trying to gain a favorable position for their attack when the shelling stopped.

"Let's go!" Duncan shouted. "They're coming! Open fire!"

The men raised their heads as German shells fell all around them. Some of them were coughing from gas that had crept into their masks but positioned their rifles anyway and opened fire at targets they could see only indistinctly. Whenever a shell landed nearby they all crouched down, their fire easing for a few seconds.

Suddenly the shelling stopped. The doughboys knew the attack was coming, so fired wildly into the smoke and haze ahead of them. Machine guns sprayed back and forth, and soon, far out in the mists, the dark shapes of moving bodies could be seen. The wind was blowing the gas away, allowing the doughboys to see German shock troops racing toward them across the field.

It seemed strangely quiet. Rifle and machine-gun fire didn't sound like very much after the shelling. But in the field Germans were being cut down. They had about three hundred yards to go to reach the doughboy trenches, but were faltering. The doughboys had been trained in marksmanship, their shots piling up the German dead as machine guns mowed them down. Unholy screams erupted in the field, then the German attack broke. Instead of retreating to the line of woods in back of them, they swooped toward the woods on their flank, woods that were supposed to be held by other units of the Second Division.

Within minutes the Germans had fled the field, but this time they didn't have time to take their dead and wounded with them.

The gas had blown away, so Sergeant Tucker tore off his mask. "After the bastards!" he shouted, going over the top.

Duncan watched in horror as the men followed Tucker. He took off his mask and yelled: "Wait a minute!"

But the whole platoon climbed out of the trench and followed Sergeant Tucker toward the woods. Duncan decided he couldn't stop them now; they were too excited and hungry for German blood. All he could do was go with them and try to provide leadership. He scrambled up the side of the trench and ran after them.

Sergeant Tucker held his rifle high in the air. "Come on, you sons of bitches!" he shouted to his men. "Do you want to live forever?"

The other platoons in the company saw what the Second Platoon was doing and came out of their trenches to run after them. Even the machine-gun crews broke down their weapons and fell in behind the main charge.

"Come back here!" Captain Harrington screamed. "Where do you bastards think you're going?"

Everyone heard him but pretended they didn't. Duncan ran past most of his men and got in front of them with Tucker. Muzzle blasts flashed in the woods as Germans fired at them. Other companies in the battalion saw that Company B was charging Belleau Wood, and they came up out of their holes to join the charge. Soon Sergeant Tucker and Lieutenant Hunter were leading the entire battalion in an attack that no commander had ordered.

They charged into the woods like wild animals. The Germans hadn't had time to dig holes and fortify themselves, and soon had doughboys all over them.

This was the moment the doughboys had been waiting for, and they ripped into the Germans with relish, stabbing and slashing with bayonets, banging their rifle butts into German faces.

The Germans fell back beneath the ferocity of the attack, but the doughboys stayed close, cutting them down. The Germans retreated into the deepest part of the forest, and the doughboys went after them.

Rifle shots rang out and machine-gun positions were set up. The forest became littered with bodies. The Germans tried to pull together and launch a counter-attack, but the doughboys fought them off from behind trees and fallen logs. When it became clear that the German attack would not succeed, the doughboys went after them, routing them again, chasing them into gullies and killing them behind huge boulders.

In the late afternoon, the Germans obtained reinforcements and pushed the doughboys back a hundred and fifty yards, but then the doughboys received a new support battalion and hammered the Germans into another retreat. As the sun sank in the sky, no one could say for sure how much of the woods had been taken by the Americans and how much by the Germans.

Tripping over rocks and bumping into trees, carrying a German rifle and bayonet that dripped blood, Duncan fired through the darkening woods at Germans crossing a river up ahead. Duncan believed he should get his men across the river by nightfall; otherwise the Germans would fortify it by morning and the doughboys might never get across.

"Follow me!" he yelled. "Across the river!"

He fired the German rifle from his waist as he plunged into the rushing water. The Germans were halfway across, swimming and dragging their wounded. They yelped as they were shot down by intense fire, their bodies carried downstream by the current.

"Forward!"

Duncan went first and the Second Platoon followed him. Behind them came the rest of Company B. A shell dropped, and a group of doughboys near the river's edge was blown into the air.

"Forward!"

The water came up to Duncan s chest as he pushed ahead, holding his German rifle high in the air. Germans reached the other side and turned around, firing at the advancing doughboys.

"Forward!"

Bullets zipped into the water but Duncan kept charging forward. The water became increasingly shallow as he ran to shore, firing his rifle from the waist. The Germans on the shore ran into the woods as the doughboys charged toward them.

Duncan was gasping for breath, and he badly needed a few moments' rest, but first he must get his men dug in for the inevitable counter-attacks. They were haggard and covered with blood, their helmets slanted over eyes that glowed like hot coals in the night, but they could afford no rest either.

"Get those machine guns up here!" shouted Duncan.

He was telling the doughboys how to deploy, pointing to boulders, trees and natural depressions in the ground, when mortar shells suddenly began to fall upon them, with machine guns opening up to their front.

"Forward!" he yelled.

The Second Platoon began another charge, but a huge number of Germans came out of the woods and counter-attacked. The doughboys held their ground for about two minutes, then retreated to the river.

Duncan went with them, seeing that his men were outnumbered. "Back to the other side," he screamed. "Hurry up — get the hell out of here!"

They moved as quickly as they could, but the German mortar squads adjusted their sights and the shells fell on top of the retreating doughboys. Duncan fired wildly behind him as he retreated. Doughboys were running like dogs with their tails between their legs, wanting to get the hell out of there. Many were shot in the back, and would soon join their dead German enemies downstream.

The doughboys paused to fire behind them as they came to shallow water. Finally they reached the river's far side and hid behind the trees. The Germans had not followed them across the river, which would become the line of demarcation for the night.

Dripping water from head to foot, Duncan slogged up the bank and collapsed behind a boulder. He looked over it and saw the Germans retreating into the woods on the far side of the river. They'd probably send a mortar barrage over in a little while, but that would probably be it for the rest of the night.

"All right — dig in right here!" he said. "Post guards and send back for chow!"

Then he reached into his shirt pocket and took out his cigarettes.

"Who gave the order to attack?" screamed Lieutenant Colonel Foster.

Before him in the command post tent, Captain Harrington and the other company commanders stood with pale, worried faces. Today had been the first major action of the AEF in the war, and there had been major insubordination.

"Well?" Foster's small frame was rigid with anger. "What the hell happened out there?"

Harrington cleared his throat. "Well, sir, I think it might have begun in my company. When the Germans fell back, my boys just went after them. I tried to stop them, but they wouldn't stop."

"Did they have leaders?"

"I didn't see any, sir."

"Were any officers among them?"

Harrington remembered seeing Lieutenant Hunter, but said, "No."

Foster was pacing in front of the map table. "Heads are going to roll for this — let me tell you! We cannot have such gross examples of insubordination again. A soldier's first duty is to obey orders! If entire companies have to be put into the stockade, that's fine with me. If officers have to be relieved of command, that's okay too. I'm going to get this goddamn battalion into shape once and for all, or else I'm going to know why!"

"But, sir," Harrington protested, "the boys were just a little eager. They saw a chance to kill some Germans, so they went after them. They've been training for so long that they couldn't help themselves. Why not just let it ride this time, sir? I doubt it will happen again."

Foster stopped cold and narrowed his eyes. "You doubt it will happen again? Is that what you said? I can't run this battalion on what you doubt and what you don't. I have to run it on discipline, and by God I'll have discipline in this battalion or else!"

A commotion could be heard outside the tent. Everyone turned to the flap, which was pushed aside. Someone somebody shouted, "Ten-hut!"

The group of officers who entered the tent had *General Staff* written all over them. Foster blanched when his eyes fell on the wide-shouldered frame of the Iron Commander.

"What's going on in here?" demanded General Pershing.

Foster and his officers stood ramrod straight. "Sir," said Foster, "I was just dealing with a serious case of insubordination."

"Stand at ease, men," Pershing said, looking around. "Insubordination you say? What kind of insubordination?"

Colonel Foster explained the disgraceful situation. Captain Harrington stood with the other company commanders, fully expecting that in the next five minutes he'd be a private again. Pershing listened closely, his brow furrowed.

"Why didn't an officer step forward and try to stop them?" Pershing demanded after Foster was finished.

"Evidently they tried, but they couldn't."

Pershing looked at Harrington and the others. "Are these the company commanders?"

"Yes, sir."

Pershing turned to them. "Why couldn't you stop your men?"

Harrington answered first. "They were too eager to get the enemy, sir. If the German army couldn't stop them, I certainly couldn't. Actually, I don't think they even heard me. They just wanted to get their hands on the Germans, sir."

"Hmmm," said Pershing. He looked at the other company commanders. "Anybody have anything to add to that?"

"It was the same with my men, sir," said Captain Swenson of Company A. The other captains nodded in agreement.

"I see," said Pershing. He clasped his hands behind his back and paced in front of the map table, lost in thought. Finally he stopped and looked up at them. "It's highly undesirable," he said, "to check the fine fighting spirit of such troops. Experience will teach them caution soon enough, but gallantry can never be taught to them. That, thank God, they were born with. Colonel Foster?"

"Yes, sir."

"I suggest you let the matter drop quietly."

"That's just what I was thinking myself, sir."

"Good." Pershing turned to the map table. "Could you please give me an idea of where your men are?"

The officers gathered around the map table as Foster attempted to explain what had become of his battalion.

It was night and Duncan lay awake in his shallow foxhole.

"Help…"

No one stirred at the cry from across the river. They'd heard it all evening and knew it was Private White, but a rescue seemed near impossible.

Duncan smoked a cigarette and wondered what to do. Private White had been wounded, was alive and delirious, but couldn't make it back. The Germans were probably letting him carry on so that his plaintive voice would demoralize the doughboys.

"Help — Lieutenant Hunter! Help me, somebody … please!"

Duncan heard movement in the woods and a few seconds later Sergeant Tucker slid into the hole.

"How are we doing sir?" Tucker asked, pushing his helmet back on his head.

"I'm wondering what to do about White out there."

"That's what I came to talk to you about. A few of the boys from the platoon want to get him."

"No."

"But sir — we just can't leave him like that."

"That's why I'm going to get him."

"You?"

"Yes, me. I led the poor bastard over there and I'm going to bring him back."

"But—"

Duncan held up his hand. "Pass the word along that I'm going alone, and everyone should cover me. You'll be in command of the platoon while I'm gone. If anything happens, use your judgment. Any questions?'

Tucker took off his helmet and scratched his matted black hair. "You're going alone?"

"I think it's best that way — less noise, less bother. I'll be in and out before the Germans know what's happened."

"The Germans might be waiting for someone to come."

"If they are, one person can get away quicker than a bunch of guys who don't follow orders so well. Anything else?"

"Be careful, sir. We'd hate to lose you."

"Tell the men to get ready, and be completely goddamn quiet. I'll be moving out in about five minutes."

"Yes, sir."

"Help me somebody…"

Duncan started unbuttoning his shirt. "Jesus, I wish he'd shut up."

"He ain't gonna shut up until somebody shuts him up, or until you get him back over here."

Tucker crawled out of the trench. Duncan stubbed out his cigarette, stripped down to his undershorts, removed his belt and forty-five from his pants and strapped them to his head.

Private White moaned on the other side of the river as Duncan crawled out of his foxhole. Breezes whistled by his body, chilling him as he made his way on hands and knees to the water. Stones and twigs hurt, but he gritted his teeth and kept going. He reached the cold mud of the river and then came to the water itself. Pausing for a few moments, he peered through the mists on the other side. There was no moon, but his eyes had adjusted to the dark. Somewhere behind those mists was Private White, and Duncan felt compelled to get him out of there.

Duncan slipped into the water and swam silently. It was icy cold and nearly took his breath away at first, but he quickly grew used to it. He was reminded of how he and Blake used to go into the woods of Virginia at night, swimming streams like this, climbing trees, and stalking animals. Sometimes they even slept all night in the woods. Their father approved of their Indian games and sometimes went with them to be their chief.

Duncan swam against the strong current, aiming for Private White's plaintive voice. It was a miracle the soldier hadn't bled to death by now. He must have one of those wounds that heals, festers and hurts like hell. As Duncan swam he scanned the shore for Germans, but there was no sign of them. Still, the Germans might be hunkered down in their holes, just waiting for him.

His hand touched bottom. He stopped swimming and crawled along the riverbed to the shore, keeping only his eyes, nose and forty-five out of the water. If anything moved back there he'd pull the forty-five and start shooting. The Germans might get him, but he'd take a few of them with him first.

"Help ... Help me..."

The cries came from a section of riverfront straight ahead. Duncan slowly emerged from the water and crawled up on the bank. He kept looking for signs of German soldiers but could see nothing yet. The voice kept calling to him and he crept silently toward it. Something moved in the woods behind the voice, and he stopped cold. He waited for a few minutes, but when the sound didn't repeat he crawled forward again. After a few more paces he saw Private White lying on his back near the trunk of a tree. White's helmet was gone, and only his head moved as he whimpered and moaned.

Duncan crept up to him and crouched beside him. "Sssshhhh."

White turned toward him and went tense.

"It's only me," Duncan whispered. "I'm going to get you out of here."

White blinked his eyes. Duncan checked him over and saw an ugly wound in the man's groin. It was just as he'd thought: a wound that coagulated. Duncan doubted White would have much of a sex life from then on — if he lived, which was not certain.

"Can you hear me, White?"

White nodded.

"Any Germans around here?"

"Don't know."

"Don't make a sound."

Duncan picked up White and draped him over his shoulders. Crouching low, he carried White to the river and stepped in slowly so as not to make any loud splashing sounds. The river went roaring past and Duncan expected a bullet in his back at any moment. He wondered if the Germans had pulled back farther than he'd thought. That must have been what happened. They were regrouping someplace farther east.

He slowly dropped into the river, laying White back so that the wounded man was floating. Then he hugged him across the chest and swam back with him. The night was silent except for the sounds of the river.

"Are you all right, White?"

"Yes, sir."

"We're almost there."

Duncan continued to swim across the river. It had been much simpler than he'd thought, but now made sense to him. The Germans must have pulled out while White was still unconscious. White regained consciousness after they left, and called for help. White and Duncan had never been in danger, but Duncan could not have known that.

He touched bottom on the far side of the river. Soldiers came out of the darkness to help. They carried White back into the woods. Sergeant Tucker brought Duncan his clothes.

"You sure got guts, sir," Tucker said. "Never seen nothing like that in my life."

Duncan spat as he pulled on his pants. "There wasn't anything to it, Sergeant. The goddamned Heinies are gone. Get the men together and tell them to get across that river. If the Heinies come back in the morning, it'll be easier to fight them over there than over here."

"But the river is a great natural protection for us, sir."

"I'm not worried about protection for us, Sergeant, because we're going to be the ones who are attacking. I just don't want the Heinies to have the river for protection. Got it?"

"Yes, sir."

"Then move out."

CHAPTER 19

General Ludendorff stood in front of the map table in a château he had commandeered ten miles behind his lines. He was alone in the room, which was lit by a single electric light bulb hanging over the map. Littered along the edges of the map table were communiqués from the front. It was three o'clock in the morning and Ludendorff was sick with worry, for it was beginning to dawn on him that the battle was lost.

After so much intricate planning and so many gains, and even though he had the best troops, officers and equipment, he realized that his great offensive had failed.

Others might not think so, but they didn't have the facts that he had. He had lost three hundred thousand of his best assault troops and hadn't captured Paris, hadn't split the French and British armies, and hadn't broken through to the English Channel.

The drive he had put into effect was slowing down. In some places it had stopped. He'd never be able to mount such an offensive again. All he could do now was hold fast and try to wear the Allies down until they realized further war was futile and they'd sign an armistice. They were sick of the war too, he was certain. A deal would be made.

There was just one fly in the ointment: the Americans. His spies had informed him that new American divisions were arriving in France every week. They were fresh, eager troops and they weren't looking for an armistice. They wanted to win the war decisively. Ludendorff wondered if he could hold back this swelling mass of soldiers. He hadn't thought they'd mean much, but now realized he'd been wrong. The Americans had fought well and defeated some of his best troops. Sooner or later they'd attack. What could he do?

Sighing, Ludendorff left the map room. He walked down the dark corridors of the château, passing guards every several paces, and went to his bedroom. As he stood in front of the mirror and unbuttoned his tunic, his hands trembled, his throat dry. He wondered whether he'd be able to sleep tonight. After four years of war, he was beginning to feel as though he was falling apart. How much more of the strain could he manage? He knew he wasn't as sharp now as he'd been when the war began.

I've got to keep going somehow, he told himself. *The Fatherland is depending on me. I dare not slack off now.*

It was night in Belleau Wood. Private Bell was tired and cold and didn't feel like getting up to relieve himself, but there was no longer any waiting. He pushed himself on to his knees and looked around.

It was pitch-black in the woods. Bell could make out only the vaguest shapes of trees and boulders. It looked eerie and haunted and he felt alone although two divisions of men were in the woods with him.

No latrines had been dug yet, so he had to find a quiet little spot. Picking up his rifle, he walked away from the front lines and angled toward a bush he saw in the distance. He went behind the bush, pulled down his pants, and squatted. Then he picked up some leaves from the ground and wiped himself.

It was as if someone had touched him with burning acid. Bell swallowed his scream and grimaced, nearly falling into the mess he'd made. The pain, almost unbearable, made him feel faint. He closed his eyes and his head spun.

As the wooziness passed he took out his bayonet and cut away part of his sleeve, wiping himself with the fabric. That relieved the pain somewhat. Breathing heavily, he stood and pulled up his pants. Mustard gas had been on the ground and he'd wiped himself with it. He'd have to see a doctor now. Where the hell would he find a doctor?

He limped back to the spot where he'd been sleeping. *What a dirty deal,* he thought. He'd been engaged in so much tough fighting and hadn't been wounded seriously, but now was tormented by that damned mustard gas. He wanted to wake up Sergeant Tucker and ask him what to do, but didn't dare. On the other hand, he didn't dare leave to look for an aid station without asking permission.

He sat gingerly on the ground, but the pain worsened. He turned on to his side and closed his eyes. Despite the pain, he began to doze off. Suddenly there was an explosion not far away, followed by several more. German artillery shells began to rain down on the Second and Third Divisions. The shelling gradually became more intense until the woods were a mass of smoke, flame and fallen trees.

Bell huddled behind a boulder, and was soon joined by Corporal Murphy.

"Holy shit," Murphy said, as the woods resounded with the din. "I don't think the kitchens are gonna get through this."

"All you think about is food," Bell muttered.

"What else is there? What's the matter with you, anyway? You look like you just et something that didn't agree with you."

"I had a little accident."

"What kind of accident?"

"I took a shit this morning and wiped my ass with some leaves that had mustard gas on them. Boy, does it hurt."

Murphy began to laugh. "You goddamn fool!"

"How was I supposed to know there was mustard gas around?"

"You shoulda smelled it."

"Everything smells the same around here."

"You know what I'm gonna call you from now on? I'm gonna call you the red-assed baboon."

"I'm gonna ask Sergeant Tucker if he'll let me go back to the battalion aid station. He must be awake by now."

Murphy shrugged. "I don't suppose even Tucker could sleep through this."

Crouched over and carrying his rifle, Bell went to look for Sergeant Tucker as shells fell throughout the company area, knocking down trees and sending debris flying through the air. Bell passed soldiers clustered in shellholes or hiding under fallen trees. They smoked cigarettes and chewed hardtack while awaiting further orders. Finally Bell found Tucker and Lieutenant Hunter lying in a shellhole.

"What do you want, Bell?" Tucker growled.

"I gotta go back to the aid station, sir."

"What's wrong with you?"

Bell told him the story, and Tucker laughed as hard as Murphy had.

"That's about the funniest goddamn thing I ever heard in my life," Tucker said. "Only a birdbrain like you would do a thing like that."

"Can I go back?"

"Do you know where the aid station is?"

"No, but I'll find it."

"Go ahead, then. Don't get lost. We'll expect you back by noon."

"Thanks, Sarge." Bell crept away, keeping his head down.

The ground heaved from the impact of artillery explosions. Duncan looked at his watch. It was five o'clock in the morning and dawn glimmered faintly behind the trees.

"The Heinies are going to attack when this is over," Duncan said. "I think you'd better find out how much ammunition we've got left."

"About a quarter of our usual allowance," Tucker replied. "I checked last night."

"Send a runner back to battalion headquarters and tell him we need more."

Two German artillery observation balloons sat plumply above the woods, directing fire on to the American positions in Belleau Wood. Half the sun had risen on the horizon, making the balloons shine pink against the pale blue sky. The German officers studied the woods beneath them through binoculars, and relayed coordinates through their field telephones.

Flying above them was a squadron of German airplanes, assigned to protect the balloons from the American air service. They knew the Americans would be along sooner or later to try and shoot down the balloons.

They were not wrong. American soldiers all along the front had seen the balloons go up in the first light of dawn, reported their sightings, and the air service had been ordered to shoot them down. As the sun became a fiery silver ball on the horizon, the 94th Aero Squadron was streaking across the sky from their base at Villeneuve.

Lieutenant Blake Hunter was at the rear of one of the vee formations, wide awake and looking around to make sure no Fokkers were sneaking up on them. His face thin and deeply lined, he had been losing weight and felt ill. Like many of his compatriots, he was worn out by the incessant round of combat missions.

The American aviators knew exactly where the balloons were, and should sight them soon. Blake hunched behind the wheel of his Spad, hearing his engine's roar and feeling queasy fear in the pit of his stomach. The sensation of fear was fairly new to him.

His former duty with the escadrille had seemed all stunts and heroics, but now too many of his friends had been killed, and he'd faced death himself too many times. He was beginning to realize that the odds were running against him, and couldn't imagine how he would get out of the war alive.

Specks appeared in the distance ahead; the Fokkers were coming as predicted, but the American pilots had their tactics all worked out. One group would fight the Fokkers, and the other would shoot down the balloons. Blake was in the group that would go after the balloons.

One squadron rose into the air to fight the German planes, but Blake continued straight ahead. His orders were to avoid a fight with the Fokkers if possible. He should try to get away if it became necessary, but was not to engage.

Balloons emerged out of the dawn like big eggs floating in the sky. Blake's group held their vee formation, heading directly at the balloons while the other Spads fought the Fokkers. Whenever one of the Fokkers tried to get away to stop the planes in Blake's group, a Spad would go after it and try to shoot it down or hound it back.

One Fokker broke through though, heading down on the Spads flying at balloons. When the Fokker opened fire from above, Blake decided he'd better ignore orders and try to stop it. Pulling out of formation, he climbed up to attack the Fokker from the blind spot underneath it.

The Fokker continued its dive while firing its guns, and one of the Spads began to smoke. Blake held the Fokker in his sights and opened fire. The fuselage of the Fokker blasted into the air, disintegrating into a thousand pieces as the Fokker fell from the sky.

Blake returned to his attack formation. Escort Spads were keeping other Fokkers busy. Balloons were straight ahead, and in the baskets beneath them, observers were gesticulating wildly.

Spads in Blake's group peeled off for their strafing run. The pilots pulled the triggers of their machine guns, and the tracer bullets ripped into the balloons. On the ground, the German crews tried to pull the balloons in but they were too late. Blake dove toward one of the balloons, firing his machine guns, and the balloon burst into flame. The observers in the basket looked up fearfully. The fire spread over the balloon and air began to hiss out of it. Blake kept firing and the balloon ripped apart. The gases inside exploded and the fire crept down to the basket, which plummeted to earth. The observers jumped out of the flaming baskets to their deaths.

Blake pulled back his stick and climbed into the sky, noticing Spads were attacking another balloon. One of the Spads fell to earth, its tail on fire. Just then, a burst of bullets tore into Blake's wings.

Blake's plane bucked like a wild horse. He pushed his stick to the side to get away from whoever was attacking him. As he dropped he saw a Fokker following him down, and behind the Fokker was another Spad. The Fokker fired at Blake and the other Spad fired at the Fokker. Blake's Spad went out of control. He struggled with his stick, but couldn't pull the Spad out of the dive. The ground was coming up fast. He heard an explosion and glanced back to see the Fokker burst into flame.

Blake looked at the bottom of his stick and saw that the control wires had broken loose. He grabbed them with his gloved hands and tried to steer, sweating profusely despite the wind rushing at him. He pulled the wires and managed to level off the Spad, but he'd never make it back to the aerodrome. He was losing altitude steadily.

Many of the struts holding up his wings had been shot away. The Spad wobbled dangerously as it glided to earth. His engine sputtered because it had taken a burst of bullets in the intake manifold. Blake was headed toward American lines, but didn't know if that's where he'd crash. He might wind up behind enemy lines, and had heard that German soldiers sometimes shot on the spot Allied pilots they'd found behind their lines.

Blake's Spad skirted the tops of trees. He pulled his throttle and tried to get some power, but his engine conked out. He heard a terrible cracking sound as part of his right wing fell away. His wheels touched the treetops and he yanked the cords desperately to keep himself in the air. The treetops dropped away, and he saw a small pond dead ahead. *That's my only chance,* Blake thought. *I've got to land in that pond.*

The Spad sank lower, and the pond widened beneath him as he drew closer. He tried to raise the nose of his Spad so that it wouldn't topple over as soon as it hit the water, but couldn't bring it off. His wheels hit the water and his speed made the Spad flip suddenly on to its back. Blake tried to leap from the cockpit but before he was clear, something slammed down on his arm.

He was dazed as the Spad began to sink, dragging him down, but the icy water revived him. He kicked his feet and his buoyancy vest raised him up. His head broke through the surface and he looked around. His plane could no longer be seen, and his right arm ached fiercely, no good for swimming. With one arm and both legs he swam toward shore.

The pond was small, he soon reached its bank, climbed on to the grass, sat down and felt his right arm. The bone had broken through his skin just below his elbow and hurt intensely, a compound fracture. Otherwise he was in reasonably good condition. *Shot down,* he thought. *Well, what do you know about that?*

He had no idea whether he was behind German or Allied lines. He should have remembered to take his compass out of the cockpit, but events had been happening too quickly toward the end of his flight. Then he remembered the sun — you could always orient yourself by the sun. It was still early morning. All he had to do now was walk west, in the direction toward which the sun was moving.

He got up and began walking, holding his aching right arm with his left hand. Soaking wet, feet squishing in his boots, he tried to ignore the pain in his arm that threatened to overwhelm him.

It was a fairly warm spring day, and once he got moving he didn't feel so cold. He made his way through a beautiful forest where birds sang and no signs of war presented themselves. This realization troubled him, because Allied positions had been bombed thoroughly that morning. In fact, he could still hear shelling in the distance. Either he was very far behind his own lines, which was unlikely, or he was in German territory.

He hoped that a miracle had happened, that he was behind his own lines, and feared that he would faint from pain. If he reached safety, he would probably go to a hospital for a while. That meant he could stay out of a plane for a couple of months and get away from the damned war. He'd have more time to spend with Danielle.

He walked for a long time, finally arriving at a narrow dirt road running east and west. He turned west, blood soaking his sleeve. He'd give anything for a nice rest in a hospital and then a holiday in Paris with Danielle. He was amazed that she loved him so much. Sometimes he wondered how much she'd love him if she knew what he was really like.

"Halt!"

Blake froze in his tracks and his heart sank as he saw four German soldiers emerge from behind a bush. They approached cautiously, and one raised his rifle at Blake.

My God! thought Blake. *He's going to shoot me!*

Another German slapped down the rifle of the soldier who was going to shoot. Then all the Germans got into a heated argument, pointing at Blake and pushing each other around. They were getting so angry that Blake thought they might shoot each other.

It was clear that they were arguing about whether or not to shoot him. Whenever one soldier tried to assert his authority, the other soldiers shouted him down. Blake smiled and tried to look friendly, although uncomfortably aware of the predicament he was in. One of those Germans might kill him at any moment.

He heard the sound of an automobile. Turning around, he saw a vehicle speeding toward him down the road. As it came closer he saw that it was a large Mercedes-Benz convertible, its black finish highly polished. The German soldiers stopped fighting at the sound of its approach and turned to look.

The vehicle slowed and halted. The rear door opened and a tall, dapper-looking German officer got out — a major. He wore the wings of a pilot and had a medal hanging from his throat. A captain without a medal got out behind him. The German soldiers snapped to attention and saluted. The major asked them some questions, and they replied nervously. Then the major turned to Blake and smiled.

"Do you speak French?" the major asked, his French accent sounding as harsh as if he were speaking his native German.

"Yes," Blake replied, "rather well."

"So do I." The major bowed slightly. "I am Major Rudolph Kessler of the German Imperial Air Corps. Who might you be?"

"Lieutenant Blake Hunter, American air service."

"May I introduce you to Captain Gerd Steinhardt."

"How do you do," the captain said.

"Not too well actually," Blake replied. "I believe I've broken my arm."

Major Kessler looked at Blake's bloody arm and frowned. "We have a doctor at our château." He pointed to the rear seat of the car. "Please have a seat."

"Thank you."

Blake climbed into the car. A driver sat stiffly behind the wheel, his pancake hat squarely on his head. Major Kessler spoke with the soldiers, then he and Captain Steinhardt returned to the car.

"You wouldn't be carrying a weapon with you, by any chance, would you?" Kessler asked.

"I do have a pistol here."

"They really should have taken it from you."

"Why don't you take it? I'm having a problem with my arm."

Kessler reached around and took it, holding it up in his fingers. "Crude-looking thing," he said to Steinhardt. Then he turned to the driver. "Back to the château."

The driver shifted into gear, backed around in the road, then shifted again and drove off in the direction from which the limousine had come.

"Tomorrow," said Kessler to Blake, "you will have to show us where your plane is."

"I landed in a pond," Blake said. "I doubt you'll be able to see it."

"A lieutenant named Hettel shot you down, but then he was killed himself. You were his third kill."

"I didn't see him," Blake said. It was odd, this excessive politeness in the German's tone, and it made Blake wary. He thought it best to respond in the same manner.

"He showed great promise," Kessler went on. "It is too bad."

"I believe a number of American planes were shot down, too."

"I imagine that is very upsetting to you Americans, because you've just got into the war. We have been fighting for a long time, and are more used to it."

"On the contrary," Blake replied, "I'm very used to it. I flew for the French before my country declared war."

"Oh? You flew for one of the American escadrilles?"

"Yes. And I was with the French foreign legion before transferring over to the escadrille."

"What a coincidence. I have fought against them. Perhaps we have seen each other in the sky."

"Very possible," Blake agreed wryly. "By the way, where are we going?"

"To our headquarters. We would like you to have dinner with us, but then I am afraid we must send you to a prisoner camp."

Blake shrugged. "If that's the way it has to be."

"We cannot very well let you go."

"Of course not."

The car sped past the trees, kicking up clouds of dust behind. Blake's sleeve was becoming wet with blood.

Steinhardt leaned forward and looked at it. "Nasty wound you've got there. Perhaps you had better have something to drink."

"Do you have anything?"

Steinhardt and Kessler laughed.

"Of course we have something," Steinhardt said. Reaching into his back pocket, he took out a silver flask and handed it to Blake.

"Can't unscrew the top," Blake told him.

"Of course, sorry." Steinhardt took back the flask, unscrewed it and handed it to Blake. Steinhardt was blond and wore his hat at a cocky angle. Kessler had darker hair and sported a neatly trimmed mustache. His hat was low over his eyes. *They're both rather spiffy,* Blake thought. Just as he had been before the war began to take its toll.

"Here you are," said Steinhardt.

Blake accepted the open flask and took a big swig. The fiery liquid sizzled all the way down. He took another big swig, then handed the flask back.

"Just what I need," he said.

"How many kills do you have?" Kessler asked.

"Nine."

"That many!"

"Yes. All confirmed."

"Quite impressive."

"Not after nearly four years in the air. Say, I had a dogfight with one of your most famous flyers about a month ago. He flew a white Fokker and I believe he was Goering, isn't that so?"

"Yes — Goering flies a white Fokker. You fought Goering?"

211

"Evidently. Someone in a white Fokker almost shot me down, but the arrival of additional American planes chased him away."

"Very interesting," Kessler said. "I bet Goering would love to meet you."

"I wouldn't mind meeting him also, as long as it's not in the sky. He certainly lived up to his reputation."

Kessler looked at Steinhardt. "Perhaps we should invite him to dinner."

Steinhardt shrugged. "I've never known him to turn down a free meal."

"Perhaps we can have a little party." Kessler elbowed Blake gently. "You like parties?"

"Love them."

"Then it is settled. We shall have a party."

The driver turned a corner and the steep-roofed château came into view. Nearby was an airfield and hangar. The limousine continued down the winding road and turned on to a circular drive in front of the château. A group of officers came out of the château as the limousine pulled up. Kessler spoke to them in German, then he and Steinhardt helped Blake out of the back seat and introduced him to the assembled men. Blake noticed that all of them seemed quite friendly, with the exception of one officer who frowned as he shook Blake's left hand.

Blake felt weak from loss of blood, but two officers held him up, then followed Kessler into the château and to the doctor's office. A nurse and two orderlies were there with the doctor.

"Well," Kessler said, "we'll be back for you in a little while."

The orderlies and nurse helped Blake to one of the beds and told him to lie down. They removed his jacket and shirt, remaining silent even as they saw the bone sticking through the skin of his arm.

The doctor held a hypodermic needle in the air and squirted a bit of serum out of it. "This will not hurt much."

He stabbed the needle into Blake's shoulder, and seconds later Blake began to feel dizzy. The room spun around as the doctor, nurse and orderlies gazed down at him and smiled. It occurred to Blake that the whole experience had been a dream and he'd awaken soon in his bed at Villeneuve, with all his old friends, and maybe they'd go out to shoot down some German balloons.

CHAPTER 20

"My dear, I am very sorry but it is just as you suspected, You are pregnant."

Danielle stared at him, unwilling to believe her ears. "But Doctor Saulnier, it cannot be!"

The white-whiskered old man shook his head sadly. "It is."

She raised her hands to her cheeks. "What am I going to do?"

"It might be a good idea to have a talk with your mother."

"My mother?"

"Who else?"

Danielle dropped her hands into her lap. She looked around the doctor's office, from the degrees on the walls to the immense bookcases, to the glass-doored cabinets that held gleaming instruments. "I can't believe this," she said. "It can't be happening to me."

"Surely, my dear," he said gently, "you know that babies don't come out of thin air."

"Yes, but…" Danielle didn't know what to say. She had never believed such a thing — such a disgrace — could happen to her. "My mother will kill me."

"I doubt that," Saulnier said, repressing a smile.

"If she doesn't my father will."

"Extremely doubtful also."

"Doctor, will you do me a favor? Will … will you tell my mother for me?"

The doctor raised his white eyebrows. "Me? I'm sorry, Danielle, but that is a responsibility that falls on your shoulders, not mine. And I doubt that having me break the news would make any difference."

"But I can't face my mother!"

The doctor reached over and held her hand. "My dear, you are a woman now. You must take control of this situation. You must determine what to do, and not expect others to do it for you. This is not a catastrophe. These things happen all the time, even in the best families, and everyone knows it. I suggest that you go home and tell your mother right now. The sooner she knows, the sooner you can all start working together on what to do."

Danielle was so nervous that she was wringing her hands. "I might be able to reason with my mother, but my father might shoot somebody."

"In my experience," the doctor said, "and mind you I have two daughters of my own, fathers are notoriously weak with their daughters. They will kill their sons at the drop of a hat, but they'll let their daughters get away with just about anything."

"He'll kill Blake!"

"Is that the father's name?"

"Yes."

"Then don't tell him the young man's name until you determine it is prudent to do so."

The doctor took Danielle's hand and led her out of his office. Georgette was sitting in the waiting room and got up as the door opened. Georgette could see that Danielle had been crying, and she knew the verdict. But she'd known it all along, for she knew what morning sickness was.

The two young women walked through the corridor and down the front steps of the building. It was a bright summer day but so many people had left the city already for their vacations that the streets seemed relatively empty.

"Well," Georgette said, taking Danielle's arm, "are you going to have it?"

"What do you mean?" asked Danielle. "What other choice do I have?"

"Well," said Georgette, "I happen to know a doctor—"

Danielle stopped on the sidewalk and turned to Georgette. "Are you talking about an abortion, Georgette?"

Georgette looked Danielle in the eye. She wasn't afraid of Danielle after knowing her for ten years, through all of her temper tantrums and whims. "What else would I be talking about?"

"Never!"

"Never say never."

"I said never and I meant never!" Danielle replied vehemently. "I'm going to have this child one way or the other!"

"Whatever you say, ma'am. Shall I get a cab?"

"Please do."

Georgette raised her arm, but no cabs were available. They had to wait a long time before they finally found one to drive them home.

Blake awoke in mid-afternoon, and at first he didn't know where he was. Then he saw his right arm in a cast and remembered everything. His pack of cigarettes had been placed on the table near his bed, and he lit one up. It was only a few minutes later that the nurse stopped by and asked how he was doing. He said he thought he was all right.

I might as well enjoy this while I can, he thought. *Tomorrow I'll be going to a prisoner camp, a grim prospect indeed. I might even spend the rest of my life there.*

When he and Franklin DeWitt enlisted in the foreign legion in 1914, he'd never dreamed that he might spend five or ten years in a prisoner camp. But at least he was still alive. Franklin had not been as lucky…

An aide brought him some soup with dumplings, which was delicious. Then Blake fell asleep. An hour later, Captain Steinhardt arrived with Blake's uniform on a hanger. "We cleaned your uniform, and Captain Goering has indicated that he would come tonight. I am sure you will want to look your best."

"Surely," Blake said, surprised and pleased.

"How are you feeling?"

"Quite well, actually, except for my arm."

"Nice here, isn't it?"

"Very nice."

"Belonged to a French count. He is gone, of course, with his family. Kept a magnificent wine cellar. We German pilots always get the best accommodations. I imagine it's the same with you?"

"Not always."

Steinhardt returned to his duties, leaving Blake alone. He slept for a while, then woke in late afternoon and stood to look out of the window. As he was doing so, a German ambulance drove on to the estate and made its way around the circular drive to the front of the château. It stopped, the attendants got out, and a crowd of pilots formed. The attendants opened the rear door of the ambulance and removed a stretcher bearing a man who was obviously dead. The man was carried into the château, and among those closest to the stretcher was the young officer who'd been cold to Blake earlier in the day. Now Blake knew why. This man was a friend of the pilot who had been shot down, perhaps by Blake. *Well,* Blake thought, *we can all be killed at any time in this war, but the main thing is that we all remain gentlemen. At least, I hope these Germans remain gentleman, and don't put me before a firing squad.*

Marie Giraud sat in her living room, reading a newspaper. At forty-five years old she was still trim and petite, but her hair was graying and lines becoming imprinted at the corners of her eyes and mouth. She had a large nose and had never been particularly attractive, but was deeply religious and considered almost saintly among her friends and family.

Danielle entered the living room. "Hello, Mother."

"Hello, dear. Where have you been all morning?"

Danielle leaned toward her mother and kissed her cheek. "At the doctor's."

Her mother looked up with an expression of concern. "Nothing serious, I hope."

"Yes and no..." Danielle sat on the chair opposite her mother. The fireplace was nearby and a huge oil painting of her father in uniform hung over it "Mother," said Danielle, "you'd better prepare yourself, because I ... I have some rather bad news."

"What is it?" her mother asked, leaning forward on her chair.

"I'm pregnant."

Marie Giraud paled. "Pregnant?" she asked, dazed.

"Yes, Mother...

Blake finished dressing and looked at himself in the mirror. His uniform fit loosely because he'd lost so much weight lately, but otherwise he looked fine. They'd mended his sleeve where the fabric had been torn. He'd taken a bath and shaved. Sitting on the bed, he lit a cigarette and looked out of the window. The sun had set and darkness fallen on the château. His arm didn't hurt nearly as much as before.

There was a knock on the door.

"Come in."

Captain Steinhardt entered the room. "How are you feeling, Lieutenant?"

"Rather well, thank you."

"Dinner is being served soon. Would you care to come downstairs?"

"Sure. Is Captain Goering still going to join us?"

"Yes, he just arrived."

"I've been looking out of the window. I haven't seen anyone new arrive."

"He flew here in his plane."

They descended the stairs to a hallway crowded with officers. All the chandeliers were lit and the hall was brilliant. Major Kessler stood at the foot of the stairs, smoking a cigar, his chest covered with decorations, a large medal hanging around his neck.

"Lieutenant Hunter — how are you?" he asked, holding out his hand.

"Much better, thank you."

Kessler again introduced Blake to the other officers, and he shook all their hands. One was Count Leo von Viebahn, the young officer whose friend Blake had shot down. This time he was polite, if somewhat reserved.

A hush suddenly fell over the room. Everyone looked toward the door, where a tall, lean man wearing a monocle was standing. Blake knew that this had to be Goering.

Kessler clicked his heels. "Captain Goering, may I present Lieutenant Blake Hunter of the American Air Service."

Goering smiled as he approached Blake. He gripped Blake's hand firmly. "So good to meet you."

And Blake could have sworn that he meant it, so sincere was the German's manner.

Just then a servant walked by carrying a tray of champagne glasses. Goering lifted two glasses off the tray and handed one to Blake. When all the officers held glasses of champagne, Goering raised his glass. "To men of courage everywhere!"

They heartily echoed his toast, then sipped their champagne and fell into conversation.

"I understand you flew with the French," Goering said to Blake.

"Yes, since the beginning of the war, practically."

"The French are good pilots, as are the British. But the Americans have yet to prove themselves."

"We will."

"No doubt."

Everyone started moving into the dining room, which had a long table set up at its center and clusters of candelabra along its length. Goering sat at the head of the table, and invited Blake to sit beside him. Major Kessler sat at the other end of the table.

The servants poured more champagne, then returned to the kitchen and brought out tureens of chicken consommé. Blake noticed that Leo von Viebahn was sitting across from him, and was wondering what to say to him when Goering interrupted his thoughts.

"Where are you stationed?" Goering asked.

"Villeneuve." Blake was grateful for the opportunity to postpone conversation with the young German officer.

"I am at Metz. On what day did we meet?"

"It was about two weeks ago. You're the only German pilot who flies a white Fokker, aren't you?"

"Yes."

"Then it was you for sure. As I recall, it was early in the morning, on the dawn patrol. You and your pilots flew out of the sun and attacked us. I tried to get away, but you got on my tail. I did loops and turns — everything I could think of — but I couldn't shake you. I thought you had me, and indeed you would have if more of our planes hadn't arrived and chased you away."

"I remember!" Captain Goering exclaimed. "We were returning to Metz after observing the front. We saw you before you saw us and I ordered my men to attack. I selected you for my target — don't remember why now — but I couldn't seem to get you. It's true — you did try every trick in the book. I remember thinking what an excellent pilot you were. If you were not, let me tell you that you would not be here right now."

Blake shrugged. "I was lucky then, but not so lucky today."

Goering's eyes glittered as he smiled. "Too bad we will never meet again to finish our little joust."

"Fate holds of sorts of possibilities."

"You are a prisoner. You will not fly again in this war."

"Captain Goering," Blake said, "I've been thinking about something. Both sides capture enemy aviators all the time. Why don't you trade me for one of the captured German aviators? You must have a friend or a close comrade you'd like to have back."

Goering looked at him appraisingly. "I have many."

"Surely something can be arranged."

Goering nodded. "Not a bad idea. I suppose we could give it a try."

"No!"

The cry came from across the table. Everyone stared as Lieutenant Leo von Viebahn shot to his feet, his face pale, lips trembling.

"I cannot tolerate this nonsense anymore!" Viebahn screamed. He pointed at Blake. "This enemy aviator killed Franz today, and we are treating him like a hero! Have you all gone mad? Have you forgotten that we are at war? You're acting as if it's all a game, but it is not! How dare anyone suggest that this aviator be permitted to return to his side! He should be put up against a wall and shot immediately as an enemy of the Kaiser!"

Goering stood and gazed levelly at the young man. "Count von Viebahn, would you please be so good as to leave this room."

Viebahn glanced from Blake to Goering, trembling with the effort to control himself. Finally he pushed his chair back and marched out of the room. There was awkward silence as Goering returned to his seat.

Goering leaned toward Blake. "I apologize for the bad manners of Count von Viebahn."

"I accept your apology," Blake said, "but it is unnecessary. I understand how the young man feels. I am responsible for the death of his friend, and indeed I imagine that many here in this room were friendly with the dead man."

Goering nodded. "Yes, but we are all volunteers. We know what might happen to us. And there is nothing personal in what you did. You are a soldier, and we are soldiers. You fight for your country, and we fight for ours." Goering sighed and shook his head. "I detest politics and doubt I could even explain precisely what this war is about. But I'll tell you one thing that I know — we have an unfortunate situation in our country where cowards and slackers are blaming soldiers for this war, when we only do our duty, as you do yours. It is disgusting. No — it is worse than disgusting. It is treachery of the lowest sort. I imagine you have the same sort of thing happening in your country?"

"I don't know," Blake said. "I haven't been home for so long."

"You are lucky. You might not like what you see there." Goering smiled suddenly and raised his glass. "We are getting awfully gloomy. Let us drink up and enjoy tonight's festivities, because tomorrow will come soon enough. It is not every day that two people like us have the opportunity to meet. After this war is over, you must come and visit me, Lieutenant Hunter. You have a standing invitation, as of now. We shall dine together again and remember when we were aviators for our countries during this great war."

"I'll look forward to that," Blake said, touching the rim of his glass to Hermann Goering's. *But will we both be alive when the war ends?* he wondered.

The dust-covered Citroen screeched to a halt in front of the building on the Rue St Faubourg. The rear door opened and General Hercule Giraud got out. He was a short man with a bulldog face, and his eyes were ablaze with anger as he vaulted up the steps. He pounded on the door, which was opened by Georgette.

"Where is she?" the general demanded.

His wife came down the corridor. "Hercule! What are you doing here?"

"What am I doing here? I am here to get to the bottom of this disgraceful matter. Where is my daughter?"

"In her room, but please calm down, dear. There's no reason for you to get upset. The child is pregnant. You wouldn't want her to have a miscarriage, would you?"

She led her husband into the living room and sat him on the sofa. Georgette went for coffee, and Marie Giraud sat beside her husband, taking his hand. "I should have known you would come as soon as you received my message."

"Of course I came! How could I not?"

"But you must have plenty to do at the front."

"Who is the man?"

"A young American aviator."

"Good grief! An American aviator? What kind of idiot have I raised?"

"These things happen, dear. I understand he is a very nice person."

General Giraud sat stiffly on the sofa. "He can't be very nice if he gets young girls pregnant. Well, is he going to do the right thing?"

"You mean marry Danielle?"

"What else would I mean?"

"We don't know."

"You don't know! Why don't you know?"

"The young gentleman has been missing in action since last Thursday."

General Giraud stared at the wall, then buried his face in his hands. "Oh, my God!" he muttered.

"Daddy?" said Danielle, entering the room.

Marie motioned for Danielle to go away, but it was too late. General Giraud shot to his feet and glowered at his daughter. She saw immediately that he knew, and that he wasn't happy about it.

He pointed at her. "How could you do such a thing?"

"I love him," she said simply.

"You love him?" the general cried. "What do you know of love, you silly little girl?"

"Daddy, calm down."

He began to sputter, but when Marie gestured for him to be silent he grumbled and sat down again. Just then Georgette brought a pot of coffee and cups into the room. She stole anxious looks at their faces as she poured, but could see it was too early to know the outcome.

The room remained quiet for a few moments after Georgette's departure. Then General Giraud looked angrily at his daughter. "You have dishonored me, young lady."

She replied, "Stop being so melodramatic," she replied. "You're only thinking about yourself, as usual. What about me? And what about Blake?"

"Is that his name?"

"Yes. He's missing in action, maybe even dead." A tear rolled down her cheek. "He's a wonderful man. I love him with all my heart. He is the man for me, and I am the woman for him."

"Please stop," General Giraud growled. "I'm becoming quite nauseous. I can't believe you would do a thing like this to me and your mother." He shook his head, eyeing her sternly. "There is a war on. My duty is to be a soldier, your mother's duty is to manage this household, and your duty is to remain chaste. You, young lady, have failed in your duty!"

Danielle began to cry. "I'm sorry, Daddy. I didn't mean it."

General Giraud looked to his wife for support, but she was frowning at him. General Giraud cleared his throat and sipped some coffee. "Well," he said, "I suppose we'll all get through this somehow."

CHAPTER 21

Second Division Headquarters was set up in a tent deep in Belleau Wood. The officers were clustered around the map table, trying to keep track of the battle, when someone shouted: "Attention!"

The officers snapped to as Major General Jean Degoutte of the French army entered the tent. He was commander-in-chief of all the American and French troops in that sector.

"At ease," he said. "Is General Bundy here?"

Preston Brown, the Second Division Chief of Staff, stepped forward. "No, sir, he's away inspecting the lines."

"I see," replied Degoutte, approaching the map. "Can anyone here tell me what is going on in front of this division?"

"What specifically do you want to know, sir?"

"Are you holding?"

"Yes," replied Brown. "We're holding."

"Good," said Degoutte. "It is very important that you hold. If the Germans break through anywhere on this front, there will be nothing to stop them from advancing all the way to Paris."

Preston Brown grinned and pointed in the direction of the front. "I wouldn't worry about that if I were you, sir," he said. "Those are American soldiers down there, and they haven't been beat in one hundred fifty years."

Private Bell ran around a tree, jumped over a fallen log and dived into a shell crater. Bullets whizzed over his head and his chest heaved as he struggled to catch his breath. He was hungry and his canteen was nearly empty.

"Get them fuckin' machine guns!" shouted Sergeant Tucker.

Bell raised his head an inch and looked for the machine guns. They were somewhere in front of him, behind bushes and trees. Bell raised his rifle to take a shot in the direction of the machine guns when suddenly he heard a shell whistling down on him. He hastily drew back down into the hole and pulled his helmet tight over his head. It sounded as though the shell was going to land right on him, and he swallowed hard with fear. He looked up and could see it, a gray blur hurtling down toward him. He gritted his teeth and waited.

The shell slammed into the ground only two feet away from the hole he was in. Dirt flew into the air — but the shell didn't explode. Bell cautiously raised himself to look at it. The shell was half in the ground and half out. "A dud," he muttered. "I'd better get out of here."

He jumped out of the hole and ran across the woods, while bullets zipped over his head and mortar shells exploded all around him. He saw a big boulder in front of him and jumped behind it.

Private Sullivan was there, firing his rifle.

"Sully," said Bell, "you'll never believe what just happened to me."

Sullivan wasn't listening. He was too busy firing his rifle. Bell took out his dirty handkerchief and wiped his filthy face with it. Uncapping his canteen, he took a swig of water but was careful not to finish it all.

"Move up on that machine gun!" Tucker shouted.

Sullivan ran out from behind the boulder. Bell followed him, noticing other men also advancing toward the German machine gun. They ran several steps, dropped to their stomachs, fired a few shots, and charged again. Somebody on the right screamed and went down with two machine-gun bullets in his guts. Bell jumped up and ran forward, wishing he had some hand grenades. When he thought he could see the machine gun, he dropped to his stomach again. Peering over the dead leaves, he saw bursts of blue smoke and the trembling of branches. When the machine gun fired, he saw more smoke and movement.

"It's over there!" he screamed, pointing with his rifle.

"Where?" It was Lieutenant Hunter's voice.

"Over there!"

Duncan jumped up and started running toward the machine gun. "Follow me!"

Bell and the other survivors of the platoon scrambled to their feet and rushed the machine gun. It was only twenty-five yards away, the gun barrel swinging back and forth, spreading death before it. Sullivan yelped and fell, writhing on the leaves. Bell jumped over him and followed Duncan toward the machine-gun nest. Another soldier screamed as he tumbled to the ground. Duncan fired his pistol as he ran. Sergeant Tucker and a few other soldiers fired steadily at the machine-gun nest, trying to keep its occupants down. Duncan's forty-five ran out of ammunition so he dropped to one knee to load up again.

Bell trotted around him and charged the machine-gun nest alone. He could see the long, ugly snout of the barrel. Darting to the side, he put on one final burst of speed and jumped over the wall of the embankment, landing inside the machine-gun nest.

Four Germans inside were surprised to see an American soldier in the hole with them. Bell fired his rifle from the waist and shot one of the Germans through the throat. He ran another one through the chest with his bayonet as the German soldier was trying to rise behind the machine gun. The third went for his pistol, but Bell slammed him in the face with the rifle butt. The fourth was on his feet now, but before he could shoot, Duncan jumped into the nest and fired his forty-five. The last German slumped to the ground.

Duncan took off his helmet and wiped his forehead with the back of his arm. Sergeant Tucker and the others piled into the machine-gun nest, stepping over the dead Germans.

"Let's stay after them," Duncan said. "Form a skirmish line and let's go."

They jumped out of the hole and formed a skirmish line. Duncan waved his arm forward and they moved out. An occasional shell fell to their rear, but only random bullets were fired at them now that the machine-gun nest had been silenced. Bell looked to his left and saw only fourteen men left in a platoon that once had numbered forty.

Duncan motioned with his arms to the ground and they all dropped down. "Sergeant Tucker!" he called out.

Tucker crawled up to him. "Yes, sir?"

"I'm going up ahead to see what's there. You stay here with the others and cover me."

"You sure you don't want me to go with you, sir?"

"I told you that I want you to stay here. Bell!"

"Yes, sir."

"Come with me."

Duncan and Sam Bell stood and began stalking forward through the thick brush. They were six feet apart, crouched over, moving stealthily. Bell's eyes scanned every bush and rock for sign of German troops deployed for ambush. He looked up into the trees for snipers.

"Hold it!" Duncan said.

Bell stopped in his tracks.

Duncan pointed ahead with his forty-five. "Look!"

Bell looked but couldn't see anything. "What is it?"

"I think it's a clearing. Get down."

They both dropped to their bellies and crawled forward, inching their way along the forest floor. Something snapped to their left and they stopped suddenly, jerking their weapons around toward the sound. They waited a few seconds, but when nothing happened they resumed their crawl. Finally they came to the edge of the woods. They peeked through the branches and saw wheat fields ahead of them. To the left they could see German soldiers running down the hill toward a small village.

Duncan decided he'd better not take his men into the village without orders to do so. He'd better find Captain Harrington and tell him the village was there. Taking out his map of the area, he marked the location of the village, then motioned for Bell to follow him back to the platoon.

Captain Harrington lay in a shellhole, wondering what to do next. His company was strung out all over the woods, he was low on ammunition, no one had eaten for more than a day, and it looked as though the fighting in Belleau Wood might go on forever. His company had been making only erratic movements through the woods and he had no wire communications to battalion headquarters. Maybe he should go back to battalion headquarters to check in.

Lieutenant Dirkson, his new executive officer, was lying beside him in the hole. Dirkson was smoking his last cigarette. He needed a shave, and his eyes were bloodshot from lack of sleep. Harrington knew he himself must look just as bad. Worse than the filth and fatigue was the guilt he felt for not being closer to the front with his men. But he didn't even know exactly where they were.

He heard something crash through the underbrush and drew his forty-five. Lieutenant Duncan Hunter of the first platoon appeared, running with his head low and his forty-five in his hand. Harrington waved at Hunter, and Hunter headed for the shellhole.

Duncan dropped down and crawled into the shellhole. "It was harder to find you than a needle in a haystack, sir."

"It's a wonder you didn't get lost. What's the problem?"

Duncan unfolded his map. "We've come to the end of the woods and I don't know what to do next, sir. There's a village down there —" he pointed to its location on the map — "and wheat fields over here. We saw Germans headed down into the village, but I can't tell how many of them are down there. You think I should send down a patrol?"

Harrington pursed his lips. "I don't know. A patrol might get massacred. Maybe I should see about bringing some artillery down on the village."

Duncan shook his head. "I don't know about that, sir. There might be civilians in the village, and the Germans might just be passing through."

"Sir," said Lieutenant Dirkson, "maybe I should take a run to battalion and find out what's going on. Maybe I can get some kind of wire communications back here."

"No, I'd rather keep you here with me. You never know what might happen." Harrington looked at Duncan. "I think you should make the run to battalion headquarters, Lieutenant. You're pretty good in the woods."

"Back to battalion, sir?"

"Right. Tell them our situation here. We need ammunition and food, and instructions on what to do about that village."

"Sir, maybe you should go, so there won't be any questions about what the orders are. And no one at headquarters will pay much attention to a lieutenant asking for food and ammo."

Harrington groaned. "You're right. They'll walk all over you up there. But the bastards won't dare give me any trouble." He looked at Dirkson. "You think you can hold everything down until I get back?"

"I think so, sir."

"All right." Harrington looked at his watch. "It's 1500 hours. If I'm not back in three hours, you can assume that the Heinies got me."

Harrington got to his knees, hitched up his belt, and checked his forty-five. He looked at Dirkson and Duncan. "See you later, boys," he said. "Hold the fort."

Duncan returned to his platoon and found his men huddled around Private Robert Whitewater, a pure-blooded Indian from Utah who had joined the company shortly before it came to Belleau Wood.

"What's going on here?" Duncan asked.

"He's making food," said Sergeant Tucker, "or at least that's what he said he's doing."

Duncan got down on his knees and watched. Whitewater appeared to be grinding something between two flat stones.

"It's wheat, sir," Whitewater said. "I'm making wheat berry mush."

He lifted up one of the stones, and everyone scrutinized the paste-like substance. Whitewater dabbed some with his fingers and put it in his mouth. "Not bad. Could use more water, but we don't got more water."

Private Winslow and Private Crawford showed up with more wheat. Whitewater passed out the batch of mush he'd been working on, then started on more.

Duncan tried some, putting a small bit into his mouth. The paste was sweet and chewy. He noticed Bell sitting nearby, licking the substance off the palm of his hand.

"Bell, can I speak with you a moment?"

Duncan walked back several yards from the other men, with Bell following him. The woods smelled like gunpowder and freshly cut lumber.

"Bell," Duncan said, "I forgot to tell you, but that was a great job you did back there in that Heinie machine-gun nest."

Bell looked away from him and scratched his nose in a nervous gesture. "Which nest was that, sir?"

"The one that you jumped in alone."

"Oh, that machine-gun nest…" Bell fidgeted and looked embarrassed.

Duncan smiled, thinking back to the way he'd ridden Bell when they first met. He'd been wrong about Bell, given him too little credit. Or maybe Bell had changed in this damn war. *For that matter,* he thought, *maybe I have too.*

"I'm going to put you in for corporal," Duncan said. "You're a helluva soldier."

Bell looked around as though he wanted to escape.

"Yes, sir."

"You may rejoin the others now, Bell."

"Thank you, sir."

Duncan watched as Bell ran back to the group of doughboys. Then he sat on the ground and leaned against the trunk of a tree, closing his eyes and puffing on a cigarette. It was strange that he'd come to respect and like Bell so much, when he'd thoroughly loathed him at their first meeting. But that seemed like so long ago. And Duncan had been quite a different person then.

Captain Harrington made his way through the tangled and devastated forest, in search of battalion headquarters. Whenever he found soldiers he asked them for directions, but most of them didn't know where they were themselves. He continued toward the rear, following his instincts and scraps of information he was able to gather. The forest was littered with dead bodies, many of them torn apart by violent explosions.

Finally, after an hour, he ran into Captain Shilansky of Company C, who said he'd been to battalion headquarters a few hours ago and told Harrington where it was. Harrington set out in the direction Shilansky indicated, and a half hour later saw a large group of officers in a clearing. Harrington walked toward them and saw that it was Colonel Malone, the new regimental commander, with several of his staff officers. They all looked glum. Harrington approached and saw that they were standing around an immense shell crater. Harrington looked down into the crater and saw a few scraps of canvas, some lengths of splintered wood, and a man's shattered leg.

"Looking for battalion headquarters?" Colonel Malone asked Captain Harrington.

"Yes, sir."

Malone pointed to the hole. "There it is, down there."

Harrington looked into the crater and the hair rose on the back of his neck.

"A direct hit from a 155," Malone said. "Fortunately my staff and I were in the field, but several clerks were killed instantly, and Colonel Foster happened to be there, waiting for me."

"Oh, my God," whispered Harrington, the color draining from his face. Lieutenant Colonel Foster had been commander of Harrington's battalion.

"I'm glad you showed up," Malone said. "We were just talking about putting you in command of the battalion, now that Colonel Foster is out of action."

"Me, sir?" Harrington asked weakly.

"That's right. There's no one else available right now. I'm told you've got more time in grade than any other company commander in the battalion."

"Ah, I don't know, sir."

"I do. From now on you're an acting major and commanding officer of your battalion. I'll send a few officers to serve as your staff. You might want to bring your executive officer along from your company."

"Then who'll command my company?"

"The best officer you've got. I'm sure somebody will be able to handle it."

"Yes, sir."

"Another thing, Harrington," Malone said. "Whenever you move, dig in right away." He pointed to the hole in the ground. "I don't want any more repetitions of this. Carry on."

Colonel Malone turned and led his staff away from the clearing, leaving Harrington standing alone beside the big hole in the ground. Harrington took off his helmet, crossed himself, and mumbled a prayer.

Duncan lay at the edge of the woods, peering at the village through his binoculars. He could see no movement; the Heinies had evidently passed through and set up a position farther east. Duncan thought he ought to take the village while he had the chance.

Nearly three hours had passed and Captain Harrington hadn't returned. Duncan really shouldn't take the village without orders — but on the other hand, he didn't think he should let the opportunity pass by. Finally he decided to send a patrol into the village to find out for sure if any Germans were there. After all, they might simply be hiding, using the village to set a trap.

"Sergeant Tucker!"

Tucker came crawling over. "Sir?"

"Take a few men down into that village to see if anyone's there. Don't take any chances. If anyone starts shooting, get the hell out fast."

"Yes, sir."

Tucker decided to take Bell, Whitewater and Gleason. Hunched over, they departed the woods, holding their rifles ready to shoot, bayonets in their scabbards.

Down the hill they went, passing through the field of wheat. Their eyes darted around and their mouths grew dry, because a German machine gun might suddenly open up and cut them down. Bell imagined German eyes looking at him in the shadows behind the windows of the village. The Germans probably were licking their chops, waiting for the doughboys to get closer.

The village consisted of a dozen stone houses on either side of a dirt road. The houses looked eerie to Bell. Children should be playing in the road, women hanging out washed clothing and bedding in the backyards, but there was not a soul about. Perhaps the residents of the village had fled, but were Heinies lurking behind the windows?

They slowed and drew their heads lower as they moved on to the road leading into the village. Sergeant Tucker held up his hand, indicating they should stop.

It was silent; not even the birds were singing. The only sound came from the distance — the too-familiar sound of muffled explosions and the fire of rifles and machine guns.

Duncan watched them through binoculars from the edge of the woods. On both sides of him were the other members of the platoon, ready to open fire if anybody took a shot at the patrol.

Tucker looked at the silent rows of houses and decided that they'd have to break into a few of them to make sure no Germans were inside. If he were a German he'd put his men in the houses facing the woods, because that's where the American attack would come from. He pointed toward one of the houses.

"Bell," he said, "see if anybody's in there. We'll cover you."

Bell walked up the path that led to the front door of the house. He looked at the windows but could see no movement behind them. Everything was weirdly silent — too silent, he thought. He stepped on the wooden platform in front of the door and reached to the doorknob, trying to turn it, but it wouldn't budge.

"It's locked!" he called back to Tucker.

"Kick the damn thing open!"

Bell kicked the door with all his strength, but his foot only bounced off it and stung with pain. He aimed his rifle at the doorknob and fired three times, shattering the look and wood. Kicking again, the door flew open. He dashed to the side, in case somebody inside was ready to shoot, but there were no shots.

Bell cautiously entered the house and found himself in a kitchen with a sink, counter top and icebox, but no one there. He opened the icebox and found nothing inside except a puddle of water. Returning to the door, he cupped his hand around his mouth and shouted to Tucker, "Nobody here!"

Tucker sent Whitewater into the house across the street; it too was empty. He checked the third house himself, again empty. Walking toward the edge of town, he signaled to Duncan that the town was deserted.

Duncan led the platoon into the village, and his men rampaged through the houses, looking for food and liquor. One man found some rabbits in a cage in a backyard, and others found bottles of brandy and wine. Potatoes, carrots and onions were discovered in some of the cellars. The doughboys lit fires in the stoves and began to prepare feasts.

Duncan settled himself in the living room of one of the houses and wondered whether to send somebody after Captain Harrington. The problem was that he didn't know where to look for his company commander. Had he been killed? What was the big delay? Duncan decided to stay where he was until ordered to move. Captain Harrington would return sooner or later. And if not, somebody else would arrive with orders.

A soldier brought him a bottle of wine and he took a drink. In the kitchen, a rabbit stew was simmering on the wood stove. Sitting in the living room and smelling the aromas of dinner somehow reminded him of his wife, Patricia, who lived with his two children in Virginia. He wondered what she was doing right now. It was the first time he'd thought of her in some time. He didn't really miss her, and didn't feel much of anything for her. Just a vague regret. He thought of Catherine Hawkins more frequently, and with more feeling, than he ever thought of Patricia.

A soldier Duncan had never seen before entered the living room. "You Lieutenant Hunter?" the soldier asked.

"Yes."

"I got a message for you from battalion headquarters. I'm supposed to wait for a reply."

Duncan held out his hand, unfolded the paper and saw the unmistakable scrawl of Captain Harrington.

Colonel Foster has been killed in action. I am the new battalion commander, and you are herewith appointed commander of Company B, with the temporary rank of captain. Lieutenant Dirkson is coming to battalion with me. Report your present position, and I'll have supplies sent to you along with wire communications. Good luck.

Blake Hunter, his right arm in a cast, sat in the rear seat of a Rumpler CIV as it approached the AEF aerodrome at Villeneuve. Captain Steinhardt of the German air force sat in the front seat and piloted the aircraft. Long trails of white bunting flew from its wings to identify it as a truce aircraft.

Blake, wearing his flying hat and goggles, looked over the side of the Rumpler to the aerodrome below. He could see people congregated beside the hangars, obviously waiting for him. A series of radio messages had set up the prisoner exchange. Blake had been worried that he'd need to spend years in a prisoner camp, but now, only two weeks after being shot down, he was being returned, exchanged for a German aviator. He couldn't wait to get his feet on the ground.

He saw Steinhardt pushing the stick forward to bring the Rumpler down. The nose lowered and the big bomber began its descent to the runway. Lower and lower it flew as Duncan watched the runway coming up quickly. Treetops whizzed by, then the Rumpler touched down.

Duncan felt like shouting for joy. The first thing he wanted to do was call Danielle in Paris. She'd been on his mind constantly.

The Rumpler taxied down the runway. Blake looked at the buildings and hangars, overjoyed to see them. Villeneuve was his home, and now he was back at last. Just a short while ago he'd wondered if he'd ever see Villeneuve again, and now here it was.

The Rumpler coasted to a stop. Aviators and mechanics rushed toward it. Among them was a young man in a German uniform with bandages around his head and left leg, assisted by two American aviators.

The Americans crowded around the rear seat of the plane. Two of them climbed up and lifted Blake out of his seat. Everyone cheered when Blake's feet touched the ground. He stepped toward Captain Steinhardt, who extended his right hand out of the cockpit. The propellor was still turning, sending back blasts of air and making it difficult to hear.

Blake gripped Steinhardt's hand. "Goodbye, and thanks for the ride."

"Till we meet again," Steinhardt replied.

The American officers placed the bandaged German in the Rumpler's rear seat and strapped him in. Then they all stepped back from the plane. Steinhardt waved one last time at Blake, then pulled out the accelerator. The idling Mercedes engine snarled to life and the Rumpler moved forward. Steinhardt glanced at the buildings and hangars, thinking how strange it was to be on an enemy air base. Then he accelerated down the runway, came to its end, pulled back the stick, and soared into the sky.

There was a lump in Blake's throat as he watched the Rumpler and its white bunting become smaller in the sky. He'd liked the Germans he'd met when he was a prisoner, and hoped to meet them again someday when the war was over, if they didn't kill each other first.

Pilots and ground crew crowded around and shook his hand. Captain Kenneth Marr, the commanding officer of the squadron, welcomed Blake back.

"We thought we'd lost you for good," Marr said.

"You're not that lucky," Blake replied with a laugh. "I wonder if you'd mind if I used your telephone now. I'd like to call Paris."

"Sure," Marr said. "Come back to my office. How's your arm?"

"Compound fracture, but I'm sure it'll be all right real soon."

"How'd the Heinies treat you?"

"Pretty well."

Blake told them the highlights of his experience with the Germans as they walked toward the administration building. They were astonished by his description of the dinner with Hermann Goering. Blake could see that they were viewing him with awe, as if he were a god or a hero, and he liked the feeling. They crowded around him, listening to him talk, and he imagined that newspaper reporters would be interested in his story, too.

They came to the administration building. Marr escorted Blake inside his office. "Sit behind my desk and make whatever calls you like. I'll leave you alone for a while."

"I don't want to make you leave your own office," Blake protested.

"Shaddup and make your calls."

Marr left the office and Blake sat behind the desk. He looked at the telephone and the papers spread out beside it, thinking how nice it must be to command a squadron of aviators. If his luck held out, he'd command one himself before long.

He picked up the phone and asked the operator to connect him with the Paris exchange. When the Paris exchange came on, he told the woman Danielle's phone number.

The phone buzzed in his ear, and he prayed she was home. There was a click, and he heard a female voice. "Giraud residence."

"Danielle Giraud, please."

"Who's calling?"

"Lieutenant Blake Hunter."

"Lieutenant Blake Hunter?"

"That's right."

"Just a moment, please."

A pack of cigarettes lay on Marr's desk. Blake took one and lit it up while waiting for Danielle.

"Blake?" Her voice was breathless, excited.

"Hi. I'm back."

"Oh Blake — I'm so happy to hear from you!"

"Believe me, I'm happy to hear you, too."

"We were afraid you'd been killed!"

"No, just a broken arm. I'll probably be coming to Paris in a day or two. Can I see you?"

"Of *course* you can see me. I've missed you so much."

"I've missed you, too. In fact, I've been thinking about you a lot. I've decided that I'd like to marry you. How do you feel about that?"

There was silence on the other end for a few moments. Then: "I think it's a marvelous idea," she said, her voice tightly controlled now. "You see, I'm pregnant…"

Blake stared at the top of the desk. "Pregnant?"

"Yes."

"Oh…"

"Not changing your mind, are you?"

"No — just a little surprised, that's all. Do your parents know?"

"Yes. They've been taking it rather well, all things considered. They'll be very happy to know you're back. They were going to send me to Switzerland."

"Your father probably wants to kill me."

"He did at first. Now he's resigned to the situation. He will be happy to know that you have proposed to me. That will solve all our problems."

"I can't believe you're pregnant."

"Well, I am."

"I've got to get back to duty. I'll call you before I come to Paris."

They said goodbye, made kissing sounds, and hung up. Blake stubbed out his cigarette and looked out of the window at a Spad taking off. *I'm going to get married,* he thought. *I guess it's about time.*

PART 3

CHAPTER 22

"The time has come to counter-attack," said Field Marshall Foch, standing at the map table in his office.

On the other side of the table were General Pershing, General Haig, Field Marshal Pétain and General Mangin, plus interpreters.

According to intelligence reports, German troops were exhausted, their supply lines drawn taut. It appeared that the great German offensive had stalled. If ever there was a propitious time for the Allied armies to attack, it was now.

Foch planted his finger on the map in an area near Soissons. "We shall attack here, where forty German divisions are commanded by General Boehm. If we can take the high ground near Soissons, we will place them in jeopardy. A lightning thrust will cut off their supplies and we shall be in a position to close in and annihilate them."

Foch scratched his mustache and continued. "We will attack along the front from Rheims to Soissons, with the main effort on the west. I have selected General Mangin's Tenth Army for the task, with the Twentieth Corps as the spearhead. The actual assault divisions will be the First and Second American Divisions, and the First French Moroccan Division. They will be supported by a full complement of artillery, and by approximately one hundred fifty light and heavy tanks. Two more divisions will be in immediate reserve." Foch looked up and smiled. "As you can see, this will give us overwhelming strength on a front only five miles wide. Each of you will receive more detailed orders within the next few days. Any questions?"

No one said anything.

"Gentlemen," continued Foch, "I feel that we have come to the crucial moment of this war. Now at last we are in a position to deliver the Boche a crushing blow when they are weak at the front and their government is collapsing at home. I believe that this war can be won by the end of this year, if this assault is successful." Foch gazed purposefully into the eyes of each officer before him. "Gentlemen," he said, "we dare not fail."

Blake, his arm still in a sling, climbed the steps to the building where Danielle lived. His heart beat rapidly, for this would be the first time he'd seen Danielle since he'd been taken prisoner by the Germans. She had told him on the phone that both of her parents would be home, and he'd put on a freshly cleaned and pressed uniform for the occasion.

He knocked on the door. There was no response, so he knocked again. Glancing behind him, he saw that the sidewalks and streets were crowded again, just as they'd been before the war. The citizens of Paris who'd left when the German army was threatening had returned now that everyone knew that the German war machine had been stopped.

The door opened and Georgette stood there, a nervous smile on her face. "Yes?" she said.

"I'm Lieutenant Hunter," Blake said, taking off his hat.

"Please come in, Lieutenant Hunter. Please give me your hat."

Blake had no sooner handed her his hat than Danielle appeared in the vestibule. She threw herself at him, and he drew her tightly against his chest, pressing his lips to hers.

"I love you," he whispered.

General and Mrs. Giraud entered the vestibule. General Giraud cleared his throat.

Danielle separated from Blake and introduced him to her parents. Her mother shook Blake's hand and smiled, deciding that he was every bit as handsome as Danielle had said. Even General Giraud was impressed by the dark, handsome, confident manner of the young aviator. The general thought, *Perhaps everything will turn out all right after all.*

There were a few moments of awkward silence as everyone looked at Blake, whose eyes were admiringly on Danielle.

It was Mrs. Giraud who spoke first. "We heard that you had been wounded, Lieutenant. I trust you are mending well?"

"Quite well," Blake replied, flashing his irresistible smile and noticing that the living room behind the vestibule was nothing less than sumptuous. Evidently he was marrying into a wealthy family, probably as wealthy as his own. He doubted his parents would have any objections to this match. And his marriage, unlike poor Duncan's, was for love. Who would have thought that Blake Hunter, that daring and frivolous young man, would marry for love?

General Giraud looked at his watch. "I must get back to the front," he said in his gravelly voice. "I believe we have something to discuss, Lieutenant?"

"Yes, sir."

"Come with me, please."

Blake followed the general across the living room and down a corridor to a wood-paneled office. The general sat behind the desk and invited Blake to sit on one of the two green leather chairs facing it.

"Well," said the general, "let us not waste any time. I understand that you want to marry my daughter."

"Yes, sir."

"Good. You appear to be a decent young man. I hope that you will be good to her."

"I love her, sir. I'm sure that we'll be happy together."

The general gazed at Blake, trying to perceive a glimmer of falsehood, but could detect nothing. The young man appeared sincere.

"You understand," the general said, "that marriage can be very difficult?"

"Yes, sir," Blake replied, thinking of his mother and father and of Duncan's marriage. "But I believe — and you might think this silly — that Danielle and I are destined for each other, and we'll have a successful marriage."

The general pursed his lips. "Let us hope so. Well, there is a problem, as I'm sure you know. Danielle —"

Blake interrupted: "I'm sorry about that sir. It was…"

General Giraud held up his hand. 'Too late for that now. We must deal with the problem at hand. You and Danielle must be married as soon as decently possible. Then, within a reasonable length of time, Danielle must leave for Switzerland to have the child. She has an aunt there with whom she can stay. When the baby is born, we will make certain changes in the birth certificate. I am sure you understand what I am talking about."

"Yes, sir."

"Good. Then everything is decided. Let's go out and have a drink with the ladies."

They rose and left the office. As they made their way down the corridor to the living room, General Giraud glanced sideways at Blake. "What did you say your father does?"

"He's in the railroad business."

The railroad business, the general thought. *This marriage is looking better and better all the time.*

They entered the living room. Danielle and her mother looked at them, hope on their faces.

"Everything is settled," the general said. "Let's drink a toast to the upcoming marriage. Then I must be getting back to the front."

CHAPTER 23

Everett Dewitt was walking from the French War Ministry to General Pershing's Paris Headquarters at 73 Rue de Varenne, his briefcase stuffed with papers because he'd just attended a meeting with lower-echelon French officers concerning details of the attack at Soissons. His brow was furrowed because he was considering asking General Pershing for a transfer to the front.

He felt like a coward; so many friends and former classmates were serving at the front, while he was fighting the war far behind the lines, working in the comfort of spacious offices, sleeping on clean sheets every night, dining in the best Parisian restaurants, leading a soft life while others were attacking German machine-gun nests daily.

Someday in the future, when he returned to New York after the shooting was over, and people asked him what he'd done in the war, it would be embarrassing to say that he'd worked in offices far behind the lines. Even now when he spoke with his friends, he noted an attitude of condescension toward him, because they were combat officers, while he was basically a clerk.

"Everett!" called out a female voice.

He glanced up and was astonished to see Danielle Giraud, on the arm of none other than Blake Hunter.

"How are you, Everett?" Danielle asked graciously, holding out her hand.

"Very well, thank you. How are you, Danielle?"

She touched her left hand to her face, but Everett was too surprised to notice the engagement ring on her finger. "I am fine," she said.

Blake held out his left hand. "Good to see you, old man."

"Good to see you." Everett awkwardly shook Blake's left hand, noticing his right arm in a sling. "Nothing serious, I hope?"

"Only broken. They say it'll be good as new in a few weeks."

"Crash your plane?"

"I was shot down by the Heinies."

"Sorry to hear that." Everett felt himself becoming more depressed. Everyone had wounds sustained in battle, wounds like badges of nobility, and the worst thing that had happened to him was that he'd stubbed his toe while walking around barefoot in his darkened room.

Danielle managed to wave her engagement ring in front of Everett's face again. "I don't suppose you've heard the news," she said.

"What news?"

Danielle looked at Blake and smiled proudly.

Blake grinned. "Danielle and I are getting married."

"Congratulations," Everett said, feeling depression turn to anger. Blake the combat pilot had won the beautiful woman while Everett was walking around in the dark stubbing his toes. "I hope you'll be very happy together."

Danielle touched Everett's arm. "You'll have to come to the wedding, Everett dear."

"That's right," Blake said. "After all, you're the one who introduced us."

"Yes, I did, didn't I?" Everett replied, trying to sound happy.

Danielle opened her purse and took out a little leather notebook. "What's your address, so I can send an invitation?"

Everett told her his address, then asked, "When are you getting married?"

"Sometime in mid-July," she replied. "We haven't set the precise date yet."

Everett thought it seemed awfully soon, but didn't comment or think about it further. They continued to chat for a while, then Everett glanced at his watch and told them he had to return to his office. They shook hands once again, Everett congratulated them and they parted.

Everett was furious as he walked toward the Rue Varenne. Danielle had preferred Blake to him, unquestionably because Blake was a famous aviator and he a mere clerk. Everett was more determined than ever to transfer to a combat unit. He resolved to ask General Pershing about it the first chance he got.

On Bastille Day, the tricolor fluttered in the summer breeze from the rooftops of houses and public buildings all over France. The Second Division was billeted in the villages around Montreuil-aux-Lions, taking a well-deserved rest after having been withdrawn from fighting on the Marne two days before. The doughboys were spending most of their time sleeping and caring for equipment. There were rumors about a whorehouse in one of the villages, but so far the men had been too tired to investigate.

That evening, Captain Duncan Hunter returned to his command post, a small white cottage, and hung his helmet on a peg.

"Order the platoon leaders to report to me immediately," he told Private Whitewater, his runner.

Whitewater sprang up from the cot where he'd been resting and ran out of the door. Duncan took a cigarette and looked at Sergeant Kersey, his new first sergeant.

"We're moving out first thing in the morning," Duncan said. "You'd better start getting everything together now."

"Where are we going?"

"You'll find out at the meeting."

Duncan walked back to his office, opened his map case, and took out the maps they'd given him at battalion headquarters. He spread the maps on his desk and was studying them as his platoon leaders arrived one by one. They sat on wooden chairs around the desk and when all of them were there, along with the quartermaster sergeant and Sergeant Kersey, Duncan began the meeting.

"We're moving out first thing in the morning," Duncan said. "There's going to be an attack around Soissons, and we'll be in the spearhead."

The sergeants and young officers groaned. They had thought they'd have a week of rest at least, but now it was back into the meat grinder again.

"I knew something was up," said Second Lieutenant Thorpe of the Third Platoon. "The artillery's been moving out all day."

Duncan pointed to the map. "We're headed for the forests around Retz. Once we get there, we'll travel by night to the jump-off point, and will become part of a very big battle, much bigger than anything we've been in before. Speed will be all-important, so keep your men moving. At headquarters they think that if we can beat the Heinies at Soissons, we can win the war by the end of the year."

"Bullshit," said Sergeant Tucker.

"Maybe so," replied Duncan, "but I expect all of you to give this fight your very best. Any questions?"

"Where's the jump-off point?" asked First Lieutenant Dawes of the Second Platoon.

"I don't know yet," Duncan said. "I imagine I'll find out tomorrow. Any other questions?"

Nobody said anything.

"Then return to your units and prepare the men to move out," Duncan said.

General Pershing looked up bleary-eyed from the stacks of papers on his desk. "You wanted to speak with me, Everett?"

"I know you're busy, sir, but it'll just take a minute."

"Have a seat."

Everett sat in front of the desk and looked at the Iron Commander buried under work connected with the big Soissons offensive. "Sir, I wonder if I might be permitted to transfer to a combat unit."

Pershing sighed wearily. "I knew you'd ask sooner or later, Everett. Everyone wants to go to the front and fight the Huns. But I'm afraid I need you here. I'm sorry."

"But sir," Everett protested, "you said once yourself that no one is indispensable in the army. It shouldn't be any problem to replace me. Why, I could find a replacement myself."

Pershing shook his head. "It's true that no one is indispensable, but at this time I need you here with me. The AEF has a variety of needs, and your special skills are of more use here in my headquarters than anywhere else in the army. You can't be as easily replaced as you think. I'm sorry, Everett, but that's the way it has to be. The army comes first. Also, to be blunt, I don't think you'd be good in the infantry. Although you're tall, you appear frail. Physical strength is extremely important in the war that's developed here in France. There's been a great deal of hand-to-hand fighting, and the man with the greatest physical strength almost certainly will win a hand-to-hand fight. I think you can serve the army best with your mind, which is a very fine one, rather than with your body, which probably wouldn't last long at the front. That's my final decision. Anything else?"

"No, sir."

"You may return to your office."

Everett rose and walked out of the office. Frustrated and disappointed, he made his way down the corridor to his office. *I may not get a transfer*, he thought, *but someday I'll figure a way to get to the front, and then I'll find out what kind of man I am.*

CHAPTER 24

It was the night of July 18 in the Forest of Retz. Lightning jagged across the sky and rain fell in torrents. It was so dark that the men of the Second Division had to hang on to each other's belts as they moved in long columns through the woods, soaked to their skins, tired and hungry. But they had plenty of ammunition and hoped to have the advantage of surprise on their side.

Men cursed as they slipped in the mud. They'd been on the move for two days, traversing twenty miles of roads congested with trucks and tanks. The French troops they were relieving came from the opposite direction, adding to the confusion. The American officers didn't see how their troops could make it to the line on time, but the French officers were confident everything would go off like clockwork.

The Second Division doughboys hadn't eaten all day, and their canteens were low on water. Everything had been sacrificed to speed, moving into position at night so the Germans would have no inkling of the attack that would befall them in the morning. The attack would be German-style, preceded by a brief but intense artillery bombardment, then a wild charge intended to cover as much ground as possible.

The First Division would be on the left, the Second Division on the right, and Moroccans between them. Assault troops had been ordered to advance quickly and leave behind enemy strong points to be mopped up by the second and third waves of attackers. Their immediate objective was to seize the heights above the valley of the Crise.

Duncan marched at the head of Company B, along with Sergeant Kersey and Private Whitewater. Rain dropped on to his helmet and he shivered underneath his soaking clothes. Bolts of lightning illuminated the woods for brief moments, and Duncan could see the men of the First Battalion all around him, spread out over a half mile of the attack line. He looked at his watch: two more hours to go before the attack began. He hoped they could make it to their jump-off point by then.

Wet branches slapped his face, making his scar sting. He pushed the branches out of the way and kept trudging along. The Forest of Retz was spooky and he wouldn't relish being here all alone at night. He'd read that the forest had been site of a castle inhabited by Gilles de Rais, a fifteenth-century nobleman reputed to have been the original Bluebeard. Duncan wondered if women were buried under the earth where he was marching, because not all de Rais's victims had been found.

Exhausted and confused, the Second Division advanced through the forest. The doughboys heard tanks rumbling along the dirt roads, and hoped their artillery was in position. Everyone wondered how the attack would go. The old-timers among them had seen many comrades die at Château-Thierry, and more than half of the attacking doughboys were new replacements. Not a man among them didn't wonder if he'd be alive tomorrow night at this time.

As the hour of attack approached, the order was passed down to double-time. The doughboys ran through the woods, their gas masks and gear bouncing up and down. Some men tripped and fell face-first into the muck, but their buddies helped them up and they kept going. Panic set in among some of the new replacements; they wondered what had gone wrong. The old-timers tried to reassure them and keep them moving along.

Finally they reached the edge of the woods, stopped and lay panting on their bellies, checking their equipment and waiting for the barrage to begin. Duncan looked at his watch; it was nearly 0435 hours. They'd made it to their jump-off point ahead of time.

The pitter-patter of rain and the thunder in the heavens were suddenly augmented by the roar of the artillery barrage. The ground trembled beneath them and they could see flashes on the horizon. Swarms of shells whistled over their heads, landing on the German lines straight ahead. Even through the driving rain they could see the orange and red shellbursts.

Duncan took his forty-five out of its holster and licked his lips. He'd been through this routine many times already, but he still had the metallic taste of fear in his mouth. He knew he'd never get used to it no matter how many battles he was in.

An officer from battalion rode by on a horse. "Let's go, boys!" he shouted. "Up and at 'em!"

Duncan stood up and raised his pistol high in the air. "Forward!"

The doughboys couldn't see where they were going, but raised themselves off their bellies and moved forward anyway. They emerged from the Forest of Retz and advanced across a grassy plain. Although it was still night, the German front ahead of them was aflame, as artillery barrages rained hell upon the German soldiers.

French tanks were interspersed among the doughboys, some already firing machine guns. The French Moroccans screamed their battle cries, and the Second Division doughboys realized this was the biggest operation they'd been in so far. They became excited, some shouting rebel yells while others screamed Indian war whoops. Duncan looked from right to left, shouting orders.

"Dress right!" he yelled. "Keep moving!"

The order "dress right" meant that every man should line himself up with the man on his right, in an effort to keep the skirmish line straight. The barrage began rolling back. Duncan pumped his right arm up and down in the air. "Double-time!"

He saw the barbed wire of the first German outposts straight ahead. The barbed wire had been blown apart by artillery shells, and there were huge craters everywhere. Duncan jumped over some barbed wire but one of the hooks caught his pantleg and ripped it open, cutting his skin. He landed on the ground, ran four steps, and saw a German aiming a rifle at him from inside a trench straight ahead. Duncan screamed and jumped feet first at the German, who fired his rifle. The bullet whizzed past Duncan as he kicked the German in the face with both of his boots. The German dropped to the ground, half-unconscious. Duncan rose to his knees and shot him through the heart.

He looked to his left and right and saw his men overpowering the few Germans in that forward outpost trench. "Keep moving!" he yelled.

They climbed up the rear of the trench and continued their drive. Tanks fired machine guns at the fleeing Germans. The attack had been easy so far, but the old-timers knew that German resistance would stiffen within the next mile or two. The Germans were falling back to build up a strong defensive position and marshal their reserves for a counter-attack.

The rain still fell, but the day was growing lighter. The sun was rising, although it was still heavily obscured behind the clouds.

The attacking troops swept across the fields in three waves. German mortar fire began to fall on them, but they kept on going. German machine guns opened fire on them, but that didn't stop them either. Doughboys were blown into the air and cut down by bullets, but those still alive kept charging hard. They knew that their only salvation was to keep moving.

Duncan saw the next row of German trenches straight ahead. Torn barbed wire was everywhere, and German helmets, rifles and machine guns could be seen in the trench network.

"Keep your lines straight!" Duncan shouted. "Make sure you don't shoot each other! Make sure you shoot the Krauts! Go get the bastards!"

Duncan ran toward the trench, firing his forty-five wildly in front of him. The ground rocked with explosions and bullets whistled everywhere. Men screamed as they fell to the ground, trying to staunch with their hands the blood flowing from horrible wounds.

Then the doughboys jumped into the trench and the melee began. German and American soldiers stabbed each other with bayonets and smashed each other's heads with rifle butts, grunting and bellowing as they contended in the trench, blood spurting into the air. In the darkness it was hard to see who was friend or foe, and the soldiers soon found themselves fighting on top of dead bodies that squished beneath their boots.

A German soldier lunged his bayonet at Duncan, who fired his forty-five at the soldier's face. The bolt clicked; the pistol was empty. Duncan raised his left arm to block the bayonet, and it sliced him open from wrist to elbow. In the excitement of the moment, he barely felt the pain. Rearing back his right hand, he slammed the German in the face with his empty pistol. The German's nose split apart and blood squirted out. Duncan hit him again, shattering his jaw. The German fell back, and Duncan kicked him in the groin. Duncan snatched the rifle out of the German's hands, positioned it, plunged the bayonet into the German's stomach and yanked it out. The German reeled and collapsed on top of the other German and American bodies.

The killing of the German and the pain in his arm unleashed an animal wildness in Duncan. Shrieking like a maniac, he slammed the rifle butt into a German's face, breaking cheekbones and fracturing his skull. The German fell and Duncan stepped on his stomach to charge another German soldier. The man hesitated, fear on his face, and Duncan reared back, throwing his rifle and bayonet forward like a harpoon. The bayonet sank to the hilt into the German's chest, and his eyes rolled back in his head. Duncan yanked the bayonet out and blood gushed after it.

The German sagged to the ground. Duncan looked to his left and saw a German running a doughboy through with his bayonet. Duncan raised his German rifle, took quick aim and pulled the trigger. The German shuddered as if shaken by a giant, and a dark stain appeared on the back of his tunic. He fell face first into the accumulating bodies lying at the bottom of the trench.

"Forward!" Duncan shouted. "Keep moving!"

The doughboys climbed out of the trench and charged farther into the German position as the Allied barrage blanketed the landscape before them. The doughboys followed the barrage, their ranks greatly depleted. Duncan looked to his right and left and saw that his company had about half the men he'd started out with when the attack had begun. He heard hoofbeats behind him and turned around. Astonished, he saw

French cavalrymen leaping over the trench he and his men had just taken. The cavalrymen stood in their stirrups and waved their sabers in the air.

"Make way!" Duncan yelled to his men. "Let them pass!"

The soldiers bunched together and the troops of cavalrymen thundered past. They wore bright blue uniforms with silver helmets and yellow plumes. They shouted battle cries as their sleek horses kicked clods of mud into the air. The men of the First Battalion watched in astonishment, for they'd never seen anything like it in their lives.

Duncan realized that the attack must have opened a huge hole in the German front, and cavalry was being rushed in to exploit it. *We're winning*, Duncan thought. *We've got the bastards on the run.*

"Forward!" he hollered. "Dress right and follow me!"

There was a knock on the door. General von Ludendorff opened his eyes. "Who is it?"

"Captain Beck, sir. General Boehm is on the telephone. He is under attack and wants to speak to you."

"Under attack?" Ludendorff reached for the telephone. "What is it, Boehm?"

"Sir," said the anxious voice in his earpiece. "I have been under attack since four-thirty this morning, and I thought I should notify you."

Ludendorff turned on his lamp and looked at the clock on his dresser. It was fifteen minutes after five. "Who is attacking you, and where is their main effort?" he asked, trying to sound calm although his heart was pounding like a drum.

"They are Americans and French, and they appear to be concentrating on the high ground near the Crise Valley."

Ludendorff closed his eyes and saw the map of that area in his mind, recognizing immediately the threat to Boehm's Seventh Army if the enemy took that high ground.

"Boehm, can you maintain your position in those hills?"

"I don't know, sir."

Ludendorff thought for a few moments, while trying to hold down the rising panic. He'd known that an attack would come from somewhere, and he'd been afraid that the Allies might inflict a humiliating defeat on him. But he could not permit that to happen. It would be better to give up ground than suffer a defeat.

"Can you hear me clearly, Boehm?"

"Yes, sir."

"Get out of there. Move all your troops back to our side of the Marne. I don t want to take any chances with forty divisions of good soldiers. Is that clear?"

"Yes, sir."

"You have your orders. Carry them out."

In his headquarters bunker near Reims, General Boehm hung up the phone.

"What did he say?" asked his adjutant, Colonel Hoepner.

"He said to retreat to the other side of the Marne." Hoepner shook his head. "Evidently he has lost his nerve."

"But we must follow orders. Who knows, he may be right."

"He is not right." Hoepner scrutinized the map. "He should bring in troops from another front and hit the Americans on their left flank. That would bring their big attack to a sudden halt, I can tell you that."

Boehm looked Hoepner in the eye. "Would you risk the safety of forty divisions on the success of a flank attack?"

Hoepner wilted before Boehm's stare. "I don't know," he replied. "I'd have to give it more thought."

"There isn't time for more thought," Boehm snapped. "The decision has to be made now, and the colonel-general has made it." He looked down at the map. "We will carry out our orders, but in our own way. My army will move back to the Marne, but the Americans will pay a high price for every inch of ground they get."

Carrying a captured Luger in one hand and a forty-five in the other, Duncan, bleeding from his arm and leg, led his company up the hill to the artillery emplacement.

"Keep moving!" he yelled. "Take those goddamned guns!"

The company now had only eighty men left, but they followed Duncan up the hill. The German artillerymen huddled behind the sandbags surrounding their big guns and fired rifles at the charging doughboys.

These Germans weren't front-line infantry soldiers and weren't accustomed to this kind of face-to-face warfare. Some broke and ran, while officers screamed at them and ordered them back to their positions, to no avail. The Germans who stayed in their positions leveled rifles at the attacking Americans and pulled their triggers as quickly as they could. Some of the doughboys fell to the ground, but the mass kept hard-charging.

"Hand grenades!" Duncan shouted.

The doughboys dropped to their stomachs, took hand grenades out of their pockets, pulled the pins and hurled the grenades at the German position. The grenades flew up the hill like plump birds and landed behind the sandbags. A series of ear-splitting explosions rent the air, German bodies blowing above the sandbags. Duncan leaped to his feet, brandishing both of his pistols.

"Follow me! Take that high ground!"

He ran up the hill, his remaining doughboys following close behind. A hole had been blasted in the sandbags by grenades, and Duncan ran through, his two pistols cocked, ready to shoot anything that moved.

Nothing moved. Blood and broken bodies covered the ground around the big artillery piece. The grenades had done their job. In the distance, he could see German soldiers running away.

"After them!" Duncan ordered.

His men chased the Germans around the bunkers where they'd lived, shooting some of them in the back. A few got away, but the rest surrendered. The doughboys then invaded the bunkers, capturing more Germans and finding hot coffee and sausages frying in pans on stoves. The doughboys hadn't eaten for a day and a half, and fell on the food with orgiastic intensity. One group of doughboys found a telephone station in a bunker, but the German operators had thrown a hand grenade at the switchboard before they'd fled.

Duncan watched his men running around like maniacs, stuffing themselves with food. Fatigue overtook him and he leaned against one of the artillery pieces, taking off his helmet and wiping his brow. He felt the pain in his arm and leg, and knew he ought to find an aid station. But there wasn't time. He had to get his men moving again.

Private Whitewater brought him a loaf of bread and two fried knockwursts. Duncan sat at the base of the cannon and began to eat. His men found the German water tank and were filling canteens. Some had confiscated Lugers from dead German officers. A group of doughboys arrived wearing the ivy leaf patch of the Fourth Division, and they too joined in the feast. The German prisoners huddled in a circle, watching the mayhem around them, fearful that they'd be shot at any moment.

Private Whitewater pointed to Duncan's left. "What army is he in, sir?"

Duncan looked and saw a man with an upturned mustache, wearing the uniform of an officer in the French foreign legion. The Frenchman had a big smile on his face and shook hands with every doughboy he met. He spoke with one of them, and the doughboy pointed at Duncan. The officer strutted toward Duncan, who rose to greet him.

The Frenchman, his eyes glittering with joy, held out his hand. "It is an honor," he said in a thick French accent, "to serve on the field of battle with such companions as you!" Then he walked off, intoxicated with victory, shaking hands and slapping backs.

Duncan gnawed at his knockwurst. Private Whitewater brought him a full canteen, and Duncan drank a few gulps. He felt exhausted and didn't think he could go on. Moreover, his men had been attacking all morning and they needed to be relieved.

An officer on a chestnut mare rode into the artillery emplacement. "Who's in charge here?"

Everyone pointed to Duncan, who raised himself off the ground. The officer dug his spurs into the horse and trotted toward Duncan.

"Are you in command?" the officer asked.

Duncan transferred the knockwurst into his left hand and saluted. "Yes, sir."

"What's your name?"

"Captain Duncan Hunter, commanding officer of Company B."

"Do you think you're out on a picnic, Captain?"

"No, sir."

"Then get your men together and move them out!" The officer pulled his horse's head to the side, spurred it and galloped away. Duncan put his helmet on his head and walked toward the center of the artillery emplacement.

"I want a column of twos right here!" he shouted hoarsely.

It took a while, but the men finally formed up. They carried bread and sausages, and one had found a bottle of brandy. Duncan ordered six to escort the prisoners to an internment camp, then marched his men forward toward the fighting again.

The half hour or so that they'd spent in the artillery emplacement had caused them to fall behind their advancing front line. Duncan might be in trouble when the battle was over, because he should have sent the prisoners to the rear immediately and continued advancing with his men. But they were all tired and hungry, and he hadn't thought they could maintain the fast pace of the advance. Now, however, they were refreshed. Now he and they were ready to fight again.

They marched down the other side of the hill and saw the line advancing ahead of them. The rain had stopped and the sun was up, but a heavy cloud layer still blocked its rays. About a thousand yards ahead of Company B, the front lines advanced up a hill and disappeared. Duncan wondered whether to double-time his men so they could catch up, but decided to take his time. They'd be back in the battle soon enough. A brief respite from the war would be good for them.

"Look, sir!" cried Corporal Bell. He was pointing up to the sky, where Duncan saw a dozen tiny dots. Airplanes. He didn't know whose they were at first, but then saw them diving toward his company.

"Spread out and hit it!" Duncan yelled.

The doughboys scattered in all directions and dived into shell craters or any other depressions in the ground they could find. The planes swooped down and opened fire, their bullets kicking up mud and ricocheting off stones. Duncan pressed his face into the mud and imagined one of those big 50-caliber bullets blowing his back apart.

Airplane engines roared as they passed overhead. Duncan spotted black crosses on their wings. He was afraid they might turn around to make another pass, but they kept heading toward the American rear. He waited a few minutes, then ordered his men back into formation and moved them out again.

They marched across the field and up the next hill. As they neared the summit they heard artillery falling to their front. Reaching the summit, they looked down and saw another field with rows of doughboys lying in the middle on their stomachs. In the distance, American shells rained down on German positions.

At the bottom of the hill he formed his men into a skirmish line and ordered them to advance. After about a half-hour they reached the American forward line. Duncan ordered his men to get down, so they took out the sausage and bread they'd brought with them, to finish their meal.

Duncan left Lieutenant Dawes in charge and crawled away to find out what was going on. He saw a cluster of men toward his right and crept toward them.

"Is there an officer around here?" he asked them.

"I'm an officer," said a young man with pimples on his face.

"I'm Captain Hunter from Company B of the Twenty-third Regiment, and I just got back on the line. I'm trying to find out what's going on."

The pimpled young officer grinned. "I can tell you, sir." He pointed to the line of hills ahead. "That there's called the Vierzy Ridge, and it's the Heinie stronghold. We're gonna attack it before long."

Duncan crawled back to his company, told Lieutenant Dawes what the young officer had told him, and ordered that the information be passed along.

Lieutenant Dawes was the only other officer in the company now, and Duncan had about seventy men left out of the two hundred that had begun the assault in the morning. *They'll have to relieve us pretty soon,* he thought. *We can't keep taking losses like this.*

The shelling went on for twenty minutes before suddenly stopping. Farther down the line, a man with a pistol in his hand jumped to his feet and motioned for everyone to follow him. Duncan saw that it was Major Harrington, the new battalion commander. He was going to lead the attack on the Vierzy Ridge himself!

The doughboys climbed to their feet and followed Major Harrington, screaming their enthusiasm for the attack. They charged up the hill, and when they were halfway up the Germans came out of their holes and opened fire. It soon became evident that they hadn't been damaged much by the bombardment. Their machine guns raked the advancing doughboys and their mortar shells rained down. German marksmen found plenty of targets, and doughboys dropped their rifles as they fell bleeding to the ground.

"Forward!" shouted Major Harrington. "Follow me!" Then a bullet struck him in the chest and he went down.

The attack faltered as the doughboys wondered whether to continue moving forward or fall back. German fire was withering, and the doughboys began backstepping. Duncan thought he should run to the front of the lines and take over command of the attack, but didn't think the battalion's doughboys could take the ridge without reinforcements.

The incoming fire became more intense, and although no one ordered them to retreat, the doughboys ran back down the hill as fast as they could. Duncan found himself exposed and alone. His first instinct was to drop to his belly, as German bullets whistled around him, and mortar rounds continued to rain down. Duncan peered ahead to where Major Harrington had fallen.

The German gunfire diminished. They were conserving ammunition for the next attack. Duncan crept around dead and bleeding doughboys, making his way toward Major Harrington.

"Mother, I can't see," wailed one of the wounded doughboys.

Duncan crawled around him and reached Major Harrington, who was lying face down on the ground. Duncan turned the major over and saw the bullet hole in his forehead. Harrington was dead. He felt the major's pulse to make sure, but there was nothing. The major's eyes were closed, his face expressionless, as if he was merely sleeping.

Duncan heard hoofbeats. Looking behind him, he saw a French cavalry troop in silver helmets and yellow plumes, pointing their swords straight ahead and charging up the hill. They spurred their horses and shouted battle cries, looking splendid and unstoppable in the gray morning.

When they were halfway up the hill, the Germans opened fire. Machine guns ripped into the horses and men, and mortar shells blew them to bits. Horses whinnied with fright and pain, and men fell from their saddles, crashing to the ground. Some kept charging, holding their swords in front of them and urging their horses on. Duncan ducked his head as one of the horses jumped over him, but the Germans maintained their fire, and blood spouted like geysers from the horses.

The huge beasts stumbled and fell to the ground, pitching their riders forward out of their saddles. On foot, some of the cavalrymen charged up the hill with only their swords, but they were cut down by German machine guns. Finally the last horse and last cavalryman were shot down.

Horrified, Duncan looked at the carnage of horses and men around him. Blood ran in rivulets down the hill. Some horses twitched spasmodically in their death throes. A lone cavalryman stumbled about in a daze, his sword trailing behind him, his helmet fallen off, and blood trickling from the corner of his mouth. He appeared to be no more than twenty years old. A German rifle shot rang out, and the cavalryman fell to the ground.

The hillside became silent. Duncan covered Major Harrington's face with his helmet, then crawled back down the hill toward his men.

The Kaiser, followed by an entourage of aides and staff officers, climbed the steps to Field Marshal Hindenburg's headquarters in Avesnes. The front door opened and Hindenburg appeared, stately and dignified. The Kaiser and the field marshal shook hands.

"I know why you are here," said Hindenburg gravely. "You have heard of the Allied breakthrough."

The Kaiser looked him in the eye. "How bad is it?"

"It could be much worse. Come — I will show you precisely, Your Excellency."

They went into the country mansion that Hindenburg was using for his headquarters and entered the conference room, where Colonel-General Ludendorff was poring over the map table. With Ludendorff were general staff officers, among them Karl Ritter von Beck, who had been promoted to major.

The Kaiser handed his helmet to an aide and approached the map table. Hindenburg pointed to a sector of the line. "I believe Your Excellency may desire first of all our opinion as to how we got into this critical position."

The Kaiser nodded. Hindenburg described the disposition of German forces throughout the entire front on the morning of the attack, and said that the attack had taken them by surprise.

"It rained last night, as you know, Your Excellency," he said. "The inclement weather prevented us from seeing the Allies move into their attack positions."

"But surely," replied the Kaiser, "they did not move everything in one night. For an attack of this magnitude, there must have been troop movements for days. Surely someone must have seen something."

"There are always troop movements in combat zones, Excellency. We detected nothing unusual. Their main movements were covered by the weather. I don't believe that anyone can be blamed for not perceiving that the attack would take place."

The Kaiser's eyes went cold. "We should not have been taken by surprise in this manner," he said in a deadly tone.

"It was unavoidable, Excellency."

"Show me the present line in the critical sector."

Hindenburg traced it with his arthritic finger. "It is here, Excellency."

273

"Can we hold?"

"We must withdraw, Your Excellency, because General Boehm's army is threatened by enemy troops infiltrating into the high ground here." He pointed to the vicinity of the Vierzy Ridge.

The Kaiser looked at the map. "No," he said firmly.

"I beg your pardon, Excellency?"

"There will be no withdrawals."

"But—"

"I repeat, there will be no withdrawals."

"We have no choice, Your Excellency. If we do not retreat, we stand to lose forty divisions in an enemy pincer."

The Kaiser shook his head and raised his chin in the air. "It is not politically feasible to withdraw at this time. The home front would not stand for it. They are suffering terrible deprivations, and a defeat would imperil their will to support the war effort."

"But, Excellency," said Hindenburg, "it is not prudent to permit political considerations to overrule sound military procedures."

"No withdrawal," the Kaiser insisted. "We must hold the enemy and push them back."

Ludendorff, who had been bending over the map, stood and squared his shoulders. Everyone turned to look at him. His face had become flushed with anger, and his eyes were bulging.

"Cowards and slackers on the home front shall not dictate the course of this war!" he exclaimed. "It is because of cowards and slackers that the Imperial Army lacks sufficient supplies and manpower to turn back attacks like this one. The Americans attacked with tanks, but we have no tanks to oppose them. Why have we no tanks? Because the cowards and slackers in Berlin have not seen fit to supply the army with them. No, the Imperial Army shall not stand and be slaughtered. We shall withdraw and establish new strongpoints that the enemy will never penetrate!"

The room was silent. Aides and staff members looked at one another, surprised and embarrassed by Ludendorff's outburst against the Kaiser, upon whom it finally dawned that Ludendorff had the power of the army behind him, while he, the Kaiser, had only his prestige and the royal family.

"Can we not," the Kaiser said softly, "bring in reinforcements from another sector of the front?"

Hindenburg nodded. "That is a possibility."

Ludendorff drew himself erect again and glowered at Hindenburg. "Anything of that sort is utterly unfeasible — as I thought I had already made abundantly clear to the field marshal! Any sector of the front that we weaken will be attacked by our enemies! We shall pull back from the threatened sector to a more secure line. That is the only possibility left to us at present."

The Kaiser felt old and tired. His army was being pushed out of France, and in Berlin there was talk of revolution. To make matters worse, his wife was distraught and under the constant care of a physician.

Hindenburg noticed the Kaiser's change of mood. "The war is showing a hard face," he said consolingly.

The Kaiser sighed. "It is very strange that our soldiers cannot get used to tanks."

Ludendorff calmed himself now that he saw the Kaiser knuckling under. In a more modulated voice, he described the new defensive positions that he thought would be impregnable. They would be established in the Argonne Forest, and heavily fortified. Nothing, not even tanks, would smash through them.

In a dark corner of the room. Major Beck listened and knew that if the German army had not been able to hold the Allies at Soissons and on the Aisne, they would not be able to hold them anywhere. *Unless heaven sends us a miracle,* he thought, *this is the beginning of the end.*

The Second Division howitzers subjected the Vierzy Ridge to another massive bombardment, but there were nooks and crannies where their shells couldn't reach, and where the Germans huddled, waiting for the attack that they knew was being prepared in the fields below.

Duncan had led his company back to the First Battalion and discovered that it too had suffered massive casualties. Of over six hundred men in the battalion who'd jumped off that morning, fewer than two hundred were left. Some companies were commanded by sergeants and corporals.

After a meeting with the other surviving officers, he discovered to his astonishment that he had become the ranking man in the battalion. He left Lieutenant Dawes in charge of Company B and tried to pull the battalion back together as a fighting unit.

Fresh regiments were arriving on the line. Nearly one hundred tanks were assembling for the attack on the ridge, which was now wreathed in smoke.

Duncan's left arm was stiff from the wound he'd sustained in the first German trench, but he could still aim a pistol. Every time he moved that arm he felt pain like a flaming torch.

Medics roved through the line, bandaging wounded men and giving them pills. One noticed Duncan giving orders to the sergeant who now commanded Company D. The medic put antiseptic on Duncan's wound, then wrapped a bandage around his arm.

Duncan moved back and forth on his line, shouting encouragement to the men, asking them about their experiences, slapping them on their shoulders. Canteens full of water were brought up from the rear and exchanged for empty ones. The men took hardtack out of their packs and tore at it.

Duncan was amazed to see that the battalion had shrunk to a unit barely larger than a full-strength company. He thought of all the dead and wounded men scattered over the fields and woods between the ridge and the jump-off point in the Forest of Retz. It was incredible that so many could have fallen, and for what? A few miles of ground? He looked up to the hill and located the area where Major Harrington had fallen.

It was unbelievable that a man like Harrington could be struck down by the war, an old Regular Army soldier like that, risen from the ranks and a veteran of the Spanish-American War. Harrington had known every trick in the book. If he could be killed, so could anyone. Duncan had a premonition that he would not survive the war. *The odds are against me,* he thought. *Perhaps this is my last day on earth.*

Walking on the line, trying to give his men confidence by his manner and orders, he came back to Company B and saw Corporal Bell sitting on the ground, munching on his hardtack.

"How's it going, Bell?"

"I only got three men left in my squad, sir, but other than that I'm doin' okay."

Duncan looked at Bell and saw a bleeding cut on his cheek, his pants ragged from encounters with barbed wire, his face covered with dust and grime.

Duncan knelt beside Bell, took out a cigarette, offered one to Bell, and lit both. "Bell," he said, "if we had a few more like you out here we'd take that ridge without any trouble."

"If I were you," Bell replied, "I think I'd rather have more tanks. You can never have enough tanks, sir. They go right over everything. Why, back there, I saw a shell hit a tank, and the goddamned tank kept going as if nothing had happened. There was just a dent on it, that's all."

"I agree. You can't have enough tanks."

An officer on a horse appeared, holding his reins with one hand and waving with the other. "Get ready!" he yelled. "The barrage is going to stop soon, then we attack!"

Duncan took out his forty-five and checked to make sure the clip was filled. He rammed a round into the chamber and clicked the safety off.

"Keep your head down, Bell."

"You too, Captain."

Duncan jogged to the center of his battalion, positioned himself in front and watched them lining up, his heart beating rapidly. Shells poured down on the ridge where Germans were holed up, and he was surprised to realize that he was eager to get moving. He turned around and saw his men holding their rifles ready, waiting for the order to attack. Light-headed, he felt the old blood-lust coming over him again.

The artillery barrage suddenly ended, and the countryside became silent.

"Forward!" screamed Duncan. He raised his pistol high in the air, then pointed it at the ridge. "First battalion — follow me!"

He hard-charged up the hill, and from behind could hear men's boots stomping over the ground. He felt as if electricity were running through his veins, and screamed like a madman as he waved his pistol in the air, leaping over dead men and horses.

His doughboys shouted battle cries as they rushed forward. Germans climbed out of holes and rushed toward their fortifications. When in position they fired their rifles and the doughboys fell to the ground.

American tanks made a terrible racket as they rolled up the hill, crunching over the bones of dead men and horses, firing their cannons, blowing holes in the German fortifications. Their machine guns sprayed hot lead at the Germans, who were forced to keep low and fire without taking adequate aim.

Tanks are the key to everything, Duncan thought as he approached the barricades. A German raised his head and Duncan fired at him. The head disappeared, but Duncan didn't know whether he had hit him or not. He leaped over the barricade and saw the German on his knees, unmarked and terrified, holding his rifle like a shield. Duncan shot him in the face, and the German's head blew apart. Duncan spun around and shot another German in the chest. A third German ran at him and he shot him in the throat.

The doughboys poured into the German position, and it was clear to everyone that the Germans were hugely outnumbered. The Germans fled, and the doughboys got down on one knee, taking careful aim with their Springfields and picking them off one by one. Tanks crashed through the barricades and leveled their machine guns at the retreating Germans, who stumbled and fell to the ground, never to move again.

The Germans ran across the ridge and down into gullies and caves. The doughboys ran after them, pausing every several feet to fire their rifles. The ridge became narrow and dropped off steeply. The tanks could go no further. Germans in the caves and behind rocks fired back at the doughboys, who dropped on to their stomachs and took cover.

Duncan hid behind a boulder and peered around it. The doughboys had taken the front of the ridge, but many Germans were in the caves and gullies farther back. It would be tedious work to extricate them, but the work had to be done, cave by cave, gully by gully. They might as well start with the nearest cave and proceed systematically until all were cleared out.

He looked around and saw a sergeant he didn't know. "Sergeant — get over here!" he yelled.

The sergeant leaped up from the depression he'd been hiding in and ran toward Duncan, joining him behind the boulder.

"What's your name?" Duncan demanded.

"Robinson, sir."

"Can you round up ten good men?"

"Yes, sir!"

"Go get them and bring them here."

The lanky sergeant ran back to get the men. Duncan looked over the boulder at the first cave. It was on the side of the ridge, surrounded by bushes. Flashes of light could be seen where the Germans were firing from the mouth of the cave. Duncan licked his lips and tasted salty perspiration. His arm still ached but he ignored it. Tanks lined up on the ridge and fired cannons at the German positions, but the shells exploded harmlessly on the rocks.

Sergeant Robinson returned with ten dirty, bloodied men. Duncan was pleased to note that one carried a Chauchat machine gun.

"You know how to use that thing, soldier?" he asked.

"Yes, sir."

Duncan told them that they were going to move out on his signal and take the first cave. He split them into two equal groups, one under his command and the other under Sergeant

280

Robinson. They would attack in turn, each group covering the other — the classic fire-and-maneuver tactic. When they got close to the cave they would lob hand grenades inside, wait until they exploded, then invade the cave.

"Everybody understand what we're going to do?" Duncan asked.

They all nodded, anxious to get going.

"My group will go first," Duncan said. "The rest of you get into position and start firing."

Sergeant Robinson deployed his men and soon they began firing at the mouth of the cave. The Chauchat gunner was in Robinson's group, and his bullets flew into the cave like a hailstorm.

"Up and at 'em!" Duncan bellowed. "Take that damned cave!"

He jumped up and rushed forward like a wild bull, as five doughboys followed him. One tripped on a boulder, tumbling down the incline, but managed to get to his feet. Another doughboy was hit and fell with blood streaming from his shoulder.

"Hit it!" Duncan screamed.

They dropped to the ground and fired at the mouth of the cave as Sergeant Robinson ordered his men to their feet and led them in the next charge toward the German emplacement.

After passing Duncan's group, they continued ten more yards, then flopped on to their stomachs, but the Chauchat gunner was a little slow, and before he could touch down a German bullet tore through his stomach. He shrieked and doubled over, clutching his bleeding gut. The Chauchat gun fell to the ground and Duncan took note of where it landed.

Duncan rose and ran up the hill, his men following close behind. He veered toward the Chauchat gun, picked it up and continued past Sergeant Robinson and his men. Duncan aimed the Chauchat gun at the mouth of the cave and pulled the trigger. It bucked and stuttered in his hand as the bullets spat out of the barrel. Soon he saw German helmets in the cave and figured he was close enough to throw grenades.

Duncan and his men dropped to the ground, raising their rifles and firing at the mouth of the cave. Sergeant Robinson brought his group up and they formed a skirmish line adjoining Duncan's group.

"Hand grenades!" Duncan shouted.

They took out their hand grenades, pulled the pins and hurled them into the mouth of the cave. The ground shook with the explosions and smoke poured from the cave.

At Duncan's command, his men jumped up and ran the remaining distance toward the cave, Duncan in the lead, firing the machine gun. Like a mountain goat he went up the hill and jumped into the cave. Dead Germans were lying on the cave's floor. Farther back German soldiers were waving white handkerchiefs in surrender.

"Get out here!" Duncan yelled.

The Germans didn't speak English, but they understood his meaning. They crept forward cautiously, holding their hands high, still waving the handkerchiefs.

"Sergeant Robinson — take your men and search them for weapons."

Robinson moved forward with his four remaining men and surrounded the Germans, patting them down and poking hands into their jackets to see if they had any hidden pistols or grenades.

Suddenly one of the Germans shouted, and all of them dropped to their stomachs. Shots rang out from deeper in the cave, and the first one hit Sergeant Robinson, blasting out through the side of his head.

"Hit it!" Duncan screamed.

The soldiers dropped to the rock floor of the cave for cover. The Germans who'd pretended to surrender ran toward the deeper recesses of the cave, but Duncan aimed his machine gun at them, pulled the trigger, and cut them down.

Four men were left with Duncan, and they lobbed hand grenades deep into the cave. The explosions sent shrapnel whizzing around the confined area, ricocheting off the walls.

"After them!"

Duncan jumped up and ran into the cave. He saw movement ahead of him and fired his machine gun from the waist. The four remaining doughboys followed closely, shooting into the smoke and shadows. They stepped over dead and shattered Germans and advanced more deeply, firing every step of the way.

"*Kamerad!*" called out a German voice. "*Kamerad!*"

"Come out of there," Duncan replied.

Germans waving white handkerchiefs emerged from the darkness of the cave and inched toward Duncan. The one in front had a nervously ingratiating smile on his face, but the others looked downright scared.

"Be careful," Duncan warned his men. "They might try something."

The Germans kept coming. Duncan held the machine gun tightly and pulled the trigger. The cave echoed with the sound of exploding bullets, and the German soldiers twisted and turned as they were ripped apart. They fell to the floor of the cave, but Duncan kept firing until his machine gun was empty.

CHAPTER 25

The wedding reception was held at the Giraud home on the fashionable Rue St Faubourg in Paris. Numerous dignitaries representing government, diplomacy and the military were there. General Giraud had obtained a brief leave from the front to attend the wedding, and stood proudly as the newlyweds entered the spacious parlor.

Danielle wore a white wedding gown with the veil pushed back over her head. Her hair was golden and her smile radiant. She held Blake's good arm tightly as she walked around the room accepting congratulations. Blake's wounded arm was out of the sling, but still somewhat painful. He looked very much the dashing young aviator as he flashed his winning smile and shook hands with the guests.

One old gossip hid her mouth with her fan and whispered to a friend, "The bride's tummy appears a bit large, wouldn't you say?"

"The marriage *was* arranged rather hastily," her friend replied.

Everett DeWitt happened to be standing behind them. He frowned and looked at Danielle's belly. Could she really be pregnant? No, it was impossible. Danielle wouldn't do anything like that before she was married. She had been one of the most strait-laced women Everett had ever known.

"I don't believe we've met," said a voice to Everett's left.

Everett turned and saw an officer wearing aviator wings. He was about Everett's age, had a ruddy complexion and appeared half-drunk.

"I'm Lieutenant Everett DeWitt," he said, holding out his hand.

"Lieutenant Hamilton Fuller. What outfit are you with?" He was looking at Everett's left breast pocket, which was devoid of combat ribbons.

Everett said: "I'm with the General Staff. I imagine you're in Blake's squadron?"

"Yes, the Ninety-fourth Aero. I envy you, old man. Must be nice to be back where the bullets aren't flying."

"The grass always looks greener," Everett replied with a sardonic smile. "I wish that I could see some action."

Fuller's eyebrows rose in surprise. "It's really not much fun. You should feel lucky you are where you are."

"I feel like I'm not really in the war," Everett complained.

"To hell with the war." Fuller took a large swallow of his drink.

"That's what I say," added another aviator standing nearby.

Fuller pointed to Everett. "This feller here is on the General Staff but he wants to go to the front. Can you imagine?"

"He doesn't know when he's well off."

Everett thought the two aviators condescending, because they were real fighters and he sat behind a desk, but smiled and chatted with them anyway. He doubted they really wanted to change places with him. Men like them were usually contemptuous of desk jockeys.

"Everett, dear…"

Everett spun around and found himself looking into the lovely blue eyes of Mrs. Danielle Hunter, with Blake at her side.

Everett bowed slightly. "Congratulations to both of you. I hope you'll be very happy together."

"Thank you, old man," Blake said, shaking Everett's hand.

Danielle bent forward to kiss Everett lightly on the cheek.

A thrill passed through Everett's body at the touch of her lips. He looked at Blake and wanted to kill him. He was still crazy about Danielle, he realized. Or maybe he was just a sore loser? Whatever, he was sick and tired of taking a back seat, whether in war or in love.

"You must come to visit us when we get settled," Danielle said.

"I certainly will," Everett replied.

The newlyweds continued their little stroll, shaking hands and accepting congratulations. A waiter walked by with a tray of drinks, and Everett took one, gulping down half of it. *I can't stand him,* Everett admitted to himself, looking at Blake's broad back. *I wonder why it is that I can't stand him? Is it because he stole Danielle from me, or is it simply that I can't stand him?*

Everett wondered how his dead brother Franklin could have been so friendly with Blake Hunter. He didn't seem to be the kind of person Franklin would like at all.

CHAPTER 26

On the night of July 19, the Second Division was relieved and moved back from the front. In its two days of fighting at Soissons it had advanced seven kilometers, captured three thousand prisoners and seventy cannon, and sustained five thousand casualties out of the eight thousand doughboys who had begun the attack.

It was placed in reserve for several days, and a special letter of commendation was sent to every command in the division from Mangin, the French general they'd served under at Soissons. Part of it said:

You went into battle as to a party. I am proud to have commanded you and to have fought together with you to deliver the world.

On July 25 the Second Division marched to the Nanteuil-le-Haudouin area, where the doughboys were packed like cattle into trains. Also on that day, Major General John A Lejeune, a Marine officer from Louisiana, was appointed the new commander of the division.

The next stop for the doughboys was the beautiful city of Nancy, considered by travellers before the war to be a miniature Paris, and for centuries capital of the Duchy of Lorraine. The doughboys were billeted in homes throughout the city and began a period of rest and recuperation. New replacements arrived, and leave was granted to as many men as possible.

Duncan wrangled some leave himself, and immediately set off to find Catherine Hawkins. A French doctor told him that the 349th Ambulance Corps was stationed in Châlons-en-Champagne. Wearing a soft soldier's cap and carrying his field knapsack, Duncan hitch-hiked north on roads cluttered with troops, tanks, trucks and horse-drawn artillery. He had no difficulty finding a ride, but the going was slow.

The scuttlebutt along the road was that the Germans were falling back steadily all along the front, and the war was entering its final stage. The sun was hot and dust rose in thick billows along the road. The air swarmed with flies attracted to the field latrines and garbage pits dug throughout the area.

Duncan reached the hospital in Châlons just as the sun was setting. He found the headquarters of the 349th Ambulance Corps and learned that Catherine Hawkins was on duty, but should be returning soon. Duncan told the woman at the desk that he'd wait for Catherine in the canteen, and requested that she be told he was there.

The hospital reminded Duncan of the one in Paris where he'd been treated for the wounds to his face and scalp. It had dark, gloomy corridors and smelled of antiseptic. Nurses and doctors ran back and forth, and soldiers groaned in the wards. Duncan was glad that he wasn't a patient anymore.

The canteen was set up cafeteria-style, and was nearly full. Duncan passed down the line and received a slab of boiled beef and some vegetables, plus a few slices of bread and a cup of coffee.

He sat at a small table for two along the wall and proceeded to dine. Doctors and nurses talked and laughed around him, and he thought of Soissons, the battle for Vierzy Ridge, and how Major Harrington had been shot through the head.

Duncan was troubled by the exhilaration he'd felt during the fighting at Soissons. It was true that he'd been tense and scared, but he also had to admit to himself that in a strange way he'd enjoyed the give and take of battle, and found pleasure in leading his men to the little victories they'd won.

It gave him a tremendous feeling of accomplishment, and he thought that war had brought out the best in him: courage, leadership abilities, and a talent for sizing up a situation quickly and taking appropriate action. *Maybe I should make a career out of the army,* he thought. *I'd rather be a professional soldier than anything else in the world.*

He finished his meal and sipped his coffee. At around eleven o'clock, while still musing on the battle for Soissons, he felt a cool hand on the back of his neck.

"Hello," said Catherine.

Duncan stood and turned around. She wore a tan cotton dress belted at the waist, and she filled it out beautifully.

"Hello," he replied.

"Have you been waiting long?"

"A couple of hours."

She sat down with her cup of coffee, raised it to her lips and looked at him with her dark oriental eyes.

"I'm so happy to see you," he said, leaning toward her. "I think of you all the time."

She placed her cup inside the saucer. "I've thought of you quite a lot, too," she said softly. "Sometimes I thought I'd never see you again, because I knew that your division was taking heavy casualties at Soissons. I see your arm is bandaged. Are you all right?"

"Yes, it's fine."

She touched the bandage with her hand and smiled sadly. "You men go through such hell in this war. I really can't understand how you do it."

He shrugged. "It's simple enough. We're trained to follow orders automatically, regardless of circumstances."

"That's crazy."

"I suppose it is."

"God, what a war…" She raised her cup to her lips again, then gazed into his eyes. "Oh Duncan," she sighed.

"What's wrong?"

"I wish you hadn't come."

"Why not?"

"Because you're only going to leave me again."

"I'll be back."

"But one day you won't be back, Duncan," she said sadly. "The Germans will get you, or you'll survive the war and return to your wife in America."

He placed his hand over hers. "There's no point in worrying about what might happen in the future. Neither one of us can say for sure that we'll be alive tomorrow. We might as well make the most out of every moment that we can be together."

She shook her head. "I worry about you too much. I don't want to lose another man. I couldn't bear it."

He squeezed her hand. "Stop thinking about those things."

"I'd think about them less if I hadn't met you. I don't want to be attached to anyone. The separations are too awful."

"Catherine," he said earnestly, "you've got to take one day at a time and not worry about tomorrow. We can't possibly know what will happen tomorrow, but we can make the best of today."

She touched her fingers to the scar on his face and smiled. "Duncan, let's be honest with each other. I really don't mean very much to you."

"That's not true, Catherine!"

Her gaze met his in challenge. "Would you divorce your wife and marry me?"

"I…" He couldn't finish the sentence. Dropping his eyes from her, he reached into his shirt pocket and took out his cigarettes. He held the pack out to her, then lit both their cigarettes.

She laughed bitterly. "You just failed the acid test, my friend."

He looked down into his empty cup of coffee and took a deep breath. "I can't divorce my wife."

"You told me you didn't love her very much." There was no bitterness in her voice, just fatigue.

Duncan couldn't look at her. "That's true, but it's a complicated family situation. I could never divorce her."

She touched her hand to his cheek. "At least you're honest, Duncan. Another man would lie and say he'd divorce his wife, then back down when the time came. So I want to be just as honest with you. If I can't have you completely, then I don't want you at all. I don't want to be somebody's temporary girlfriend. This will be our last night together, Duncan, and then I never want to see you again."

General Pershing stood with his back to the map on the wall of his office at Chaumont. In front of him were his corps and division commanders, gathered for the meeting he had ordered. It was early in the morning and the bright summer sun shone through the oversized windows. Lieutenant Everett DeWitt and the other General Staff officers stood on either side of General Pershing.

"Gentlemen," began the Iron Commander, "I have good news. I attended a meeting with Marshal Foch in Paris yesterday, and he has finally given permission for the AEF to function in the future as a unified army under its own commanders, answerable only to himself instead of local French or British officers."

The generals smiled and some clapped their hands lightly. They'd been waiting for this opportunity for a long time: to fight as an American army instead of reinforcing the French and British armies.

Pershing held up his hand and they became silent. "This was a very difficult decision for the marshal to make, because British and French commanders don't want to give up their American divisions. They say that we American commanders are too inexperienced to control and direct an army far larger than any that has served under the American flag. Let me tell you that it took a great deal of persuasion to convince the marshal to give the AEF this chance, and it would be terrible for American prestige and the morale if we were to fail."

"We won't fail, sir!" said one of the generals.

The other officers nodded. A shared sense of mission spread over the room. Pershing turned to the map and aimed his pointer at a section of the line.

"General Foch has given us a mission, to test the effectiveness of the AEF as a unified fighting force. I'm sure that all of you are familiar with the Saint-Mihiel salient. It has been an ugly tooth sunk into the French line for two years. The time has come to flatten it out, and that is what we are about to do. As you can see, the enemy position runs along the Meuse River here. The Germans have heavy guns that interrupt the French railroad system and highways in the vicinity. The terrain is generally wooded and rolling, with the highest points in the center of the salient and toward the east. We will have adequate artillery preparation and supplies. There can be no excuse for failing to take our objectives."

Pershing explained the attack positions of the divisions and corps, and described the tactics of the operation. Eight American divisions would participate in the battle, and General Lejeune was pleased to learn that the Second Division had been chosen once again to spearhead the attack.

CHAPTER 27

The doughboys moved into their positions around the Saint-Mihiel salient during the night of September 11. At one a.m. on September 12 an artillery barrage of twenty-eight hundred guns began.

The Germans were taken by surprise and went deep into their holes. The bombardment continued for four hours, blasting apart the German fortifications and driving many German soldiers insane. Their sector became a hellish mass of exploding shells, burning supply dumps, star signals and obliterated villages.

At five a.m. the doughboys attacked fiercely, and the Germans fell back. The doughboys pushed forward throughout the day, and by nightfall had captured all their assigned objectives. Nearly sixteen thousand prisoners had been taken, along with four hundred fifty guns. Casualties among the doughboys numbered about seven thousand.

The German army was on the run and the doughboys stayed after them. The doughboys wheeled to the northwest and charged into the Argonne Forest, where the German Imperial Army intended to make its last stand.

The terrain favored the Germans. They organized their defense along four lines of fortifications, each backing up the other. On the heights of Montfaucon, Cunel, Romagne and Mont Blanc, they could see everything in front of them. These natural defenses were augmented by concrete pillboxes, dugouts, and machine-gun nests containing as many as a hundred machine guns. A dense network of barbed wire provided additional fortifications for every position.

By September 25, more than six hundred thousand doughboys were fighting in the Argonne Forest. They didn't know it, but they were in the biggest battle the world had ever seen.

The doughboys threw the Germans out of their first-line fortifications, and on the night of September 28, Germany's List Regiment found itself with a ragtag conglomeration of other units atop Mont Blanc. Exhausted, hungry and demoralized, the German soldiers huddled in their bunkers and pillboxes as American artillery shells fell upon them. Rumors proliferated about revolution breaking out in many German cities. Word was passed along that the civilian population was starving, the Empress had suffered a heart attack and the Kaiser was going to abdicate.

"To hell with this war!" said Sergeant Lofhausen, in one of the concrete bunkers. His uniform was torn and his face was covered by a thick growth of beard. He sat on an ammunition case and smoked his last cigarette. "We're only fighting for the millionaires anyway! They get richer and we die for them. What the hell is the point of it all? I tell you, boys, I'm ready to throw down my rifle and go back home."

"I'll go with you!" said Private Steiner. "The war is lost anyway."

Private Kiesel grunted. "Where's the goddamned Kaiser?" he asked. "I'll tell you where the goddamned Kaiser is. He's back in Berlin living in the lap of luxury, while we don't have anything to eat."

Lofhausen puffed his cigarette. "To hell with the Kaiser, Hindenburg and Ludendorff! To hell with this war! Why should we die in a war that's already lost? Let the Kaiser, Hindenburg and Ludendorff die. They're the ones who want this war."

"That's enough!" said a murderously low voice in the corner.

Everyone looked and saw a gaunt figure with an upturned mustache and eyes burning like embers.

"I will not tolerate treasonous talk in my presence," the soldier declared, standing up. He pointed at Sergeant Lofhausen. "You be quiet, or I will see that you are silenced for good."

One new replacement, only sixteen years old, turned to one of the old veterans and whispered: "Who the hell is that?"

"That is Private Hitler," the veteran replied. "He goes crazy when people say the kinds of thing Lofhausen is saying."

Sergeant Lofhausen, a brawler from the riverfront of Bremen, got to his feet and threw his cigarette to the floor. "Let us see you shut me up."

Hitler suddenly dashed across the room and leaped on Lofhausen, knocking him to the bunker's floor. As soon as Lofhausen landed on his back, Hitler began punching him hard with both hands in the face. Lofhausen managed to block a few punches, but most of them got through. His nose bled and his lower lip split open. Heaving with his belly, he pushed Hitler off him. Hitler tried to regain his balance, but Lofhausen reached up and grabbed Hitler by the throat, squeezing with all his strength until Hitler's eyes bulged. Hitler joined both his hands together in a massive fist and brought it down on top of Lofhausen's head. Lofhausen was stunned and loosened his grip. Hitler punched him again, splitting his upper lip open, but Lofhausen punched back wildly, landing a blow on Hitler's eye.

The two German soldiers stood toe to toe and threw punches from all directions. Lofhausen was stronger but Hitler was faster, able to duck Lofhausen's blows and land more of his own. A hard overhand right from Hitler dazed the burly sergeant, who began to backstep. Hitler went after him, punching again and again with all his strength. He jabbed Lofhausen in the stomach, causing Lofhausen to lower his guard. Then Hitler slugged him twice in the face, Lofhausen dropped to his knees, Hitler reared back his leg and kicked Lofhausen full in the face. Lofhausen went flying and landed on his back, out cold.

Hitler stood in the middle of the bunker, breathing hard, hands balled into fists. "Anyone else want more of the same?" he cried, spittle flying from his lips.

No one moved or said anything.

"This war is not lost unless we think it is lost!" Hitler shouted. "The will to win is everything. We may be retreating, but the army is still intact and capable of winning battles. Cowards and weaklings should keep their mouths shut and do their duty. If they did, the army would not be in the situation it is in today!"

Hitler returned to his seat in the corner and looked about him defiantly. Two soldiers bent over Sergeant Lofhausen and tried to revive him. The bunker was silent except for the sound of shells exploding overhead.

The next day the Second Division arrived on trucks at the foothills of Mont Blanc. General Lejeune called a meeting of all brigade and division commanders in a section of the forest affording a clear view of the mountain. It was a sunny day with a few puffy white clouds, and in the background the continuous sound of artillery bombardment could be heard.

General Lejeune, short and dark, of French Creole parentage, had fought in the Spanish-American War, the

Philippine uprising and in Mexico. Prior to assuming command of the Second Division, he had led the division's Fourth Brigade, composed entirely of marines.

He pointed to Mont Blanc and told his officers: "The Second Division has received orders to take that mountain. On it is located the enemy's main line of resistance. When we take it, a principal segment of the Hindenburg Line will be broken and the enemy will be compelled to evacuate the surrounding territory. We don't think they'll ever be able to reform after that." Lejeune pointed down to the map table that had been set up on the ground. "Our assault will consist of a frontal attack by the Fourth Brigade on the left half of the objective, and a simultaneous oblique attack by the Third Brigade on the right half. As you can see, this plan utilizes fully the salient position on our right and avoids an attack on the Bois de la Vipère and several other strong points."

Lejeune continued to describe the details of the attack, mentioning the artillery bombardments, supply problems, and procedures for handling prisoners. Then he looked at his officers. "I have told General Pershing that I feel no doubt whatever about the ability of the Second Division to overcome any resistance on that mountain. Are there any questions?"

No one spoke.

"Return to your units and prepare for battle," said Lejeune.

At three o'clock the next morning, as the doughboy artillery pounded Mont Blanc, Duncan stood with Company B in the wooded foothills, preparing to assault the eminence before them. He looked up at the explosions on the crest of the mountain, and thought that there was always one more hill to take, then a river, a forest, a village and another hill. Would there be no end? Colonel Malone had said that if they took

Mont Blanc they could throw the Germans out of the Argonne Forest, but Duncan didn't believe it. He was beginning to think that the war would go on for ever.

A star shell was fired into the air, the signal for the attack to begin. The Third Brigade moved up the left face of the mountain in a vast wave. At first the going was easy, the men leaning forward against gravity and trudging up the rocky incline, carrying their rifles with bayonets fixed. American artillery continued to shell the crest until the doughboys were halfway up. Then, suddenly, the American artillery stopped, and the doughboys double-timed in their mad dash to reach the German fortifications before the Germans could come out of their holes to shoot at them.

Duncan held his pistol in his right hand and ran at the head of Company B. "Follow me!"

The doughboys surged up the hill as the Germans dashed to their barricades, opening fire with rifles and machine guns. Some doughboys dropped and rolled down the hill, but others kept running toward the summit because they knew their only hope was to get inside those fortifications and engage the Germans hand to hand.

Duncan had read enough military strategy to know that the attack wouldn't have been ordered in the first place unless the doughboys outnumbered the Germans by almost three to one. The experts believed that was what it took to overwhelm a strong defensive position like Mont Blanc. So the Second Division would probably take Mont Blanc sooner or later and a third to half of its doughboys would be wiped out. Those were the mathematics of the game that the people on the General Staff played.

"Keep rolling!" Duncan shouted. "Over the top!"

Like an ocean wave the Third Brigade leaped over sandbag fortifications and landed behind them. Duncan found himself standing in front of a German soldier no more than sixteen years old. The boy lunged toward him with his bayonet and Duncan shot him between the eyes. The top of the boy's head, and his helmet, flew into the air. Duncan shot another German, fired at a third and missed, fired again. That bullet found its mark, and the German soldier fell, bleeding, into the bottom of the trench.

It was the usual bloody chaos inside the trench, with men grunting, burping, farting and trying to kill each other by any means possible. Soon the bodies of dead Germans were outnumbered by those of doughboys. Duncan decided to advance to one of the more heavily fortified German positions.

"Follow me!"

He scrambled out of the trench and ran into no-man's land, holding his pistol tightly. The rest of the company followed him, but some new replacements were slow. Sergeant Tucker kicked them in their asses or slammed their arms with his rifle butt. "You heard the captain!" he bellowed angrily. "Get the hell going!"

The frightened soldiers climbed over the sandbags and followed the rest of the company. Ahead of them the Germans were opening fire with rifles and machine guns. Tucker looked ahead at the charging company of doughboys. It was the last thing he ever saw. A bullet sliced into his chest and he toppled backward like a rag doll, landing on his back in the mud and blood at the bottom of the trench.

On the chalky ridge Duncan was aware that huge numbers of his men were falling before the intense enemy fire. If he and his men continued their charge they would be wiped out in the next fifty yards.

"Hit it!" he screamed. "Get down!"

The men dropped down on the flat rock at the top of the ridge. The sun's rim appeared like a red line on the horizon as a hail of bullets flew over doughboy heads. Duncan was trying to figure out what to do, but the first few German mortar rounds that fell made up his mind for him.

"Back to the trench!"

The men turned around and crawled back as mortar shells exploded all around them and machine-gun fire ricocheted off the rocks. Some of the new men panicked and jumped up to make a mad dash for the trench, but the German machine guns cut them down.

The rest slithered down the mountain and, when they came to sandbags, vaulted over to the safety of the first German trench. As soon as Duncan landed he called for Private Whitewater.

Whitewater came running over the dead bodies at the bottom of the trench. "Yes, sir!"

Duncan pointed to his right. "Battalion headquarters is over there. Tell Colonel Malone that we need machine guns and mortars over here. Tell him what we're up against. Got it?"

"Yes, sir."

"Get going!"

Whitewater climbed up the rear of the trench and ran off in the direction Duncan had indicated. Duncan marched down the center of the trench. "Fire back!" he ordered. "What the hell do you think you've got those rifles for?" Then he saw a soldier kneeling over a body in the middle of the trench. "Hey — what do you think you're doing!"

It was Private Bell. "Sir," he said in a strained voice, "Sergeant Tucker is dead. I carried him back here."

Duncan moved toward Bell in huge strides and dropped to one knee beside Sergeant Tucker, whose eyes were wide open and glazing over. His chest was a mass of blood.

Bell shook his head in wonderment. "I never thought he'd get hit."

Duncan looked at Tucker's face and fought hard to restrain the rising scream inside him. He bit the inside of his cheek as he bent over and closed Tucker's eyes. *Goodbye, you crusty old bastard*, he thought. *You taught me how to be a soldier, and I'll never forget you.*

CHAPTER 28

"Wake up, Blake!"

The voice sounded far away, down a long tunnel. Blake rolled over to get away from it.

"Come on — let's go!"

Blake felt himself being shaken. He opened his eyes and saw Lieutenant DiPietro looking down at him.

"What's going on?" Blake asked sleepily.

"We've got to go up."

Blake looked at his watch. "So early?"

"Yes. Are you awake?"

"Not yet. But if you keep talking I will be."

"Hurry up."

DiPietro left Blake's room. Blake pushed the covers away and swung his feet around to the floor. It was six o'clock in the morning and the sun was just coming up. He reached for his package of cigarettes and lit one, hoping it would help clear his head.

He'd been flying missions every day for nearly two weeks, often twice a day. His hands sometimes trembled uncontrollably and he never seemed to have any energy. He put on his clothing and boots, grabbed his flying hat, stumbled down the corridor to the latrine, took a leak, then washed his hands and face and rinsed out his mouth.

Outside, mechanics were pulling the airplanes on to the field. A cool autumn breeze was blowing. Blake buttoned up his sheepskin-lined jacket as he made his way to the briefing hut.

Most pilots from the squadron were already there. A cook was serving coffee and buns. Blake got a cup of coffee and a bun, then sat on a rickety wooden chair. Other pilots arrived and sat down, munching buns and sipping coffee as they waited for Captain Eddie Rickenbacker to show up. Rickenbacker had become commander of the Ninety-fourth Aero only three days before.

When Rickenbacker arrived the briefing began. He told them that they were going on a strafing mission in the Meuse-Argonne sector and pointed it out on the map. The Germans were holding on to fortifications on some critical high ground, and the squadron had to attack them. Blake was half-asleep and missed a lot of the details, but he'd been on plenty of missions and knew more or less what to do.

The briefing ended and the pilots gulped down the remainder of the coffee and buns, then made their way out to the runway. As they approached the planes they shook hands and wished each other luck. Separating, they climbed on to the wings of their planes, strapped themselves into the cockpits, put on their long-eared hats and adjusted their goggles.

The sun was a big red ball hovering above the horizon. There was a scattering of wispy clouds in the sky, tinged with pink. A mechanic turned Blake's propeller a few times as Blake flipped on the ignition. The engine sputtered and roared to life, making the Spad tremble. Blake tested the engine and all his controls. Everything seemed all right and the coffee he'd drunk seemed to be taking effect.

Two by two the planes took off. Blake waited for the signal, then moved on to the runway with Lieutenant Fuller beside him. The two pilots straightened their planes out and blipped their engines. When the ground officer gave them the high sign, they pulled out their throttles, roared down the runway in tandem and lifted into the sky.

Spads circled and formed two vee formations above the field, then began their journey to the Meuse-Argonne sector. Blake sat with both hands on the stick, listening to the monotonous drone of the engines, glancing around at farmland and trees. The flight was supposed to take about an hour and Blake, like the other pilots, was anxious to get the mission over with so he could go back to bed.

It was a beautiful morning and the sun gleamed on the metal fittings in his cockpit. He thought of Danielle, who was now in Switzerland with her aunt. He hadn't seen her for a month, and often found himself yearning for her.

In his imagination he saw her lying in bed, golden hair. He wished the war would end quickly so he could be with her always. There had been a time when he'd loved the excitement of war, but now nothing could compare with his love for Danielle.

He looked around the sky to see if any German planes were up there, but couldn't spot anything. Unfastening the top button of his jacket, he took out the gold locket and chain that Danielle had given him. Inside was her picture with a demure smile. *What incredible beauty,* Blake thought. *And she's all mine.*

He closed the locket, buttoned his jacket, and gripped his stick with both hands again as the squadron continued to make its way toward the Argonne Forest. Soon the pilots heard the faint rumble of artillery, which became louder as they drew closer to their objective.

They saw smoke on the horizon, and in the open fields below were columns of soldiers marching toward the front. The roads were choked with vehicles and troops. Vast quantities of soldiers and supplies were moving forward in never-ending streams to engage the Germans.

Finally Squadron 94 reached the battleground and could see long thin lines of doughboys charging German trenches and fortifications, shell explosions like white mushrooms covering the landscape. Blake couldn't help thinking how spectacular it all was, that war had a way of dwarfing everything in human existence.

The squadron changed course and headed for a range of mountains. Soldiers could be seen advancing up the sides in long skirmish lines. The mountain was covered with smoke, networks of trenches and fortifications. Pilots circled, then flew away from the mountain, turned around, and formed one long straight line, Span behind Spad. Captain Rickenbacker's lead Spad dived toward the trench below, other planes following at fifty-yard intervals. German anti-aircraft batteries opened fire, and German machine gunners swung their barrels around and fired at Spads descending toward them.

Blake eased his Spad down, keeping wings level, wincing whenever an anti-aircraft shell landed close by, but his hand was steady and his engine howled as he sped toward the trench. Inside it, German soldiers could be seen scattering to escape the machine-gun bullets of the American planes.

When Blake was in position he pressed his trigger lever and his twin Vickers machine guns barked viciously. Hot lead spat out as Blake kept firing into the middle of the trench, running Germans ripped apart by his guns. He passed a bunker, fired into another length of trench, fired into a mortar squad, and at the end of the trench dueled with a German machine-gun nest. German bullets rippled through the fabric on his wings as he pulled the stick, lifting the nose of the Spad and climbing into the sky.

The formation was breaking apart, individual pilots selecting targets and doing their best to dodge anti-aircraft and machine-gun fire. Blake spotted a howitzer emplacement and angled toward it. German soldiers scrambled madly to hide behind the sandbags as he opened fire. Some Germans were struck by his bullets and flung forward to the ground.

Blake yanked back his stick, climbed away from the howitzers, turned around in the sky, and came back for another pass, firing at the emplacement again and watching Germans run for shelter.

At the end of his run, he soared into the sky again, deciding to make another pass at one of the front-line trenches. Leveling off, he glanced around to make sure that no other American planes would be in his way, and no German planes were attacking. Anti-aircraft shells exploded nearby as he bit his lower lip and continued his dive toward the trench. German machine-gun fire ripped through his fuselage, but he was committed to the dive and could see German soldiers in the trench dashing for cover.

He pulled his trigger and the Spad shuddered as its machine guns fired. Their bullets ripped open sandbags and cut down fleeing German soldiers. Some Germans lay down in the center of the trench, but bullets descended on them like angry bees and punctured their backs. They writhed and screamed as Blake roared over them and climbed into the sky again.

He leveled off at two thousand feet and looked around for more targets. The sky had become darker with anti-aircraft fire, and German machine gunners on the ground were spraying bullets all over the sky.

Blake saw a huge machine-gun nest with forty or fifty machine guns in it. Again the little voice told him to get the hell out of there, but he had been on so many missions that his responses had become automatic. He angled his Spad to the left and dived sideways toward the machine-gun nest, opening up with his twin Vickers.

The German gunners swung their weapons around, but Blake was a fast-moving target coming at an unusual angle. His bullets zipped across the machine-gun nest, and many Germans fled from the onslaught, but some valiant ones stayed, firing back at the Spad.

Blake heard bullets whistling by him, some of them slicing through the canvas of his wings and fuselage. He saw German soldiers leaping away from his bullets and running to trenches nearby, while others fell bleeding around their weapons.

Blake came to the end of the nest and gripped his stick to pull it back and climb away. Suddenly his plane was jolted by a bullet that tore away part of his propeller. Splinters flew back at him and he ducked as he pulled the stick. The Spad began to climb, but without its usual speed. The German machine gunners who hadn't fled kept Blake's stricken plane in their sights, their triggers depressed.

Bullets ripped apart Blake's wings and fuselage. One bullet hit him in the back and flung him forward against his dials. His body pressed against the stick as the Spad carved a huge parabola in the sky, pulling out of its climb and falling to earth.

Blake felt as though his back and chest were torn apart. Blood burbled out of his mouth and the earth spun around underneath him. He tried to sit erect and bring the Spad under control, but he knew he couldn't do it. He tried to take a deep breath but the blood clogged his throat and he started to cough. *Oh, my God,* he thought. *I'm going to die...*

He looked at his dials but saw only blurry images. Bullets continued to rip into his plane as the engine sputtered. A bullet hit him on the shoulder and would have knocked him out of the cockpit if he hadn't been strapped in.

The sky and earth became dark. Blake could feel the wind on his face and heard humming in his ears. He tried to think of something to do but his mind was fading fast. His lap filled with blood, and fierce pain sent him into convulsions.

"Danielle," he whispered, as his plane fell out of the sky.

The Spad crashed into the side of a mountain and burst into flames, its wreckage cascading down the slope, a mangled and burning body trapped inside.

CHAPTER 29

On October 6, Everett DeWitt, recently promoted to first lieutenant, was returning to General Pershing's field headquarters in the Meuse-Argonne sector after attending a meeting with officers of the Fourth French Army. Everett's mission had been to deliver in person General Pershing's complaint that the French soldiers were not keeping up with the doughboys, and the American left flank was becoming exposed.

"We have been in this war much longer than you," the French general had told Everett, "and we have learned to be economical with our men."

Everett told the French officers that General Pershing believed the attack could succeed only if the Allied armies moved quickly, before the Germans could adjust their tactics and fight back. The French officers argued that rapid mass attacks had been too costly in terms of casualties, and they preferred to move more deliberately, outmaneuvering the Germans in a series of pincer movements.

Now Everett was returning to General Pershing with the results of the meeting. He figured that Pershing would use one or two of the new divisions to cover his left flank.

The battle in the Meuse-Argonne sector was costly, but appeared to be going well. The Second Division had finally taken Mont Blanc Ridge, although it had suffered horrific casualties, and the rest of the AEF was assaulting the fourth line of the Hindenburg fortifications. General Pershing and his senior staff believed that once the fourth line was broken, the German army would either retreat into Germany or surrender.

Everett drove over a narrow dirt road that cut through the middle of a forest. In the distance he could hear an artillery bombardment, and the sound brought a bitter smile to his face. The war would probably be over by the end of the year, he thought, and he wouldn't have fired a single shot.

He drove out of the woods and saw rolling fields and hills. A large group of doughboys, comprising perhaps two battalions, were moving across the road ahead in columns of twos, heading for the front. Everett slowed down and stopped twenty yards from the column nearest him. Some of the soldiers looked at his little Renault blankly. They were tired and dirty, their shoulders bearing the insignia of the First Division, also known as the Big Red One because that was what the patch looked like.

The Big Red One was a Regular Army division and had seen some of the toughest fighting in the war. Now it was going to the front again. Everett assumed that they had been pulled out of one sector and transferred to another.

One of the doughboys from the Big Red One pointed at the General Staff license plate on Everett's little car, and his buddies smirked. Everett knitted his eyebrows together and took out a cigarette. *There it is again,* he thought, *that goddamned contempt. Even the buck privates detest me.*

He felt his cheeks becoming warm. He wanted to give the doughboys a talking-to, but he'd never commanded any troops since he'd been in the army and wasn't even sure of how to bawl them out. Besides, the doughboys' commanding officer would probably tell him to get the hell out of there. None of the combat soldiers, be they privates or officers, had any use for staff officers.

The Big Red One troops passed over the road and across a field toward a forest in the distance. The road was clear now, but Everett kept looking at the soldiers. *I wish I were going with them,* he thought. *I'd like to be a real soldier at least once before the goddamned war is over.*

He looked at his watch. It was one o'clock in the afternoon. He ought to return to General Pershing's headquarters, make his report and get some lunch, but kept looking at the doughboys from the Big Red One. A dangerous thought began to glimmer in his mind. *Why don't I go with them?* he asked himself. *Who's to stop me?*

He knew that his presence wasn't vital at headquarters. When the Iron Commander received more reports, as inevitably he would, about his weak left flank, he'd take appropriate action. Sooner or later Everett would make it back, and he'd tell General Pershing that his car had broken down, or that some other calamity had befallen him. They were in a war zone and anything could happen. There was no reason General Pershing wouldn't believe him.

The Big Red One was moving farther away. *This might be my last chance to see some fighting,* Everett thought. *What the hell — I might as well do it.*

He pulled the keys from the ignition, dropped them into his pocket, removed his soft cap, and put on the helmet he always carried with him in case of danger. He also carried a forty-five that he'd last fired a few months ago. He climbed out of the car and looked at the doughboys from the Big Red One. *Here goes,* he thought as he double-timed after them, sucking in huge drafts of air.

The grass on the ground was yellowing and trees were turning red and gold. It could have been just another sunny autumn day, entirely normal, but far in the distance smoke could be seen and sounds of battle heard.

Everett reached the end of the column and fell in, adjusting his helmet. One of the doughboys turned around and looked at him curiously. The doughboy evidently wanted to ask who he was, but when he saw Everett's rank he decided to keep his mouth shut.

Everett tagged along at the end of the column, thinking of his few weeks of training in the fields and forests of Georgia. A city boy, he'd always felt out of place in the woods. The country had always felt as alien to him as Mars.

They entered a forest and continued marching along. The trees somewhat muffled the sounds of the artillery bombardment ahead. Huge portions of the forest had been ravaged by an intense bombardment a few days ago.

Somebody shouted for the column to halt and take a break. The doughboys sat in old shell holes or leaned against the trunks of trees, opened their packs and took out cans of beans and packages of hardtack. Everett sat with his back against a boulder and wondered how to get something to eat. The doughboys moved away from him and looked at him as if he were a ghost.

A buck sergeant examined Everett for a few moments, then walked ahead and disappeared behind the trees. A few minutes later he came back with a young first lieutenant. The sergeant sat and rejoined his men, but the lieutenant advanced toward Everett, squinting at him against the bright sun. Everett stood up and smiled.

The lieutenant grinned. "Hello there. I didn't know you were with us."

Everett grinned back. "My car broke down on the road back there and then I saw your outfit. Hope you don't mind if I tag along for a while."

The lieutenant looked at Everett's collar insignia, which marked him as a staff officer "Headquarters is that way," he said, pointing to the rear.

"I know, but I thought I'd take a look at the front. May I know your name?"

"Lieutenant John Simpson."

"I'm Lieutenant Everett DeWitt."

Simpson hesitated for a moment, as if undecided as to what to do. Then he said tentatively, "You don't look as though you've got anything to eat."

"As a matter of fact I don't."

"Well ... I've got a few extra things. Why don't you come up to the head of the column with me?"

"Thank you very much."

Everett followed Simpson to the head of the company column and sat down with Simpson and two other young officers. They gave Everett beans and hardtack, which he ate with gusto. He learned that the units weren't two battalions, as he'd thought, but the remainder of a regiment advancing to take a village up ahead.

When Everett was almost finished, the order came down to get moving again. He gulped the remainder of his food, threw the empty can away and returned the fork to the officer who had lent it to him. The brigade resumed its march and Everett took his position with Lieutenant Simpson at the head of Company G.

Everett was exhilarated to be moving into battle. He'd wanted to be in the infantry at the beginning of the war, but the procurement officer, who was a friend of the family, had told him he'd be of more use as a staff officer. Now it was going to happen at last, but beneath his enthusiasm was a shimmer of fear. He advised himself to be careful, then nothing would happen to him.

The brigade came out of the forest, crossed a field and entered another forest, which was another scene of widespread destruction. Every tree was bare of leaves and most were shattered. Trenches and shellholes were everywhere. Everett had to watch his step so that he wouldn't fall. A terrible odor pervaded the area, and in one of the trenches Everett saw the bloated, greenish body of a German soldier. Everett's eyes bugged; he gagged and looked away quickly. But then his eyes fell on another dead German.

"What a stink," said one of the sergeants.

"A dead Heinie is a good Heinie," said a doughboy.

The woods looked like a nightmare landscape as they advanced. The sounds of fighting came closer and Everett's fear increased, the sudden reality of war bringing thoughts he had never considered before. It was easy to imagine the gruesome fighting that had gone on in these woods. What a terrible way to die. And for what? He wondered why soldiers fought so hard. Why didn't they just pull out and to hell with it?

"Skirmish line!" somebody shouted.

Lieutenant Simpson turned around and cupped his hands around his mouth. "Let's go, Company G — skirmish line!"

The brigade spread out in a long skirmish line in the woods, with officers in front, running back and forth, giving orders. Everett was surprised at how docile the men were. They did what they were told as if resigned to their fates.

"Forward!"

The skirmish line moved through a forest strewn with fallen trees and pocked with holes. They joined a large number of doughboys ahead and squeezed closer to fit in among them. Officers ran around shouting at the men to form three skirmish lines. Everett and Company G were part of the second line. The mass of men continued through the forest again and after a while arrived at a field beyond which was a town under bombardment. The doughboys lined up at the edge of the forest and waited for the bombardment to stop.

Everett lay on his stomach and studied the town, which appeared quite large, evidently an important commercial center. Several roads led into it, and Everett remembered something his old friend Georgie Patton had told him. *The key to victory is control of the road net.*

The town seethed with smoke and shells bursting inside its perimeter. Many buildings had been destroyed but a surprising number still stood, although badly damaged. Everett estimated that several thousand people had lived in the town, now evidently abandoned.

The bombardment lessened and a few minutes later ceased entirely. Whistles were blown and doughboys got to their feet. Officers appeared in front, pistols in hands.

The first wave moved out, running toward the town. After a brief interval the second wave followed, then the third. Everett was wild with joy — at last he was a real soldier. Men around him whooped and cheered, their battle cries echoing across endless rolling fields. Everett shouted with them, holding his pistol tightly in his hand and thinking that one day he'd tell his grandchildren about this magnificent charge.

Then German mortar shells began to fall on the doughboys, but they landed too far back. Then more mortar shells fell, and they were too far forward. That was the usual mortar tactic.

First fire over the target, then fire short, then split the difference and hopefully land on target.

Only three hundred yards separated the doughboys from the town when the full weight of the mortar barrage rained down on them. Groups of men were blown into the air but the soldiers kept moving. Everett became frightened, disoriented. The German machine guns opened fire and doughboys were cut down like wheat before a scythe. Everett was horrified; the picture was suddenly changing. Instead of a heroic charge, he found himself in the middle of widespread slaughter. He wanted to run back to the woods, but would need to fight his way through the doughboys behind him. The shame of them seeing him run away was too much to bear. Now he understood why everyone followed orders; it was too humiliating not to. Better to be dead than branded a coward.

His whole body was shaking with terror and he was afraid his knees would give out. The German fire increased in intensity, and doughboys were falling to the ground everywhere. One of the sergeants with whom Everett had eaten lunch an hour ago was shot through the throat. As he fell to the ground, blood spurted out and streaked Everett's pants. Everett thought he'd faint, but somehow he kept going.

"Keep moving!" shouted Lieutenant Simpson. "Into the town!"

I know what I'll do, Everett thought feverishly. *I'll fall down and pretend I'm dead. Then, when things quiet down, I'll sneak away.*

Doughboys screamed all around him as they were hit with bullets, and mortar rounds continued to blow other doughboys to pieces. Everett took a deep breath and fell down, skinning his knees and hurting his elbows but managed to get down and make himself still except for his trembling legs. *That looked so false,* he thought, aghast at what he'd done. *What if somebody noticed? I could get court-martialed, my family disgraced.*

But in that wild, headlong charge, nobody noticed him go down. Doughboys ran past him as Everett peeked up at them. German fire was ripping them apart, but still most of them kept charging toward the town. Everett wondered how they did it.

He closed his eyes and buried his face in the grass, trembling all over. *I'm a coward,* he thought, sobbing. *Whatever made me think that I'm a soldier? I'm nothing more than a clerk with the insignia of a lieutenant. I was a fool to come here today.*

He looked up again and saw dead and wounded doughboys all around him. Some of moaned and tossed convulsively on the ground. *If only I had been shot, too. Then at least I could have kept my honor.*

He raised his tear-stained face to the sky and saw puffy gray clouds. It became clear to him that he'd never be able to live with himself after this shameful day. *I might as well shoot myself right here. I'm a disgrace to my name and my family, because fundamentally I'm yellow, a coward.* He closed his eyes and cried bitterly into the grass.

He imagined his ancestors looking down at him sniveling on the ground. His father and grandfather had told him stories about generals, colonels and captains who'd been in his family and fought for America ever since the French and Indian Wars. He could see them all now, as clearly as he had as a boy, in their strange uniforms, representing all the armies that the United States had ever put into the field. His own father had been with the Rough Riders on San Juan Hill, and Franklin too had gone into battle, his death tragic but heroic. They had made the DeWitt name a proud one in America, and now he was letting them down.

Quaking, still terrified, Everett forced himself to stand, because he finally realized that death in battle was preferable to disgrace in battle or suicide. He wiped his eyes with his sleeve and ran slowly at first, then with more purpose toward the shattered skirmish lines ahead. Pointing his pistol at the sky, he fired once to give himself courage. Suddenly, somehow, a savage cry tore up from deep inside him, wrenching him free of all restraints, and of any thought of fear or safety. "Take the town!" he screamed, racing forward across the bloody and ravaged land.

The skirmish lines were faltering under withering fire. Officers and men fell to the ground in huge numbers, but more than half of the original regiment still charged forward into the bowels of hell.

Everett ran at top speed through the slowing skirmish lines. "Forward!" he hollered, oblivious to his chattering teeth and the tears pouring down his face. "Always move forward!"

Somehow he found himself in front of everybody. He imagined all his ancestors looking down at him from the heavens and smiling in satisfaction. He waved his pistol wildly in the air and ran toward a brick wall, behind which German soldiers were firing.

"Keep moving!" he cried again. "Always keep moving!"

He leveled his pistol and fired toward the stone wall. German helmets bobbed around in back of it, and he shouted: "Kill me, you bastards — I don't even care…"

He jumped over the wall and German soldiers swarmed all over him, but he spun and dodged, firing his pistol as quickly as he could pull the trigger. A German bayonet slashed his chest and another cut his shoulder, but none of the wounds were deep and he barely felt them. When his pistol was empty he hurled it into a German soldier's face and yanked the man's rifle and bayonet away.

The rest of the brigade stormed the wall and joined Everett, who had become crazed with the violence of the battle, stabbing and butting every German who landed in his path.

"Kill them!" he shrieked. "Kill them all!"

He had the added strength and sharp instincts of a madman. No rational German could stand before him for long. One German officer fired a Luger at him but Everett was a fast-moving target and the bullet missed. The officer fired again and this time the bullet hit Everett's helmet, ricocheting off. It was like being hit over the head with a hammer, and Everett dropped dazed to his knees. The German officer was going to fire again, but a doughboy ran him through with his bayonet.

Everett tried to clear his head as the doughboys pushed the Germans back. Other doughboys charged into buildings and cellars. Everett tried to get up to go with them, but his legs buckled and he fell to the ground. He tried again, but couldn't make it.

Somebody was bending over him. "Are you all right, son?"

Everett looked up into the face of a middle-aged officer. "I think so."

"You just lay still there, and a medic will be with you directly. What's your name?"

Everett was aware that the side of his face was wet. He touched it and looked at his fingers. They were covered with blood.

"I said to lay still now," the officer said. "Who are you?"

"Lieutenant DeWitt…"

"You're not in my battalion. What are you doing here?"

"I don't know, sir."

The officer smiled. "Well, whatever it is, welcome to the Big Red One. I saw what you did just now, and I'm going to put you in for a Silver Star."

CHAPTER 30

The List Regiment was among the German units falling back from the third line of defense in the Hindenburg system of fortifications. Private Adolf Hitler ran through the smoke and explosions, searching frantically for cover. Then he saw a shellhole and dived into it, only to become aware of a fierce burning in his lungs.

"Gas!" somebody shouted.

Hitler panicked when he realized that he'd inhaled poison gas. He tried to hold his breath as he reached for his gas mask. A shell exploded nearby and shook the ground so hard that he was stunned for a few moments. When his head cleared he found that everything was blurred in front of him. With shaking hands he managed to free his gas mask and put it on, but he already felt faint and everything around him was dissolving into grayness.

I've been gassed, he thought. *I'm going to die!* Terrified, he jumped out of the hole and ran in the direction of the German rear. He couldn't see anything and his chest felt as though a firestorm was inside. Shells burst around him and bullets flew in all directions. He tripped and fell, got quickly to his feet again, but dropped his rifle as he ran to safety.

His mind was filled with tumultuous thoughts and he was becoming nauseous. His legs wouldn't hold him up anymore and he dropped to his knees, tore off his gas mask and screamed: "Help — I've been gassed! Help!"

He walked a few steps forward on his knees, then fell over a dead soldier. *I should have kept my gas mask on,* Hitler realized. He held his hands in front of him to feel the way. Everything had become dark now.

"Help!" he shouted. "Help!"

He heard footsteps, and somebody grabbed his arm. "I've got you," a soldier said.

The soldier helped Hitler up and dragged him back to safety.

In Zurich, Danielle sat in the bedroom of her aunt's home, reading a newspaper. She'd been following the war avidly and knew that the American divisions were breaking the back of the German army in the Argonne Forest. She especially searched for news of the air war, worrying about Blake and thinking of him constantly. In the back of her mind was the nagging memory of the first night she'd met him, when she'd had the premonition that he was going to die.

There was a knock on her door.

"Come in?"

Her aunt entered, her face pale. Danielle saw that there was a telegram in her hands, and a wave of fear passed over her. "What's wrong?" she whispered.

Her aunt silently handed her the telegram. Danielle read it, and then simply stared at it for a few moments. She rose unsteadily to her feet, her look of disbelief turning to anguish. "Noooo!" she screamed, and with the cry still dying on her lips, she crumpled to the floor in a faint.

Her aunt called the servants and they tried to revive her, to no avail. After putting her to bed her aunt called a doctor, who arrived a half-hour later. The doctor gave Danielle an injection to relax her and keep her asleep. He stayed with her throughout the afternoon and evening, examining her repeatedly because he feared she might miscarry. When he finally took his leave after midnight, he said he'd return in the morning to check the patient again.

Danielle woke before he arrived. The injection had worn off somewhat, and her soft sobs were interspersed with Blake's name.

The doctor returned at nine, and after giving her another sedative he told her aunt that he was much encouraged. The mother and baby would most probably survive the tragedy.

In Berlin, the Kaiser sat behind his desk. Seated across from him were Field Marshal Hindenburg, Colonel-General Ludendorff, and Foreign Minister Paul von Hintze. The atmosphere was solemn and tense.

Hindenburg's face was chalky white, and he looked twenty years older. "Your Excellency," he said wearily, "the Western Front is about to collapse. If we do not get an armistice, the army will be destroyed."

"It is true," Ludendorff said nervously. "The only way to save Germany is to appeal to President Wilson at once. An armistice must be arranged within twenty-four hours."

Hintze, a former rear admiral in the Imperial Navy, couldn't believe his ears. "An armistice?" he asked. "In only twenty-four hours? I had no idea the situation was so desperate."

"It's worse than you can possibly imagine," Hindenburg growled.

"It would be impossible to obtain an armistice in only twenty-four hours," Hintze protested. "An armistice is an enormously complex matter."

The muscles in Ludendorff's face twitched. "You must do it! The fate of the Fatherland is at stake here!"

"But gentlemen," Hintze said, outraged at the demand, "such a move would be tantamount to unconditional surrender. The

German people would not stand for it. We would have revolution, and possibly the overthrow of the imperial dynasty. You must give me a few days to work this out, gentlemen, so that I can obtain better terms from the Allies. If we appear too desperate, the Allies' demands will be severe."

Ludendorff shot to his feet. "We are desperate!" he screamed. "What must I do to make you understand that we are desperate?"

The Kaiser, who'd been the calmest man in the room, raised his hand. "Kindly return to your seat, General Ludendorff."

"Yes, Excellency."

Ludendorff sat again. The two officers and the foreign minister waited for the Kaiser to speak. The Kaiser looked at each of them and sighed.

"I never dreamed it would come to this," he said softly, "but this is my decision. We will ask for an armistice, but we will not beg. The Fatherland may be in dire straits, but we are not a nation of beggars yet. The foreign minister will take as much time as he deems prudent to obtain the most favorable terms possible for the Fatherland."

"We do not have much time!" Ludendorff's voice was strident, close to hysteria. "The front is collapsing even as we speak!"

"The German soldier knows what his duty is," the Kaiser replied. "I have made my decision and it is final. All of you may return to your stations."

CHAPTER 31

On the morning of November 11, the Second Division was deployed in a forest near the Meuse River. The Second Field Artillery Brigade was shelling the German side of the river, and the Second Engineers were building a pontoon bridge so the doughboys could cross later in the day.

A new permanent battalion commander had been appointed, and Captain Duncan Hunter had returned as commanding officer of Company B. He sat in a shellhole with his new executive officer, Lieutenant Crandall from Little Rock, Arkansas, dining upon canned willie and hardtack. They and the other men in the Second Division were filling up with food now because they expected to attack before noon, and didn't know when they'd get a chance to eat again.

The woods they were in had been a bloody battleground only two days ago. The Second Division had managed to push the Germans across the river, but the woods had nearly been destroyed, and there were shell craters and broken trees everywhere. The smell of gunpowder hung in the air, along with the odors of decaying human and animal flesh.

Duncan had been shaken by the news that his brother Blake had been killed in action. He talked and joked with his men less, and arranged to be alone as often as possible. He often appeared distracted, and his men were worried about him.

Sitting in the shellhole, he munched hardtack and thought of Blake. Duncan's heart was heavy, and he found himself unable to accept the fact that Blake was dead. He had been so dashing and full of life. If there were any sense and logic in the world,

Blake would have lived and he, Duncan, would have died, for he was the dull and plodding one, the brooding fellow always hidden in the shadow of his more spectacular brother. Duncan realized that he loved his brother more than he'd ever loved anyone, despite Blake's many faults. With Blake's death he felt that a part of him had also died.

The US Army artillery fire died down and stopped for no discernible reason. Duncan perked up and turned toward the river. Through the broken, twisted trees he could see the engineers on their half-built pontoon bridge, looking toward the German side of the river, also wondering why the bombardment had ended. The other officers and men in the vicinity were wondering the same thing.

This turn of events was quite curious. A sudden halt of a barrage in progress had never occurred for no discernible reason in Duncan's experience on the front lines. He stood up, his can of meat in his hand.

"The war's over!" somebody shouted.

Duncan spun around in the direction of the voice.

He saw doughboys from his Fourth Platoon running through the woods, surrounding Major Berry from battalion headquarters. The major carried his helmet in his hand and was smiling.

No, it can't be, Duncan thought as he trudged toward the major. Other men in the company came out of their holes too. They'd heard the cry and wanted to know what was going on.

Duncan saluted Major Berry. "Do you know why the shelling's stopped, sir?"

Berry returned the salute, his smile broadening. "I sure as hell do — the war is over!"

Duncan and the other men from Company B stared at him in disbelief.

"Are you sure?" Duncan asked.

"Yep," said Major Berry. "The armistice was signed this morning. The war is over, boys! General Lejeune wants us all to stay in position and keep our heads down just in case, but evidently the fighting is finished."

There were a few moments of silence, then the doughboys cheered, ran around like madmen, slapping each other on the shoulders and jumping up and down. A few fell down on their knees and prayed. Some cried shamelessly. Duncan, however, was stunned, and stood still as a statue.

"Carry on here," Major Berry said, "I've got to pass the word along to Company C." Berry turned and walked away.

Duncan took off his helmet. If only Blake could have lasted a few more weeks, he would have survived the war. Then Duncan suddenly realized that he himself had survived the war. *I don't have to fight anymore!*

Corporal Bell ran toward him, his face flushed with emotion. "Sir!" he shouted. "The war is over! The war is over!"

The two men looked at each other, and all they'd been through together passed between them. Bell lurched forward and embraced Duncan, pressing his face against Duncan's chest.

"The war is over!" Bell said, tears flowing down his cheeks. "The war is over!"

Bell turned Duncan loose and ran off, waving his hands, his cry repeated among the other doughboys. "The war is over! The war is over!"

Duncan stumbled through the woods toward the river, where his men rushed up to shake his hand. The combat engineers on the pontoon bridges ran back and forth screaming at the top of their lungs. There was chaos and jubilation everywhere.

Duncan made his way to the bank of the river, kneeled, scooped up some cold water and splashed it on his face. Then he looked up to the clear blue sky.

My God, he thought. *The war is over.*

A NOTE TO THE READER

Dear Reader,

Thank you for taking the time to read *Bayonets In No-Man's Land*. I hope you enjoyed it!

I felt very excited and highly motivated to write this novel because my father had been a World War One combat veteran and had filled my youthful imagination with wild tales of his experiences.

He had served in the famed Second Division and was entitled to wear a ribbon that showed six stars representing his participation in six major battle engagements including the Battle of Blanc Mont Ridge.

I had served in the US Army myself so understood basic military life, having enlisted in 1954 during the Cold War when I was 19, mainly because I wanted the GI Bill for college. I served with the 71st and 4th Divisions, not the 2nd like my father, and never was in a hot shooting war.

My first assignment was the 53 Infantry Regiment in Alaska. I was an ordinary rifleman. My second assignment was the 271st Engineers, which was a combat engineer unit, which the British call sappers.

My Army background combined with tales from my father made me excited and optimistic about writing my World War One novel. I couldn't wait to get started, but first needed much research to make sure I didn't screw up anything.

I read many histories of the war plus accounts of individual battles, including biographies and autobiographies of main players, and memoirs of soldiers who'd experienced frontline combat. I wanted to continue reading more, because World

War One was fascinating, but was on deadline and finally had to sit down and write.

I wrote about World War One as it was according to history, consisting of tremendous artillery shelling, attacks against withering rifle and machine-gun fire, brutal hand-to-hand combat in trenches, poison gas attacks, plus the air war where pilots jousted as in medieval times, riding in airplanes instead of on horses.

I'm very pleased with this novel and hope readers enjoy it as much as I enjoyed writing it. If you are able to leave a review on **Amazon** or **Goodreads**, I would be very grateful.

Len Levinson

Sapere Books is an exciting new publisher of brilliant fiction and popular history.

To find out more about our latest releases and our monthly bargain books visit our website:

saperebooks.com

Printed in Great Britain
by Amazon